I AM HOUSE

Madonna R. Fowler

Valleyheart Press
Los Angeles, CA

Published by

Valleyheart Press

ValleyHeartPress.com

Designed by Bookwrights

ISBN: 978-0-9862263-0-4 (print book)
ISBN: 978-0-9862263-1-1 (ebook)

For Gerrie, my mother,
who taught me how to listen to houses.

There are only two ways to live your life.
One is as though nothing is a miracle.

The other is as though everything is a miracle.

— Albert Einstein

Introduction

Houses, it turns out, know everything. They see with their windows, hear with their roofs, and know their new owners before they come up the walk. Houses are the beasts that carry our burdens, able to recognize the others, not in bodies anymore who travel through their walls and hover near the living. Actually, houses can talk. Sometimes they whisper.

I AM HOUSE is the beyond all odds story of a tear down estate and a human, both deeply affected by alcoholism, who meet and save each other in the worst of times. Using her last eight hundred dollars as a down payment, Kathy O'Brien signs a contract—and goes for it. This is the house she's always wanted. It just needs a little work. Excuse me? A little work? Most would have said, "Bring a bulldozer!" But Kathy walks past those voices, convinced that if she moves into the place, she'll bring it back to life. After all, this is her dream.

Doesn't everyone have a dream house? Could the idea be hidden in the mind, stored just this side of "doubt?" Or it could it be that actual place driven by that seems beyond reach?

"Could I ever own a house like that?" The thought persists, knocking on the door of the subconscious, followed by another that hurries in asking—

"Why not live here? What's stopping me? Is it only money, or is it something buried, deeper, inside?"

Will unexpected victory arrive for Kathy as she does battle with an army of fears and seemingly impossible odds? What will happen when she discovers buried toxic waste—chromium six and mercury—behind her house, and faces foreclosure as the worst financial crash since the Great Depression sets fire to the world? Lastly, how will she defend herself from something even more destructive—the inner messages that stole her ancestors' dreams and kept them small—the voices that torment her, taunting—"Whoever told you that you deserve something this great? Who do you think you are, anyway?"

Preface

I hadn't thought of writing this part of my life for anyone else to read. It took three friends saying the same thing to me in one week to change my mind. Over dinner in a café, I broke the news to Gina. Things haven't always gone her way, especially lately. She's toiling at a nonprofit, writing grants while visions of the Great American novel swirl in her head. A few years ago she and her husband lost their house to foreclosure. I wanted to break the news to her, but hesitated. Finally, like a balloon about to burst, I let it out.

"Another house?" But Gina already knew. I wear a look when I buy real estate like some people do when they fall in love.

"Uh-huh. My dream house."

"How many do you have?"

"Three?" Even I couldn't believe what I was saying. "Gina, my dreams are coming true."

"I'm glad someone's dreams are coming true," she said, measuring words, fork glued to her fingers. "How did you find—"

"My car drove me to it."

She swallowed, scanning the room and the inside of her head at the same time.

"Kathy, you *have* to write this down. You have to tell the *Times*. Three houses in one year?" Her eyes rolled to the ceiling. "When was it—a year ago you were at a food bank because you had no groceries?"

The second friend, Dorrie, is my neighbor. She hasn't dated since her husband, Bill, died eight years ago. My second house and hers share a common driveway; gaze across at each other like two old friends.

We happened to meet in my front yard.

"How's it going with the new place?"

"It's hard, but…" I didn't want to admit the whole truth about the big house. I wanted to dress it up, skip the hard core part about stuffing newspapers into the holes in the walls.

"It's tough, but—"

"But it's yours."

"Yeah, it's mine."

"And you don't have—anyone? You're not married!"

"There isn't a man on the horizon."

"Three houses in one year, Kath. Remodeling two before you bought the last. I watched you," she shook her head. "I watched you. I said, 'How's she doing this?'"

I shrugged. "It was time. I had to."

"And you have no money!" She laughed.

Then I laughed, because it was true.

The third invitation arrived like a roll of parchment sealed in hot red wax. This was the closer. I'd staked claim in an Italian restaurant on Ventura Boulevard with Karina. She and her husband own a condo. Buying that property was, she says, the best thing they ever did in that marriage. The union was cold and lacking in other areas, but damn it, they were joint tenants on 2,200 square feet overlooking the esteemed Valley City Estates and a nine hole golf course.

After I told my tale she surveyed me across white linen. Like Gina's, her fork hesitated, unemployed. Antipasti glistened untouched on a heavy plate between us. Her head shook, too, the same way the others' had.

"And you got into it for eight hundred dollars? You are amazing!"

"God is amazing," I said. "I just, I don't know. It was time to do this. I lost a lot of people this year—three of them. I started to think, 'What am I waiting for? What is this, a rehearsal? I've got to go on. I'll learn the lines later!'"

"How did you buy three houses?"

"I don't know. I just did."

"And how do you know how to remodel and decorate them?"

"I don't know. I guess…they tell me?"

Karina leaned in, dipping a breadstick in pesto, pointing it at me like a stiletto.

"You *had* to do it, Kath. You *had* to—Because you—are 'The House Whisperer'."

CHAPTER 1

In The Beginning

She considers a field and buys it;
From her profits she plants a vineyard.
She girds herself with strength,
And strengthens her arms.
She perceives that her merchandise is good,
And her lamp does not go out by night.
She stretches her hands to the distaff,
And her hand holds the spindle.
She extends her hand to the poor,
Yes, she reaches out her hands to the needy.
She is not afraid of snow for her household,
For all her household is clothed in scarlet.
— Proverbs 31:16

I AM HOUSE

I am house
I am home

I was in my sixteenth
Winter the day she was
Born January the eighth
Away far where soil freezes

Not like here
Where the sun
Blesses burns punishes
Roofs and paint

She is on her way I
Said to the Spanish on
My right I feel her
The baby has no idea

That we houses know
Our owners years
Before they come
Up the walk

October 30, 1965 8 o'clock at nite

Dear Diary,

I did a secret thing. I put a message in a cocacola bottle inside the big hole in the kitchen. Then I plastered it up. Maybe someone will find my message in the little bottle in the wall, maybe a hundred years from now. Then they will know exactly what I was doing today.

This is my message.

My name is Kathy O'Brien. I am plastering a wall. I want to be playing football on our street with Peter and Terry. But I half to be here in this scary grey house on Clark Street. It stinks like cats and old people. The walls are a black stripe where the person touched the walls. I will have my own house one day. I will have a horse. In my backyard. He will be a black stallion with for wite feet and a star. I will be very happy. I will have my dog and a cat and maybe a turtle. And some fish. It is Halloween tomorrow. I hope I get a lot of Hershey bars for trick or treat. Thanks for reading my message.

Sincerely,

K. O.

November 1, 1968 7 o'clock at nite

Dear Diary,

It's kind of weerd when it happens. Like today at the old house. I gues when I like a house I half to go to the bathroom rite away. Empty houses usually do not have toilet paper. At leste there was some newspaper on the floor. I krumpled it up so it was softr.

When you're in an old house you do what you half to do.

My parents bot this house so they could fix it up and sell it. It smells like no one had the windows open for a long time. A blind lady lived here. It has oak cabinets in the dining room with mirors behind them. We are going to refinish the cabinets. We are going to take the mirors out. They are not originel. My job is to take the nobs off and save them in a jar.

I reely like this old house anyways. I don't know why. I know it is sik and it wants to get better. Every time we come here I half to go to the bathroom.

Maybe your stomak knows you like a house before your head does.

November 3, 1965 7 o'clock at nite

Dear Diary,

Dad says if we fix up two houses in a year and sell them we will be rich. He says if we fix up three houses in a year we will be very rich. I want to be very rich.

Mom says if you sit real quiet for a long time in a house the house tells you what it needs. Its like the house is sick and you are the doctor. You sit there by yourself and you walk around and you watch the light threw the windows. You watch the inside of the house like I watch my angelfish in the akwarium. Then you go home and think about the house and you go to sleep and then you go back there and you know what to do. A house is like a person or a dog. It has a job to do and it wants to do a good job. Mom says houses make you happy or sad it all depends. They should feel cozy and open at the same time. She says there should be something alive in each room like a plant or flowers in a vace. She says if you take care of a house the house will take care of you.

When we bought this house my dad walked around hard in his boots to see if the floor kreaked. He crawled under in the basement. He lifted up a corner of linoleum in the kitchen to see if there was wood under it. He found mapal. He was very happy then. He said he struk gold.

I got to do the cutting in around the corners of the walls and celing tonight. My arms are sore. You half to cut in and then you can roll paint. Otherwize you have holes in the color by the edges. Painting is not as easy as you think.

November 4, 1965 8 o'clock at nite

Dear Diary,

Mom says a house has to have gardens. Mom says a home without gardens is like a picture without a fram. Today we turned up the gardens. No one dug there in a lot of years. The dirt was as hard as a driveway. I jumped up and down on the shovle like a pogo stick. We made a pile of bulbs. They look like old ded potatos but Mom says they are irises. They are heavy so they are alive. Ded bulbs are lite. We found little ones she said they are krokusses. We put pork chop bones and dry leafs and more ded leafs and nitro-humus in each hole where we planted the bulbs. We broke the iris apart because they grew all over each other. We planted them in the back of the garden close to the house because they are tall. We put the krokus in the front because they are short. Tomorrow we will plant baby evergreens right next to the house so there will be green even when there is snow. They will keep the house warmer in the winter and cooler in the summer. We dug up a lot of grass to make the gardens bigger. Most people make gardens to close to the house then it looks crowded like a person with to tight of clothes. We put even eggshells and ashes from the fireplace in there in the holes. Now the roots can have dinner whenever they are hungry. We took our gloves off. Mom says you half to touch the bulbs with your hands. When they feel your skin they know you mean buziness. We covered them with dirt but not too much. Iris want to be close to the top. Then you put wood chips on so the plants have a blanket when it gets cold. Then you water and water until the sweet smell of the dirt comes up. Every time we come here we will water. But we will not see the flowers in the spring. Someone else with more money than us will own this house by then. And we will be fixing up the next one.

CHAPTER 2
The Deal

I AM HOUSE

I am house
I am home

I was born of an
Idea when war was in
The air and fear of an invader and
His army of brown shirts drifted across the ocean

Huddled in normalcy
Crouched bent weak from
Surviving the Depression
They warned my first one

You could lose everything if
You build that house but
She drew plans
For me

Big
Windows
Corner Light high
Ceilings to defy anything small

February 4, 2005 5:00 a.m.

I dreamt I bought an old mansion. I didn't know how it happened. I'd bought it sight unseen. I should say, it became mine—sight unseen. I went there and no one knew that I was the owner. It had a big theatre in it and a vast open living room. The foyer was a lobby. Objects from my past were on tables, ready to mount in glass cases like a museum; an old iron that had been used to press costumes; a miniature car and toys; things that had been left, discarded.

People were milling around like the show would start soon but they didn't know when? I was unrecognized. Then one man's voice rang out, "Kathy?" He cornered me to share his ideas for the remodel. I was busy getting away from him and the others who wanted their questions answered about what I was going to do with the place? I needed to be anonymous, to take a day before I started solving problems; while I took it all in, wishing that they would leave.

There was a family living upstairs—an older man with a white beard and his two sons. I stood at an apron farm sink and finished washing dishes that had been left in cold grey water, looked out a window at a pond that needed water, was too shallow. It was full of baby koi fish. Other mansions surrounded this one. The grounds were vast, like a park.

"Those were the days when they built places like this," I mused as I walked the yard.

When another young man who reminded me of an angel appeared next to me, I confessed, "I can't believe I inherited this place, that this is all for me?"

February 4, 2005 8:30 p.m.

I hadn't been up to the mountain in a long time. With no dogs, well, it's different without dogs. They say when you go out in the desert or up on the mountain, you take a gun or a dog or both. Today I didn't have the gun, either. Weeds that were at my knees last time were staring me in the face. Anise seven feet tall waved as I walked by.

There was no plan to go that high. Today, for reasons I could not understand, I had no choice but to go into a wild place. Above the trail, grass invited, green as a pasture under live oaks. I crawled, pulled branches, slipped often scaling that hill, catching my breath under the oldest tree until I was scanning my neighborhood, the San Fernando Valley.

I had to get far away. I couldn't be around people, be on that moving map. I wanted direction, a sense of a shape of—what is to come. Something's been knocking on my door, telling me that things are about to change.

On soft new growth, in a place that only the deer know, what was revealed stopped me, cold. Not in words, but in a way intuitive, with events "mapped out," it went like this: I would only be in the second house another nine months or so. It was to be made ready to be a rental. I would be moving—not far—but it would be like traveling to another country. Things would shift—jobs, plans. This would put me to the ultimate test. I was being readied to walk into a bigger life, another world.

Moving? But not far? Another world? What did this mean? I'm home now at the kitchen table, making a list of things to do around here before whatever-it-is happens. I still have some boxes, unpacked. Maybe I should leave them that way?

My jeans are stained green and brown from the climb. There's dirt under my nails. I kind of like that, having some of the mountain still on me.

July 29, 2005 7:00 p.m.

Was it vacant? I'd never seen it before. I'd patrolled those streets for decades. Why had I never noticed that house? Veiled behind trees and bushes, it looked abandoned. The walls hadn't seen paint in forty years. The roof was missing wood shingles. I made my way up the curving stone walk, wedged my business card in the door.

"Feel free to call me any time with real estate questions," I scribbled on the back. What I really wanted to say was, "Are you alive in there? Do you need help?"

I knocked. No answer. Either no one lived there or the person who did was struggling. One of the living room windows was cracked, with an opening big enough for a cat to walk through. Inside, a grand piano squatted, its ebony lid raised like a car's hood. Small house, I guessed. Two bedrooms, one bath, sandwiched on an odd, triangular shaped lot.

If a house can look homeless, this one did.

August 13, 2005 10:00 p.m.

I went to look at another house today, the third this week. I think it's the one. Oh, my gosh. I can't believe I'm going to do this. It's in the same neighborhood where I saw that really old one, where people keep horses in their yards, near the bridle trails that go up into the mountains.

I'm going to write an offer on it. It's really beautiful, with two stories, three bedrooms, two and a half baths, 1850 square feet, on a 6750 lot. The address? 619 South Spring Street. I could lie in bed and see my stallion down in his corral in the back yard. I could sit at the top of the stairs and admire black granite kitchen counters. It's an adult-all-dressed-up and ready-to-go-party-house.

August 15, 2005 9:00 p.m.

The son of a bitch seller refused my offer. It was $9,000 under asking, contingent on the sale of my two houses, which I know I could move very fast. I'm writing another offer—full price.

August 16, 2005 10:00 p.m.

That seller wrote "REJECTED" in red ink on page one—across all the numbers. I drove by the place three times today. My car gets sucked over there. I'm cruising it! I don't stalk men, but I'm all over 619 South Spring Street. I totally saw my friends and me partying over there. I wrote full price and he said, "No."

Shit.

August 17, 2005 9:00 p.m.

Someone told me once that God has three answers when you don't get something you want:

1. "Yes."
2. "Not now, I'm working on it."
3. "I have something better."

I can't imagine anything better than 619 South Spring Street.

September 9, 2005 11:58 p.m.

I think I have a cricket in the house. Maybe I have two or three here in the family room. They're playing shrill songs on strange violins—Their salute to fall, cooler weather, change—and risks.

First risk: Showing up at Harry Winston's in Beverly Hills. I was on the hunt to try on my dream ring. Sometimes your subconscious needs a shot in the arm, proof that the thing—whatever it is—exists. I was sure they wouldn't have it. The surprise? They actually let me inside. A burly Latin man in a navy sports jacket that stretched tight over his arms fumbled with the lock. An even bigger man stood up next. Two gorgeous women with perfect long hair were sitting behind identical desks like Afghan hounds.

This was an act of courage. I was in old jeans and a T-shirt. Even worse, the mortal sin, my nails weren't done.

"It has three ovals," I described to the brunette on the left, feeling as small as Dorothy talking to the wizard.[1] "I saw it on a billboard at Christmastime a few years ago." They nodded in unison. When one woman disappeared, I asked the first door man, "So, how's your day going?"

He seemed pleased that anyone was interested. "Really good. 'Yours?"

Yes, they did have it. My diamond ring came out in a flat black satin box. The three stones fought each other for light and position. It slid easily on my right hand, thank you very much. Whoever said that seven karats is too much should be shot? I'd need a size 5.5. The ring was a six.

She explained why it was set in platinum. "E' quality diamonds absorb what they're around."

"I can relate."

"Now, yellow diamonds, they set in gold."

"The price?"

"Twenty-seven thousand dollars."

"Okay, fine."

"Yellow diamonds, a bit more. They are rare."

"Of course. I'll keep that in mind."

"If not now, maybe later?" My helper, my accomplice, surmised as I relinquished the ring to its velvet cushion.

---

1. *The Wonderful Wizard of Oz*, Frank L. Baum.

Crossing the intersection I spotted a silver haired man in an opalescent blue Mercedes roadster. Once upon a time, his $100,000 car was shapeless metal. Once upon a time, way before that, my diamond ring was black coal.

September 11, 2005 3:30 p.m.

Second risk: Pruning the live oak. It was ceremonial, like trimming the first curls off a baby's hair. It takes vision to prune a tree. You have to see it hundreds of years from now. The deal is you have to not screw it up. After this I have an even greater respect for what The Creator does. It's not what's added that matters, it's what's removed. Think about it. He never says, "Whoops! 'Cut too much over there!"

One day when I was I was eight or nine, Uncle Horace and I walked up to a fruit tree.

"You have to prune it so a bird could fly through it." He pointed, frowning at tiny branches growing up through the center. "These are called 'suckers,'" he said. "They 'suck' the life out of a plant. If you want a lot of fruit, these have to go."

Today I got rid of the live oak's suckers. Now the grey skin is wrinkly and exposed, open to light. I stepped back, grateful that I'd been allowed to practice on common apple, persimmon, and nectarine, so that one day when I was in front of the Rolls Royce of trees, holding branch clippers, I would know what to do.

After I dropped the shears I lay on my back, looking up through her branches into open sky. I swear I heard the tree sigh. This opened the door to a vision: I let myself see the perfect house. I let myself think bigger, better than 619 South Spring Street. *Bette*r than Spring Street?

Out loud, I described my imaginary place to Him:

"It's a big, double-sized lot, with old trees or room enough to plant big boxed ones. I see hardwood floors, doors opening to the yard—pool, pond, stables with turnout corrals. There might be a guest house that I rent out to help pay the mortgage. Gracious, grand, open as a loft, cozy as a cottage, I will dance there, fantasize, sit by the fireplace. Friends and I will play croquet on the lawn, dine around a table under an umbrella, eat and laugh, raise glasses.

"I want to be able to fix it up just that way I want it," I added, to the One who hears all, wondering if He was listening? "I dare You to bring this to me. I don't think You can do it. I fucking dare You!"

September 15, 2005 8:00 p.m.

I was early at the Board of Realtors meeting. This is a rare occurrence. I was only there to sniff out the new listings, to see if my future house might be on the roster? Today the buyer I was looking for—was me. I claimed a seat next to Jack Whiting, who used to be my partner, until he went "corporate" with Keller Williams.

"Morning," he said, handing over a copy of the morning's caravan. Around us other brokers were grabbing hot coffee in paper cups, fondling donuts on napkins.

"Morning," I said, laying my wish out, front and center.

Third risk: Going public with a vision:

"We need to be on the lookout for a character 'fixer' big lot, equestrian zoned, near the horse trails."

Jack's eyes zoomed in on me over his readers.

"For a buyer?"

"For me. I want to bring my horse home."

"What price?"

"Eight."

"Hundred?"

"Right. Like I'm going to get into an estate for eight hundred dollars?"

September 16, 2005 4:45 p.m.

I don't know why I made a left on Birchwood. Long week, tired, not thinking, I drove past that contemporary two story for sale at a million three, past the Old Spanish that faces the park, the one that I used to sit in front of and pine over like an unavailable man. Another right, and there it was—the old house, the same brown house where I'd left my business card in the door a few weeks before. *I'd forgotten all about it.* Today it had a long green Dumpster in the driveway. A man wearing a surgical mask and an orange poncho was carrying things out of the front door. Lamps bristled stiffly above the debris.

Cue the realtor. I parked, smoothed my jacket, adjusted my pearls; spoke into the rear view mirror like it was a camera.

"This is my guy," I murmured, strapping holster to hip.

"You're working too hard!" I grinned, as we met on the walk.

He'd just placed his dad in a home. Mom was inside, wavering, not healthy.

"Finally I can throw out what my 'packrat' parents have accumulated! 'Finally!"

Salt and pepper, well-heeled forty plus, he didn't look away from my eyes. This was a lot to do and he was tackling it. As he spoke the mask slid down to his neck. It made him look like a doctor.

I said I'd stopped a few weeks ago for a few reasons: 1.) I wanted to know if whoever was in there was okay? 2.) I was wondering if they needed real estate help? 3.) I was interested in it for myself?

"The house needs everything, that's obvious," he sighed. "The back of the roof is 'thatch,' six inches deep with tree droppings from the past twenty years."

"Hardwood?"

"No, 'cement. My Dad lived for the past thirty years on

cement because he didn't want to spend money on carpet. 'Depression mentality."

"I get it."

We made our way to his car so he could give me a business card. Butch Connolly was a commercial realtor in San Diego. Yes, he would like a current market analysis.

Then I set sight on the man and fired.

Because in that second—in the loudest silence I ever experienced—*I knew that nothing was going to come between me and that house.*

"I can market it for you, but frankly—I'd rather buy it—myself."

"You've never been in this house."

"...That's correct."

Across the street, almost to my car, he tossed this, spiraling, arching high as a football.

"The best thing about the house is the lot." He waved up, past the roofline. "It goes all the way back to the horse trails."

Heart be still.

September 18, 2005 12:45 a.m.

This is one hell of a full moon. I hayed all the horses in the dark while the wedding reception was in full swing. Sixty people were dancing under a tent, glued around tables with yellow plastic tablecloths, under at least a trillion desert stars.

Everyone was busy partying and feeding time on the ranch had come and gone.

I drifted out of the crowd, tied up my long skirt, and used almost all of what was left of the hay. Horses nickered, inviting, standing near empty feed bins to show me, the feeble human, where to toss the flakes. Even in the moonlight I could see ribs.

Last was my horse. I filled Tyson's manger, hugged his neck, felt too much bone for winter coming on. His coat was dry and dull. He looked at me like he had something to tell me that he knew I couldn't understand. Something wasn't right. Mary and John always feed him well. What was going on?

"Do you want to come home?" I asked Tyson while he ate hay and the DJ played disco and glasses clinked and people laughed, loud and often. I leaned on the stallion and vowed, "I'm going to do something. I'm going to do something about this."

Two hours and one hundred miles later, when I was back in the city checking messages, I heard one from Butch.

"We're placing both my parents in a home. Yes, we're going to want to sell."

September 19, 2005 9:00 a.m.

I called Cooper today. Every girl needs a tall, dark, handsome mortgage broker. Boyfriends come and go in L.A., but a good lender, now that's hard to find. I leaked my secret. Unbelievably, the little two plus one on the tiny lot turned out to be a four plus three, 2750 square feet, on over a quarter of an acre, zoned for three horses.

"I want this house," I confessed, like Cooper was a priest. "I'm going to write 'no contingencies.' If I have to sell the other two later, I will."

For a time all I heard was silence while his fingers worked a calculator.

"We'll pull equity out of the others—it's going to be around four K a month."

"Iwanthishouse."

"I'll fax pre-approval over to you in five minutes."

"Cooper, do you think it's a good idea to buy a third house?"

"It's always a good idea to buy a third house, Kathy."

With Cooper's blessing I mounted up, signaling the troops to follow. This Queen was about to claim her kingdom. And she was going to need all the help she could get.

CHAPTER THREE

In Escrow

I AM HOUSE

I am house
I am home

Long before
This happened
The rot the rain
There was land

Near a river
Overflowed ponds
Shallow places
Where tadpoles swam

Cows grazed
I wanted to be born
There when I
Was a stack of lumber

Pieces parts waiting
All summer that winter
On palettes to
Be made whole

September 19, 2005 9:00 p.m.

It was dark in the office. Seventy desks, empty. Seventy computers, off. Seventy phones, silent. Even the late staying workaholic brokers had gone home. It was just me writing under a lone green accountant's lamp.

This house makes me feel like I am reuniting with a castle that I was forced to leave a long time ago. How is it that the worst house I've ever seen calls to me? Everything logical warns, "No! It's too far- gone! Run!" But something that flies above all is waving a banner that says, "This is the one! Free the David from the stone."

Michelangelo claimed the block of white carrara marble for his David after another artist had tried to sculpt it and failed, pronouncing the marble as flawed. The block lay untouched in a stoneyard for over forty years. Only Michelangelo knew that the boy with the sling was trapped in there. All he wanted was to free the David from the stone. Is Riverview my block of marble? Am I sent to free the life inside?

I picked up a pen, scratched a "9" and five zeros.

Another self, sitting very close, hissed, "Do you have any idea what you're getting us into?"

My hand trembled.

"No," I said. "I don't."

Terms: $90,000 down payment, $810,000 balance amortized over thirty years. I crossed out "physical inspection." I know it needs everything. I checked an "X" on buyer to cover cost of termite. I know it'll need tenting. Forget the home protection plan.

Just give me the keys.

September 21, 2005 5:00 a.m.

I mined my wallet for gas money, found four quarters.

"I'm trying to buy a new house and I only have a dollar for gas!" I relayed to the man behind the counter.

"Hey, if you can buy it, go for it!" he shrugged.

I know the man but have never asked his name. I see him every week when I fill up the tank after dance class. He's Russian, low profile, works a couple jobs, too. My guess is he's got apartment buildings, units, but keeps it quiet.

The red "E" light was off on the way home, a rare occurrence. Waiting in my mail box was a new equity line from Washington Mutual. I'll have $50,000 for improvements, $90,000 down. I can get in with a roof and maybe some plumbing. Cooper had worked his magic.

I cashed an $800 money order that I was going to send to the IRS, and had it reissued for the deposit. It's all the money I have. And, wow— *Like I'm getting into an estate for eight hundred dollars.*

"Will you be sending more money?" Butch inquired in his mannerly-proper-almost-English way. He could have said, "Eight hundred dollars down on a million-dollar estate? Are you crazy?"

"I'll get more later," I told him over my shoulder, galloping away.

"Bold," I decided, is not your average four-letter word.

September 22, 2005 4:45 a.m.

The house is bad. It's soaked in alcohol. Buying this house is like marrying an aging movie star—in rehab. Anything this dead will probably not live long and/or stay sober. Or will it? Could it? Vines thrust themselves through stucco. There's one an inch thick growing into the living room. Yes, the roof is a foot deep with droppings and pine needles. It's near the freeway and you can hear it. 'Bottom line? It needs a quarter of a million dollars.

Most people would say, "It's a tear down!"

"I can't show you everything because my Mom is still here," Butch, my host, confided in a low voice as he pushed the heavy entry door open ahead of us into a foyer that led into a living room that was as large as a ballroom, where a flat white marble fireplace stared at us blankly from the opposite wall. Under deco ceilings hand plastered, raised in the center, we filed along bookcases past a blue satin diva of a couch burdened with piles of old drapery, flanked by two yellow mohair chairs. The floors were raw concrete edged with lath, green carpet fibers from thirty years ago clinging from tacks like fur from long-dead animals. I'd been in garages more livable.

Around the corner we emerged into the library, the "head" of the house, with its own curving brick fireplace backing the one in the living room, under a vaulted beamed ceiling that belonged in a hunting lodge. Where was that stag's head? This is where men sank deep into leather chairs, bit off cigar tips, discussed whatever it is that men talk about when they're free of women's gazes.

"And, not to be missed—" Butch chuckled, pointing to a Dutch door, at what I thought was a closet, "The wet bar." He stepped inside, opened the top half of the door, exposing a ledge on the bottom half, and—viola—instant bar!

We were still cracking up when he pushed on a flimsy door with glass louvers which led us outside onto a rounded patio, our 'welcome mat' to the side yard.

That's when I stopped. Sprouting green and determined, two feet of fresh grass topped the rear roof like a fur hat. Was I in Switzerland? Where were the goats, grazing? I turned to him with an "are you seeing what I'm seeing" look?

We couldn't hold back. Neither of us could stop the flood of laughter. I thought I was going to fall down. I needed something to hold me up. I looked for a tree, anything, to lean on.

The sound of our voices boomed off the walls, echoing, "HA, HA, HA—" ricocheting in waves.

"My knees!" I choked, doubling over, panting. "Can you believe this?"

"My dad says, 'Hey, it took us *years* to develop this patina!'"

After we collected ourselves, his hand rested on another French door under the thatched roof.

"This—is going to be hard." He made a face. "Are you up for this? It's the worst of it. I mean, the whole house is bad, but this—"

The feeble half glass door sucked us into a room that could have been in a Halloween haunted house. We pawed our way through low-hanging cobwebs into a room with open beams like the library. The entire East wall was made up of dusty cracked French windows.

"This was my dad's workroom," he explained, looking at a pegboard wall full of tools and a raised table stacked with boxes and plastic bags. "He was an inventor. I mean, he is an inventor, and he used to play music. We have crates of scores, see?" He patted bulging cardboard.

The next room housed a twin bed and a dresser, more tables, and pile after pile of things wrapped and unwrapped, the debris of decades. A greasy dark patch on the wall testified to where the man had rested his head.

"How did he stay warm?" I puzzled as I noticed that most of the windows sagged, could not close.

I froze in the doorway of a bathroom where water was dripping into an ancient shower next to a crude Plexiglas window that was cut out, open to the hallway, shedding light on blackened walls.

"All rightie, then," I said turning away, instinctively holding my breath. "Okey-dokey."

An about face brought us back through that bedroom, and out a door into the backyard. We should have been armed with machetes. A jungle of overgrown wisteria and bamboo defied us to make our way to the pool, which, unbelievably, was perfect.

"They never swam in it, but they kept it pristine. It's a diving pool, twelve feet deep, see?" In all the degradation, the water sparkled, clear as an aquamarine. I looked down, feeling the backs of my knees tingle like I was about to fall. Holy cow. Twelve feet. No kidding.

"This is not a kiddie pool!"

"The shallow end is five feet deep!" he said, leaning on the corner of a small peaked-roof shed covered entirely with half-milled bamboo slats. "On a hot day, I'm sure you get the idea. See? He has a fridge in here. 'Party Central.'"

A 1950s round-top Frigidaire rested under the termite eaten roof. A familiar scent met my nose. It was "Gramps'" garage—motor oil, paint, and cold drinks on hot afternoons.

"Go get orange sodas from your Grandma." He'd growl.

There I was, eight or nine or ten, running across the lawn, past the apple tree, up the wooden stairs to the kitchen.

"Grandma, could I have some sodas?"

My grandmother would take a break from rolling a piecrust or washing dishes and hand over the prizes—two ice cold bottles. Back in the garage Gramps would pop the lids on the handle of the old drawer, the one filled with baby-food jars of nuts and bolts. Side-by-side, we'd sit in folding chairs.

"Gramps, tell me about the time you drove the milk wagon." I'd say.

"Oh, I was about your age and I had to take over. I was all by myself. I had to drive that horse—he was a big dapple grey, a Percheron—all the way up Lake Shore drive—back to the barn in Bay View."

"I'm going to get a horse one day," I'd promise. "And *you're* going to teach him to drive."

"We'll keep him in your garage," Gramps collaborated. "And you can ride him over here to visit."

"He'll be black, four whites and a star."

"Lotta chrome," Gramps nodded, surveying his kingdom, the yard, fruit trees. "Get a horse with a lotta white on him—A lotta chrome. So you can seem him in the dark."

"This was the 'Tiki House,'" Butch chuckled, stroking some of the bamboo, not knowing he was pulling me back into the present. "Gilligan's Island!"

We had come to the end of the property line. On the other side of the rusty cyclone fence stretched a twenty-foot pile of lumber, branches and discarded cement pieces, backed by uneven mounds of soil. Beyond that stretched eleven acres of open field spotted with a few dedicated trees.

Called "Cow Field," because legend has it, a rancher used to graze his longhorns there, the "field" wrapped itself around the back of fifteen other properties, some with pipe horse corrals jutting out into the meadow like piers on a lake. A quarter of a mile away at the other end was the old Cow Horn furniture factory, which spread out flat and grey as a prison. In the thirties, it really was a furniture plant, manufacturing baby rockers and cribs. Then one day someone got an idea to use radio and then television, the new wonder media, to make commercials for the cribs. The commercials did so well that quickly there was more return in making film products than wooden ones. Everyone still calls the company "Cow Horn," even though the official name was altered to "Cow Horn Productions."

"I used to ride my horse back here on the trails," I told Butch. "I don't know, thirteen years ago, when I boarded him nearby. I'd look at these corrals, right here—at this yard—and say, "Wouldn't it be great to live—there"?"

"If it weren't for Cow Horn, it would look like a park."

"I heard they have one of the baby cribs, bronzed, in the lobby?"

"True," he said. "I saw it."

"I guess in Hollywood, even companies 'want to direct?'" We broke up again, hanging on the wire mesh like two monkeys at the zoo. It was right about then that something serious happened to my stomach. Trying to sound causal, I asked, "Do you mind if I use the restroom?"

"It's not the best, but I think it works," Butch ventured as he took much too long to lead us up the overgrown driveway through a side door, into a service porch longer than my first apartment in New York. I happened to look up at the ceiling. A hole large enough for a grown man to fall through was a gaping a full view of the attic. Water-stained wood glared down at us.

"They never fixed the roof after the big earthquake, so this is what happened to the plaster. The water ate it away, like cancer."

I was about to say, "Could we hurry?" when Butch rounded the corner, opened yet another door into a bathroom with the same hot, stale scent as the one I ran from with black mold. "When did that bomb go off?" I worried, seeing a wall chiseled away, exposed pipes, charred wood.

"Only the finest decorating touches here!" he quipped, his hand displaying galvanized intestines, a door grooved deep from the incessant scratching of a dog, with grey electrical tape crisscrossing ancient linoleum.

"They held this place together with gaffer's tape," I muttered.

"Where's Tennessee Williams when you need him?" I teased, at our last stop, the kitchen. When turquoise was the color du jour, this early 60's remodel must have wrapped its walls around some gala parties, women in flared hemlines making dramatic turns, cigarette holders in hand, lively chatter, a piano playing favorites, Frank Sinatra crooning from the record player. They were thirty-something, immortal, floating high on dry martinis, and a world of possibilities. There was plenty of time to do it all, at least once, wasn't there?

"There's a reason the house looks this way," Butch said, holding his hands out. The left was smaller, fingertips shrunken from the joints up. "I was electrocuted in the backyard one day.

They sent me out to start the barbecue. I started playing with a rake and the power lines. I was eight. Seven out of eight doctors told them to amputate. They went with the eighth. They didn't have medical insurance. It took all they had. After that my dad drank and didn't come out of the house for eight years. I left when I was sixteen." His voice trailed off as he took a long look out of the window. "I dodged tumblers full of vodka in this kitchen," he added, with the intimacy shared only between strangers. "—By my mother."

Then I understood. It hadn't all been about parties and swing dancing. It was about survival.

"I grew up in alcoholism, too," I confessed, staring down on degenerating linoleum, at more silver tape wrinkled as elephant skin. "Alcohol burned us to the ground."

He nodded, head bowed, like he was praying over a grave.

September 24, 2005 9:00 p.m.

"Another house?"

There was no easy way to say it. So I said it.

"Peggy, I'm buying another house. I'm moving."

She chewed on the information. We were at the base of her driveway, where we'd solved at least ten million issues over the past twenty years. Across the street from my first house and my second, there was something about being there with Peggy, the way she took a literal stand— always barefoot, no matter how cold it was—that made the insurmountable, well, surmountable.

"Where?"

"The horse district."

She needed the whole scoop. A master of details, skilled in relaying facts, Peggy's thirty years in a bank had served her well. She knew the players and their numbers.

"When are you moving in?"

"First week in November."

"I'm happy for you," she said. "I know you wanted the other one, which was it?"

"Spring Street."

"You were mad about that."

"This is so much better. It's everything on the list."

Enter another neighbor, Sally, who lives four houses down.

"Kathy's moving," Peggy announced.

Sally cocked her head. "Far?"

"The horse district," we chorused.

"Don't forget us." Peggy said.

"How long have we been standing here in this driveway?" I asked.

"When did you move in?" was Sally's question.

"85."

"Twenty years," Peggy nodded. "Wow, twenty years."

"You know what's funny?" I confessed to the two women who had become aunts, friends, and mothers. "I'm buying my third house and I don't even have money for peanut butter."

September 25, 2005 10:00 p.m.

Today a hand-sized package wrapped in blue tissue paper was waiting on the front stoop, trussed up in a pink ribbon. The card read, "Now you'll always have peanut butter." It was signed, "Peggy and Sally."

Inside was a jar of Skippy Super Chunk—my favorite.

September 26, 2005 5:45 a.m.

I don't know what to do. Is this house temptation or gift? In the quiet I wrote a letter to God. "Spell things out for me! You made me blonde. You have to make it clear! Here I am with two novels almost complete that hardly anyone knows about. I thought that You wanted me to get busy publishing? If I buy this house, that'll be delayed. What would You have me do? I can let this deal pass. I can walk from this. Make it clear! Spell it out in black and white!"

I burned the letter outside on the patio under the last of the fading stars. When I came in, I flipped the Bible open. It fell to Romans 15:13.

Now may the God of hope fill
you with all joy and peace in
believing, that you may abound in
hope by the power of the Holy Spirit.

Oh yeah, the Holy Spirit will bring clarity and make the way safe. Of course He will. He's got wings.

September 26, 2005 11:30 p.m.

A pigeon landed on my car today. I saw it hovering, suspended, like it was deciding where to go. Then it zeroed in on my roof and—bingo it came in like a helicopter. I was at a stoplight downtown, on Alameda and 20th Street. I opened the sunroof to see it better. Then the bird tilted its head like it wanted to see me better. It looked right in at me! It's said that when an animal makes eye contact with you, it's trying to tell you something. In that moment it becomes your totem, your teacher, and its traits are given to you.

"Maybe it's injured?"

I reached up and, for a moment, held powdery soft feathers until it slipped out of my hand, unfazed, wings slapping in low, easy swoops.

A pigeon landed on my car today? 'Interesting.

I drove home still not knowing. Should I buy the old house? Did the bird know something? Was Someone trying to deliver a message (on a pigeon, no less!) There were a lot of cars downtown. Why did he pick mine? Deep inside my cave, combing Rocky, my cat, on the family room floor, the phone rang. Who knew I was hiding out?

Teddy. She got my message about "Do I buy the 'Biggest Fixer?'"

"You gotta do it! But you do it different than you did the other two. I've bought fixers. I moved in; 'took a year to do it. When I had money for cement, I did a driveway. When I had money for windows, I got 'em. I stayed a year in one place with bare plank floors and a Porta Potty. 'And that expensive plumber? Forget him! You get three quotes, you go with the best. Remember, FOR TWO YEARS, IT'S GOING TO SUCK! Hey—" She decided, "The worst that happens is you sell one of your houses!"

Ten minutes later as I walked into the real estate office, another phone rang.

"Kathy," Butch's voice said, "I don't think that house is livable. The neighbors are offering me seven seventy-five. What do you think about eight?"

I stopped to check my breathing. A one hundred thousand-dollar *reduction*? Forget nine? How about *eight*?

"Eight's my lucky number!" I stuttered. "I'll negate the prior offer, FedEx a new one."

Eight hundred thousand on the twenty-sixth of September. Two plus six equals eight. Close of escrow scheduled for November the 8th— of course.

Later, when Teddy and I were walking into Bob's Big Boy, we ran into another "good witch" pal, Abby, who was on her way out.

"The eighth? Eight represents eternity," Abby smiled in a magical way, flipping her dread locks over a shoulder. "—And unlimited abundance."

Then I shared about "Mr. Pigeon."

"Pigeons survive in environments where nothing else could live. They *flourish* where anything else would die. Cackling, she reached over, shaking my shoulder. "A pigeon? On your car? In traffic? I mean, *on* your car?"

"Like the effing Holy Ghost!" I laughed.

"Did I tell you the place has a library?" I mentioned to Teddy as we settled in a booth.

"Oh, I can see you up there, on the tall ladder, the one with rolling wheels. I can hear it— "Sh-h-h-h…" "Kathy?" she acted out, pointing, "Could you get me that book way up there?' I can see you with your glasses on, 'Sh-h-h-h…sliding along—'"

"Teddy," I cautioned, like I was clutching a door knob but not opening it, "It's got vines growing into the living room as thick as your finger! No one's done anything to that house for forty years!"

"Good. No layers."

"What?"

"When you paint, it'll be easier. No layers."

Opened to: *…he saw heaven being torn open and the Spirit descending on him like a dove.*

October 1, 2005 10:36 p.m.

"Kathy!" Butch's voice called, sounding an alarm. "Come over to the house, quick! My mother fell last night and broke her ankle! They took her to the hospital. She's not coming back."

"I want you to know I haven't been sticking pins into little dolls that look like your mother!" I joked, offering my hand half an hour later as he ushered me inside.

"She fell walking across the lawn to the neighbors," Butch explained as he led me to the doorway of the master bedroom that I hadn't seen. Surrounding a hospital bed were pyramids of medication containers. They seemed to multiply as we watched.

"She takes a lot of medication."He said.

"I see."

"It's easy for her to get confused."

"I'll bet."

"I need to tell you something else."

"What's that?"

He blinked, facing me with a deal breaking look.

"The place has rats."

"Really?"

"A lot of them."

"No kidding? And they don't pay rent?"

He laughed, relieved.

"Good. I'll make ratatouille."

We signed off on the tailgate of his SUV with addendums holding him harmless from pestilence, plague, and decades of neglect. It was "as is" on a whole new level.

Staring down at all of those zeros was like looking down at the ground from 29,000 feet.

October 2, 2005 4:00 p.m.

I got scared—again. I needed a sign. A big sign. The "go." The green light. Tossing, turning, wrapping, unwrapping, under my blankets, I was running, under attack from the fear that I didn't have enough "army" to fight this war.

I got up, patrolled the kitchen, lit a blue candle, and did my nails. Then I followed an urge to go outside.

In my robe out on the sidewalk I lingered, looking up to Heaven.

And then I saw it.

A shooting star.

A shot. A flash. A blaze of burning white. Did I really see it? Yes, I did. It reassured me. I calmed down instantly. Someone was in charge of the universe, and all those stars. It was pretty amazing that it turned up just then, in that neighborhood of the night sky like a signature: A private showing by special invitation from a big time Co-Signer.

CHAPTER FOUR
Thanksgiving

I AM HOUSE

I am house
I am home

The feast is in
The yard men eat and
Laugh I could
Fly

Free now if my feet
Were not concrete I
Have new life a roof
But I am afraid

I will never be the
Same I was used to infection old
Timbers water soaked
I tell her stop hurting me when

She walks in me late
At night after
The music
Stops

October 19, 2005 11:30 p.m.

It was the property line stand off. Still legged, hair up on our backs, we squared. One day Edith Goldstein, my new next-door neighbor, and I may be friends, but not tonight. I happened to be at the big house when I heard scuffling, women's voices, and then there they were, three of them crowding my front porch.

Assembled were Edith, her partner Jasmine, and another woman named Scarlett. There wasn't much chitchat. Edith wanted the lowdown. She stood much too close, delivered the first punch, an uppercut.

"Are you single?"

(Why? You wanna date me?) "Yes," I said, dodging the blow.

"Do you want to build onto the fence?"

(You mean the broken-down thing between our houses that Butch told me you were supposed to finish with the money they gave you—and you didn't?) "Maybe?"

"About that pile of wood and stuff in the back—" she began, glancing down at the ground like she was talking about a relative they'd kept chained, in the cellar.

(Ah, that pile? The mound Butch mentioned that you were supposed to have hauled away after the fence you were supposed to finish was done?) I played dumb, dancing backwards. I wanted her to work for this.

"Oh, yeah, what's up with that?"

She thought "we" could haul it away?

I caught her with a warning pop on the shoulder. Bam! "How much of 'we' am 'I'?"

"About half."

"I see."

I stood my ground, gloves up over my face.

Edith dove in, pummeling.

"You'll have Dumpsters and you could, well, whenever you have one, I know these workers, I pay them ten dollars an hour—" She took a breath, dropping her fists.

I could have landed one on her chin. I should have hit her. For some reason, I didn't. Was it kindness? Or did I not want her blood on my gloves?

"I'll think about it."

"Or we could ask the city to pick it up?"

Fat fucking chance. Was she smoking crack? The City didn't care about Cow Field. It wasn't an official 'park.' That land was as discarded as an old tin can—Los Angeles property left over from when the freeway was built. Pick up our trash? I don't think so.

"Do you have any more questions?"

(God forbid you should ask me how I am or how the remodeling is going?)

"Hey, I'm from New York," Edith squirmed, twisting a long red braid, her voice rasping like a chain dragging on gravel.

Saved by the bell, they flew out on their broomsticks. Two minutes later I called Butch.

"They were the second offer, the $775,000. But I wanted you to have it. She's bitter she lost out. That pile of junk? I'm having another Dumpster delivered. After I fill it with my stuff, you can use it for the yard, anything you want."

October 20, 2005 7:00 p.m.

He pulled up in a ten-year-old white Ford pickup. Worn pointed cowboy boots stepped out under equally faded Levi's, attached to a deep voice that came from Texas or someplace where buildings and words aren't close together. A few minutes in that vacant house with him and I knew Gregg was my carpenter, my man.

"I'm not closed escrow yet, 'haven't moved in. They still have some things to clear out. Unbelievably, he trusts me to have keys so I can get a start," I said, leading him to a shaky makeshift wall dividing the master suite's barely painted, "cabinet" which connected to the bathroom through a sawed-out hole in the wall. This evidently, made grabbing towels easier.

"It isn't a bearing wall," Gregg appraised, barely concealing his amusement. "It's easy to take down."

I watched his fingers make contact with plaster. The house warmed to his touch like an animal. Wood, I could tell, obeyed him.

Our next stop was the round cement slab outside of the library.

"Could you make a covered porch with a beamed ceiling that looks like an extension of the library?" I asked, handing him a photo of a screened veranda I'd torn out of a magazine years before. "Roof's going on in a week. We need to be done—before."

Gregg did something with his lips that made me wonder if he was no stranger to chewing tobacco—and nodded. A carpenter's tape hit the floor with a clang.

"A door here and here," I demonstrated. "I don't know how to do these things. I've been up too many nights at three a.m. lately. I've never taken on a project this big. I feel like I'm going to break. I can't do this by myself."

"Oh," he grinned. "You can do anything to a house. Anything you want."

October 28, 2005 10:00 p.m.

Cue the next actor, Gregg's friend Lucio, the plumber. Lucio comes from Mexico, where they build everything out of nothing. If Gregg is "The Man," Lucio is "The Other Man." After he crawled up in the attic, flushed a toilet or two, he unrolled "the map"—at least the way he saw the next attack.

"We lay new pipes incoming, in the attic. Sewer pipes I have to cut through the slab."

Photos of open-heart surgeries flashed through my brain, ribcages pulled apart, tubes, everywhere, bodies taken close to death.

"*Through* the slab?"

"We cut, dig a trench, almost three feet deep, cover it up, pour new cement."

"What happens with the old pipe?"

"We take it out. Or we leave it, bury it."

I was feeling faint.

"Through the slab?"

"It's very dirty. But it has to be done."

"Of course. Of course," I agreed, wondering how I could afford food with a house this diseased? My home needed open heart surgery and operations are expensive. I don't even have the funds to pay the five thousand dollars for closing costs. I'm walking blind.

Lucio's warm brown eyes took me in like a surgeon's. I looked down at his hands. They were holding a broken piece of galvanized pipe that he'd pulled easily out of one of the walls. Those hands told me that Lucio could do the impossible. Pipe, I could tell, obeyed him.

"When can you start?"

"Tomorrow," he said. "I can start tomorrow."

October 29, 2005 11:00 p.m.

A third actor called his lines in from offstage today. It was an improv. I didn't expect to hear Butch's voice.

"Could we close escrow early?" he asked, sounding defeated. "I'll pay your PITI until the day we were supposed to close."

"Why?" I asked, realizing that the amount would equal five thousand dollars. "You want closure?"

"Exactly," he exhaled. "I've got too many things going on."

Close early? Was that me, wondering how I would ever pay my closing costs?

October 30, 2005 9:00 p.m.

Sally and Robert, her husband, walked in like they forgot their hazmat suits. She held a bottle of Clorox spray in front of her like a loaded revolver. Robert toted a brown paper bag full of bagels. If she was the sniper, he was the Red Cross.

"I heard the place has rats," she stated, her eyes darting like a wild animal.

"It did. A lot of them. But not anymore. Not after they tented it."

"Are there, you know—bodies?"

"No."

"Droppings?"

"Oh, yes!"

"Where would that be?"

"Where the stove was."

"Show me." Sally gritted her teeth as I led them around the table in the living room stacked with paint cans, blue tape, sandpaper, rollers and brushes. Their eyes widened as they took in the slick greasy black rectangle on the kitchen floor where a stove had squatted which was coated in hair and, yes, droppings.

"The Connollys had plenty of friends here." I sighed. " My guess is not all of them had names."

"Canyoubelievethis?" they said in unison.

"Did they live here long?" Robert questioned, his fist tightening on the bag.

"Forty years, I think. The neighbors called it the 'Addams' Family's House' because they never saw them in the light of day."

"You really did it this time!" Sally said. "I take my hat off to you."

Robert offered the bagels on the run behind him, like a baton, saying something about how they hoped I liked blueberry. Tour over; we stood at their car taking in the dry façade of the old house.

"Be sure to spray before you sweep," she said in a maternal way. "I'd spray twice if I were you."

October 31, 2005 12:15 a.m.

It feels like days since I've written in this journal. I make fits and starts, see moments of things completing, touch new paint, smell fresh plaster, go back and forth to the house sometimes late at night when the workers' radios are quiet, feeling more ghost than human, listening to what the house has to say.

But today felt real. We stacked wood. We carried cement. June, Arturo, Victor and I kicked butt. The "pile" out back is gone. With one feeble dolly (I would have killed for a good wheelbarrow;) "Or even a sled!" June joked) one more mountain got moved by a couple of real- life Davids. There wasn't a Goliath in the house.

When June and I drove up to Avis in the morning and asked some men to help us, a man named Roberto came along with a man named Victor. Roberto took one look at the debris behind the shed and decided he had another moving job he had to get to. Arturo, a third man, replaced him. Arturo looked too slight to work hard. I judged him wrong.

At lunch time we ate burritos on the planter around the shade tree in the side yard. Arturo and June found out they were both grandparents. With a warm Español accent, Arturo said aging was "psychological." His teeth were very white, his eyes so blue they looked fake. Arturo didn't take any lip from wooden beams and chunks of cement. About an hour into it, he found a baby grass snake and held it up. I asked him to let it go in the grass. He lowered his hand for a gentle release.

Victor was tall and lean, like the Indian in *One Flew over the Cuckoo's Nest.* He lifted pieces to his shoulder for the long trek down the driveway, walking in a regal way, defying gravity. He mentioned he'd painted a lot of homes around here. In our broken Spanish, we tried to make them feel at home. They were curious about the people who had lived there, and why the place had grass growing on the roof?

The Dumpster filled in no time. The new branch clippers I bought came in handy. I would have, well, my kingdom for a wheelbarrow, like I said. On and on the four of us worked, armfuls tossed, piled high.

I applauded the two men when we returned.

"They were all puffed up, proud." I told June at sunset, as she and I leaned on the same cyclone fence Butch and I had hung on, admiring freshly cleared land.

One of Edith's horses and a goat reached through the corral pipes, sniffing at the new open space, ears flicking back and forth, until the goat made a sound like a loud sneeze and trotted away, fat belly waddling, tail erect.

"Are you going to tell your new neighbor about this?" June prodded, watching the spotted horse reach his neck farther to catch a whiff of fresh ground.

"No, I want her to notice all on her own."

The next task was moving the boxes of books from the living room to a bedroom on the west side of the house. It was part of the deal: Butch said, "You get the house, but you have to give twenty-five boxes of books away." I kept a 2003 thoroughbred stallion directory and a World Atlas. The rest are on their way to charity.

"You know," June confided as we stacked the last box, "I started praying to God for money like you said you do, like He's my—'rich boyfriend.' You told me it's working for you, so I—and the first time I did it, two minutes later, the phone rang. It was you, asking me to help you with this job! That was fast!"

"Yeah, He works fast sometimes," I said. "It's almost scary."

It was dusk when I found the "thing." I didn't know what it was at first. Deep in the cobwebbed back room, I moved something, and there it was, layered in plastic bags, wrapped in gauze like a mummy, soaked in red bandages. It had to be blood. It was a human head!

"Oh, no!" I tried to call June but no sound came out. "June!" I managed a yelp.

"What is it?" she asked when she ran up and froze at my side.

"I don't know!"

"Is it blood? It looks like a head." Take off the bandages!"

"You take off the bandages!"

She squirmed. "It's your head!"

"Fuck!" I lifted cotton wrapping, cracking it off in sections.

"Is it blood?"

"Heck if I know. Hold my hand."

June obliged. I peeled more fabric with my other hand.

"Holy shit! It's clay. Red clay!"

"It's a bust of someone—Human size. What are you going to do with it?"

"Well," I stepped back, breathing again. "It's going to make a really bad ashtray!"

Then it came to me. I knew exactly what to do with a human head. Cross the street and donate it to my kitty-corner neighbor's collection. That man, Stewart, had a yard full of dead bodies, along with zombies crawling out of his cellar. Word has it that he is a big time director. With him, this holiday was a major event.

"I'll take it to my neighbor. He's over-the-top into Halloween."

At arm's length I carried the man's head quickly across the street into Stewart's open garage, anonymously donating it onto a workbench next to a bloody vinyl severed hand and foot, walking past the living room window where an entire skeleton family seated at a café table were dining on succulent eyeballs and brains on the half skull, with a black cat and rat begging below.

There's nothing like clearing body parts out of your new house on Halloween. Come to think of it, it is my house. I closed escrow today, but I was too tired to celebrate or do anything about it.

November 15, 2005 10:35 p.m.

No kidding it's twelve feet deep. When I came back from work the pool was almost drained. The pump was sucking air. It wasn't supposed to be working. I unplugged it when I left for the day. A dry pump is a dead pump, means I could owe the rental place for a new one. Who the hell? I pulled the plug, was running down the steps into the cement canyon when over the edge, an old man's silver-bearded face appeared.

"How's it going? How's the pool?" It was Tony, my across-the-street neighbor, the one I shook hands with about two weeks ago, the man who has six cars parked around his house like a wagon train. The person who Butch disclosed has a lot of tools.

"Someone plugged the pump back in! It was almost dry!"

"It was me."

My face melted hot and my underarms began to burn.

"I didn't want it to run out of—"

The man cut me off with a gaze that told me he was no stranger to dealing with beautiful, strong-willed women.

"Wasn't it nice of me to do that?"

I bit my tongue so hard I could taste blood. One day Tony Manicetti and I might be friends, but not today. The man has tools. I have a decrepit house. Today was no day to burn a bridge I hadn't even crossed.

"Thank you," I coughed.

"You're welcome," he answered with a hat- tipping nod. "Why are you draining the pool?"

"I want to bring my horse home. I want stables."

"Your horse doesn't do the backstroke?"

Above us roofers were stripping the last of the petrified wooden shingles. These were the destroyers, heavy-boned, low-browed men sent to make way, to clear. With long-handled scrapers they decimated, while younger men raked below, sweeping, carrying buckets up a ramp into a high-sided truck in the driveway. Parked in front of that truck was another for the crew of tree trimmers. Both crews passed each other, never touching, in a choreographed dance.

When the old man and I were at the mouth of the driveway, Edith and Jasmine appeared, leading matching Appaloosas. One horse stared, mystified at the stream of water flooding out of the long hose, flowing down the street.

"Hello, ladies," Tony greeted.

"Hello, Tony," they smiled. I detected history between them, but couldn't get a clear read. They'd been neighbors for a long time.

"Water hazard!" Edith chimed, as her horse backed up, nostrils wide. "It's about time these horses learned how to not be afraid of water!"

"You can make them cross the river all day. It's okay with me," I said, easing the door open between us.

Eagerly she grabbed her reins, set her left foot in the stirrup. I counterbalanced her weight, holding the right stirrup down. As she swung her leg over, searching, I guided calf and boot into place. Then I patted her knee.

"Have a nice ride," I said.

And Edith and I were done. Dispute settled.

"You know, I wasn't in the greatest of moods the day I came over—"

I looked up at her, heard words coming out of my mouth

that I thought someone else was saying. "Well, there were a lot of feelings that day—"

"Yes, there were."

Down the street they went, hooves clomping as the water from my pool streamed out, down the gutter, towards the sewer.

"New roof?" Tony appraised, using a cane to hold up part of his weight.

"New roof."

"New roof 's a good thing. 'You going top of the line?"

"Top of the line. 'Down to the bone now," I said as we took in bare joists rising like the ribs of a dinosaur. Then I decided to let the man have the last word. It was the least I could do.

"You're going to be okay." Tony said on his way across the street. Turning, he repeated, "You're going to be okay," as if he was sure that I somehow didn't believe it? I watched him make his way, tapping his cane up red brick stairs that twenty years ago he would have taken two at a time.

In the backyard I spilled bags of corn chips into two big wooden bowls, salsa into smaller ones, spread the food out on top of garbage cans, and waved men off the roof, out of the trees.

This was my housewarming. In fractured Spanish I thanked everyone. They didn't seem to mind drinking out of a hose. I felt guilty that there was no money left to buy cokes.

As the crews ate and laughed, I wandered inside to feel my house. Through the crawlspace in the master bedroom closet I looked up through the ceiling at open sky, at clouds tinted red with a setting sun.

"I'll never see this again," I marveled, as one last worker carried a dresser drawer past me—with a rat trap inside.

November 25, 2005 11:40 p.m. Thanksgiving

Today some of my soldiers came back—on a holiday. The tree guys were here, and so were Lucio and his merry band of men, Poncho, his assistant, and Angel, his son.

"Why are you here?" I asked my plumber.

"Because we are working to finish your house!"

When I asked Señor Ortiz why he and his men were here, he said the same thing. Then he mentioned that I shouldn't worry about money.

"Three months, six months, you can pay me."

I bought lunch for everyone in gratitude. Senior Ortiz's men ate twice. He didn't know I was going to feed them, so he brought food, too. An unbelievably handsome man who is married to the unbelievably beautiful woman who lives next to Tony crossed the street when I was eating my lunch on the lawn. He thanked me for the chocolates I'd left, saying, "The house is looking so much better."

Lucio said it was a lucky day when he could work in the sunshine with his friends. Laughing under the second new side porch that Gregg finished, sitting on wooden flats and rolls of tarpaper, they all ate their fill of El Pollo Loco chicken.

So this is what Thanksgiving can feel like?

At dusk when all the workers had gone, I brought the cats over to inspect their new home. This time they explored the backrooms and the living room, too. Last time Rocky wouldn't take a step out of the crate. Magic ventured out first, rolling in plaster dust, pretending to mark corners, letting everyone know that he was claiming his turf.

Then it was my turn to be alone on a quiet stage without the radio playing Spanish songs. Peggy was right. A glass block wall between tub and toilet would soften sight lines. And why not sleep in the library?

But tonight the house dared me to love it, turned a dark side of its face in a warning.

Change is hard. Even for houses. I could feel every timber defy me.

"You're going to be okay, house," I said, borrowing Tony's pledge. "Takin' you back to the studs, but you're going to be okay."

Tonight I'm snug as a bug on a foam mattress on the floor of the second house, the perfect one, with satiny hardwood floors. Here it's all done, finished, smooth as a silk dress. Where I'm going I'll be wearing burlap—and I'm not looking forward to it.

Cover me, I'm goin' in.

CHAPTER FIVE

Fever

I AM HOUSE

I am house
I am home

She sits alone in
The small place
A plate one
Knife a fork

She fears my dark corners
Long hallways I am
Sick cannot warm
Air or water

In the dark like a lover
I whisper I was not always
This broken I waited
Still as stone for you

Do not give in to the fever
I beg you to live
You who risked your bet
On me the long shot

December 1, 2005 5:30 a.m.

Dark. Found my glasses by the bed. Where am I? Don't remember how I got here. Was I in a blackout?

First night in my new house.

Piece of foam mattress on the floor.

Cathedral ceiling.

Made it through the night. The cats had their meltdown at 3:00 a.m. Magic paced and cried and moaned under the covers, biting the bedspread. He lost it. Rocky tried to nurse on my hair, made incessant circles. When can we go home?

Oh God, we are home.

The door to the living room is open. Magic is off, exploring. My eyes are dry, tired. I can't believe I have to go to work today. The freeway is so loud, it's like trucks are in here. They can't finish that sound wall fast enough.

Memories of yesterday override. I'm ashamed. I'm in an emotional hangover. I cracked yesterday, cut her down, attacked because she put belongings out at the curb for the trash—Things that I didn't want to throw away. Peggy doesn't know when to leave well enough alone. And I don't know when to shut up. She wouldn't come to the door when I went over to her house to apologize. Ella, my friend, packed dishes and watched me cross the street to Peggy's house.

"I just ruined a friendship," I confessed. "Peggy and I've been friends for twenty years. I wouldn't have come to the door either."

My confidante smiled benevolently, patting my back.

"It's going to be okay. 'Meet you at your new house?"

We slid behind our steering wheels and made the last trip to Riverview. Next to me in a crate, Magic and Rocky yowled like caged tigers. On the back seat were boxes of my journals.

"This is all I need," I realized. "My writing, my animals—" as I followed Ella's red tail- lights.

It was a surprise attack. No time to sweep. She dropped an old rag of a Persian rug on the floor in front of the bath onto freezing cement. Dust curled up around the edges like witches' fingers.

"Welcome home," was Ella's blessing.

Then she left and I walked a castle made of stone. Would I ever be able to warm it?

I'll go back to the other house tomorrow to clear the paint cans in the driveway. Everything else, my entire life, is stacked, barricaded eight feet high in two back bedrooms here. The movers said they'd never had anyone "work in" with them for eleven hours straight.

As Ella made her departure, she said she was able to "see" people in different ways.

"I "see" you walking through the living room when it's all done in an ivory flowing kimono. I see a man in uniform. I don't know what that's all about."

It's light now. Something hot, maybe an infection is burning in my chest. The sycamore across the street at Stewart's house is the color of whole wheat toast. Which reminds me—I don't have a stove.

No heat. We're out in the woods, now, Babe.

December 3, 2005 2:30 a.m.

He offered a bucket for my stool. Enter the fourth player, my painting "general", Sebastian.

"No, thanks," I said, sitting on a six-by-six header.

The morning was cold. I pulled my collar up around my neck, Gramps' wool fedora low on my brow. In the service porch under those gaping holes, I spilled the beans.

"I had enough for a lot of the remodel, and then the first rental house needed a new sewer main. It cost fourteen thousand. If you want to pick up your tools and put a mechanic's lien on this house, it's okay with me."

For a second Sebastian looked like he dodged a bullet. Was he seeing a destination that I couldn't?

"If you could do what you want with this place, what would you do? What do you need?"

I picked up a thin piece of molding, led him to the first battleground, my bath.

"I have a claw foot tub in the backyard that I got out of salvage. It goes here, pedestal sink the corner, tile up to here." I scratched the stick along foiled wallpaper.

Two bathrooms later, we were in the backrooms.

"Do you need to keep these acoustic ceilings? There's plaster under there," he motioned. "And you need heat and air. It's cold in here."

"FORTY-SEVEN DEGREES."

"We can do this, no problem. You need to rent this out. You need the income."

Didn't I ask for a guesthouse that would help me pay my mortgage? Yes, let's fill the barn with calves to be fattened, sheep to graze. In spring, there would be meat—And the spring after that.

"Income would be a good thing," I chuckled. Imagine my home taking care of me? Could it return the favor?

"Let's do it." Sebastian rallied, at the last stop, the kitchen.

"What?"

"Let's do it right. So we don't have to come back."

"But—"

"I have a $100,000 equity line on my house. I'll pay for it. In a year, you'll refi, pay me back."

Something sharp, an arrow, hissed past my beating heart.

"You would do that?"

"Kathy, it's not about the money. I want to help you. I mean, you're a woman, alone, doing this on your own—"

"I was up at three, four, doing the numbers."

"I know. You're just like me. But sometimes, we need help." He surveyed the immense living room. "When it's all over, it'll be a palace."

"You were meant to have this," he mentioned as we were almost out to his truck. "Didn't I tell you when we were painting the other two; that you were going to buy another house—A really big one?"

"And I said, 'I don't think so!'"

"You did! You said, "I don't think so!" And I said, 'You're going to buy another very big house—and we are going to paint if for you!'"

We shook hands on our deal. Sebastian blessed me with—"When it's supposed to be yours—"

"Nothing comes between?"

He nodded, dropping his clipboard onto the passenger seat with finality.

"He already has it in His hands for us."

I waved as he drove off, knowing already that as good as all that sounded, I was going to wait for it to be provided by Someone with an equity line much bigger than his.

December 5, 2005 5:00 a.m.

I let the cats out. It was time. It was Sunday. I was home. The sun was smiling. I unbolted the side door. They ventured out, flattened, exposed, creeping up the driveway like they were under fire, snaking past the pile of debris—shredded bookshelves, pipes, mounds of old plaster—until they were at the front door.

Right about then Lynn, my next-door neighbor who lives in the old Spanish, appeared. I didn't want him here. I didn't need anyone to drop by. I was talked out, busy filling trash cans. He helped me lift a particularly heavy bag into a can. It wasn't that I don't like him. It was that I didn't want to take the time to make small talk with anyone. 'So much to do, so little time. But there he was, grinning, pencil thin, in my driveway. We chatted about garbage and horse manure and how much it costs to have it hauled away.

"Your cats are out, do you know that?"

"Yes."

"Aren't you afraid they'll run away?"

"No."

"Are you sure?"

"Yes, I'm sure."

"That's a pretty bad cough you've got. Have you been to see a doctor?"

"No, I've been a little busy." I changed the subject. "When was your house built?"

"37."

"Mine was built in '39. Maybe they're friends, huh?"

Lynn seemed amused. "Maybe?"

As we were hauling the last can out to the street he confided, "When I was twenty-seven, I bought a ranch and rehabbed it while I was working full time. Looking back on it, it was the best time of my life."

"You're right," I said, wiping both hands on my jeans, "It's a very romantic time."

December 6, 2005 11:00 p.m.

The day ended with a stop at Valerie's for a deep soak in her bathtub, water up to my chin. I don't have friends with deep pockets, but it pays to have friends with ample bathtubs. One day I'll have hot water, but not yet. I didn't expect to run across an old friend, a sponge named "Frosty," who my Auntie Joyce gave me as a Christmas present with bath salts years ago. There he was in a box mashed in between a buff puff and a razor. I started talking to the sponge. Tom Hanks had "Wilson." I have cellulose.

No arms left, orange carrot nose off to one side like a prize boxer after too many fights, he's best pals with a pumice stone. I helped Frosty the Snowman stand up on my stomach. It had been a while since we'd seen each other. Frosty seems to turn up when the-you-know-what is hitting the fan.

"So, how are YOU?" he asked, waking up.

My thoughts went to Peggy, how I'd hurt her.

"I did a bad thing."

"You know you can hug her in your heart—anytime?"

Bingo. Why is my voice coming through a puppet, so smart?

"And you can talk to me more!" he suggested, small head tilting.

(I hate it when sponge heads are smarter than my own.)

At that moment, curious about the conversation, Marmalade, Valerie's geriatric yellow tabby, appeared, a furry head over the top of the porcelain.

"Lions! Wild beats!" the sponge remarked.

"Harmless," I said. "That's Marmalade. He runs the place."

"Where are we?"

"We're at Valerie's house in Toluca Lake because I think I have—"I coughed, "Pneumonia—and the house I bought doesn't have hot water."

"You must've got a really good deal on that one!"

Laughing, choking, I told the sponge, "Yes, I got a really good deal."

December 7, 2005 8:00 p.m.

I had to have an angel's trumpet. There's one at the Mother house, the first house, sent to me as a sprout wrapped in brown paper. That one's grown into a tree now, too big to transplant. I needed one for Riverview. So I turned to Jacqueline, guardian of my favorite off-the-track nursery, way down near the airport. Senora Jacqueline has great plants. They come with her good "vibe," and her secret compost. A little bit of her magic comes along with every growing thing. Wrapped in a straw hat with a red scarf tied under her chin, wearing a long sleeved cotton blouse and gloves, she stopped watering flats of marigolds, and stood up tall, waving when she saw me.

"What kind do joo want?" she asked, leading the way down aisles of Angel's Trumpets, trees with dangling pointed flowers folded like batwings, waiting to open and release their perfume after dark.

"Not white. Yellow," I said. "They smell the best."

"Jes, they do," she said, turning a single five gallon pot towards me.

"How much?" I asked, stifling a cough.

"Seventy-five. But for joo, fifty."

"Ese a dangerous plant," she warned. "Joo eat it, joo die. Joo smell it, joo live forever!"

Then she cracked up. Jacqueline giggled often, her joy of taking care of the plants overflowing. Everything around her, water, words, settled soft, soaking like her rain making nozzle, healing the day.

One day I'll need a saw to trim this tree. For now, it's sitting where I'll plant it—on the southeast corner of the house to help shade the back wall. I baptized it in a stream of water, eager for a night when I'll breathe in her leathery blooms and feel like I'm getting a heavenly injection into the vein of my soul.

December 8, 2005 10:00 p.m.

"You can't tell me you're living in that house!" he snarled.

It was 6:30 in the morning. No need to take a number. No contractors were at the counter. No one was stirring, not even a mouse. I'd wrapped my burning throat in scarves, dove into my sheepskin jacket (the one I keep in the rear of the closet in case I might have to fly to the Antarctic or Alaska on short notice), and drove to the Department of Building and Safety. Last week when I stopped there for a permit, I thought David, my inspector, was good looking, maybe even a head turner? Suddenly, he was looking different.

"I'm living there," I wheezed. "And I don't have hot water until you sign off."

Metallic scales began to crowd his neck, fingers grew webbed. The "Creature" sprayed, "You can't be living there!"

I leaned over the counter, swallowing hard so that I wouldn't cough in the man's face.

"Could you please sign off so they can turn on the gas?"

Claw fingers grabbed a pen. He scratched something on a piece of paper, pushing it back at me, dripping in green slime.

"No one was there yesterday to let me in!"

"I'm sorry."

"I have a whole new development on the hill that I have to inspect, and I waited forty-five minutes for your plumber!" Gills were flapping wildly behind his ears. He definitely looked like a fish out of water.

"I know," I croaked. "I'm sorry."

December 9, 2005 7:35 a.m.

Fever broke sometime early this morning, before dawn. Sheets, soaked. I hope I never have to go through a night like that again.

"Maybe I made a mistake? Maybe I bought a house too sick to make well? Maybe I dreamt too big? Too real?"

No one in my family has ever lived in a place like this. Maybe this house is only for "rich people?" I am up against, slipping into a crippling belief, suffocating under a low glass ceiling—the unspoken creed of generations before me—telling me that I'm not enough—that I can only go so far.

Great-Grandma Gronski's basement apartment had a ceiling so low that we'd stoop to get through the doorway. To her, it was a penthouse. She used to live in a real "cave" in Michigan, a place carved out of a hill, when they came over from Poland, while Great-Grandpa worked in the mines.

My parents' first house was like my "Mother House," a small cottage. Then they built another on the empty lot next door. That house, the second, was my mother's "silk dress." It was the third one, the big estate, the place with the long green lawns that broke her. It needed more than they had. After they moved in she was homesick for the second house, the one she'd made perfect—just for her—with French doors on the kitchen cabinets, black-and-white checked gingham skirts along the bathroom vanity.

It was in that last house where life got so good, she tried to kill herself.

Check this out—I invested in an old bungalow, bought the one next door, made it exactly the way I wanted it—with French doors on the kitchen cabinets. And then I bought the third, the big fixer. Was this fever burning something off of me? *Out* of me? Do I literally have to walk *their* path before I can forge one of my own?

I kept a blue candle burning in the kitchen most of the night. My trusty cats held vigil on the bed. I couldn't get to the hospital. No strength. Gasping, lungs shrieking, I made the decision to live.

"Help me, help me, Lord," I think I said. Then I rolled over, flipped the New Testament open, blind. The first words that I could make out were, "Repent, therefore, and be converted, so that times of refreshing may come in the presence of the Lord."

"I could use two scoops of refreshing right about now," I thought. And then everything went black.

December 9, 2005 10:00 p.m.

"That is the most beautiful thing I have ever seen!"

My head was shaking like a bobble head doll in the back of a car. Lucio installed the kitchen faucet. Let there be water!

There's more! He'd cleaned the sink and put those orphan drawers back in their place, wiped the dusty countertops. I dragged home after work, weak, feverish, not knowing that for the first time since I moved in, I don't have to wash dishes out on the lawn with a hose in a bucket, retrieve the lost silverware later, out of the bushes.

Cautiously, I stalked to the bathroom. Voilá—A new tub faucet! I turned the left handle, held my hand under the spout. It sputtered, spat, then cold washed into warm—and turned hot!

There is no feeling in the world like stepping into a steaming hot bubble bath in your own house, in your own tub, for the first time.

No feeling in the world.

December 11, 2005 10:00 a.m.

Last night was the first night the house and I really slept together. We'd had trysts. I'd thrown that makeshift bed down on the floor in the fever to end all fevers. When I peeled that foam up I was shocked at what I found. I had soaked through six inches and the wool rug under it. Even the slab beneath the carpet was wet.

Oh, my God.

But when I woke up today, high on my real mattress and box spring that I somehow managed to drag into this room, on clean sheets, as I spied out the window at puffy white clouds spray painted on a blue sky, at sycamores, Chinese elms, spreading, turning golden, I knew I was home.

"Maybe I can live here?" I thought, falling back one more time onto the bed, arms out like a child making an angel in the snow. "Maybe I can make it? The other two are rented. I have nowhere else to go!"

Wrapped in my robe, I decided to walk the grounds. Mrs. Dennison, my neighbor three doors down, was trailing a Jack

Russell puppy on the street. Bald head shining, she waved, "I am so happy to see you! The 'Hello' chocolates were such a nice gesture! I've been singing your praises all over town!"

"You can be president of my very meager fan club!" I yelled, calming a cough. "You don't want to get near me, I'm—"

"You are so sweet and you're doing such a good job with this house."

We two women needed each other right then for safe harbor. I was in no danger of being judged by her for a major skin breakout, old bathrobe, worn socks, and slippers. No way was I looking down on her for sporting old jeans, and a flannel shirt with holes in it.

"Be careful of the yellow tomcat," Mrs. Dennison cautioned. "He beat up the last house cat I had. I came home one night and the tom had my cat pinned in the driveway, saying 'What's my name?'"

I coughed, laughed, turned away, and coughed again.

"Have you seen a doctor?" she asked, holding the renegade puppy taut on his leash.

"I'm…getting better. Besides, I don't like doctors."

"Me, neither," she confirmed. "You know, building a fire in the fireplace might not be a bad idea. I heard you can't use the furnace?" The dog was wiggling in her arms by then, distracting, showing a pink belly like a baby's. "I wasn't going to get another dog. Then, well, through a series of events—"

"I get it. That's my life—Through a series of events!""

Mrs. Dennison didn't want to leave, but the dog, biting on the leash, was tugging hard. As we parted I felt an unexpected loneliness, a pull to be back with family, to be in the "old country," the Midwest, where Autumn fell into Winter's arms and woke up properly as Spring. My cousin Brad told me they were having their first white Christmas in years. I was secretly embarrassed to feel longing for a past life, for my lost love soldier boy, included, when Someone who wasn't human gave me a castle, a cathedral, a whole new life for an eight hundred dollar deposit.

Maybe that new life began two nights ago when I lay here and decided not to die.

CHAPTER SIX

Four Coconuts

I AM HOUSE

I am house
I am home

She cannot see
Bodies of their lost
Hopes in the
Corners abandoned

Her skin soft
Burns from their acid
Past must be washed out
Ground into the soil after

The rot
The rust
The rain
The rats

Dreams and regrets wander
Here like wolves
Must be set
Free

December 14, 2005 4:00 a.m.

"Okay, so you go to the vegetable market and you get four coconuts full of liquid," he made a shaking motion next to his ear with his hand. "You know where to get those?

"Yes."

"Take one and put it in each of the farthest four corners of the house. North, South, East, West. Put a pan or a bowl under each. They might explode from absorbing."

"It's like I'm wading through their—I smudged with sage, but—"

My chiropractor x-rayed my body on the table with his gaze.

"You need to take some Epsom salts baths, as hot as you can stand, often. It'll help soak the toxins out. Every bath, twenty-five per cent of toxins get released. What's with this house?

"It's not like it's haunted. It's—I should see a watermark, like after a flood. I'm wading through something, their alcoholism, what they left. It feels like the house I grew up in."

"How many houses do you have now?'

"Three."

He turned his head at an odd angle. "That's too many. You don't have pneumonia. You have a lung infection. Lungs are about grief. What are you grieving?"

"I don't know. Life?"

"Life?"

"The thing about getting what you want is then you have it."

December 15, 2005 11:00 p.m.

This is the truth. I don't want to write this. I'm afraid of the kitchen. I only sit at one part of the counter. It's not a big room. I hold up in that spot. Six feet away is too dark, too far. A little frosted-glass lamp that they left is my only light. I eat frozen microwaved chicken stuffed with spinach every night. I figure it's protein and vegetables all in one. I haven't cleaned the fridge. It's in the service porch. It doesn't fit in the kitchen—because nothing fits.

I am afraid of the living room. It's so huge.

"How huge," you ask?

"Thirty-two by thirty-two feet to be exact."

No sofa. No chairs. Sawhorses hold up plywood tables heavy with cans, tools, rope. You never know when you'll need some rope.

"Why don't you go somewhere and sit on a sofa?" Valerie proposed.

Do people do that? Sit on a couch? Watch TV? I forgot.

And I'm afraid of the bathroom, the dark hole left from where Lucio stripped sink from vanity, an open wound left without sutures. I know nothing lives in that "wall cave," but it might.

Lastly, I'm afraid of the backrooms, far away, damp as caves. I have to traverse under the biggest, blackest holes in the service porch ceiling to get back there, to the awkward jostled pieces, clothes stuffed into closets, my sofa tipped up on its side, my Wedgewood stove. Everything I own, my armoires, are jammed tight, disgruntled, in limbo.

No bare feet here. The idea is you wear slippers or shoes, take them off only when sitting on the bed. Dirt rules, at least for now. I'm making paths, one safe place to the next. Will there ever be enough me to fill this house?

"I can't find God in this house." I confessed to Frosty, both of us coated in bath suds. "I can't find Him, anywhere."

December 16, 2005 8:40 p.m.

I guess it's "Home?" Am I "Home?" I ate real food tonight. I have an appetite again, after not wanting to eat for a week. I picked off of a barbecued chicken, tasted potato salad, cheddar potato chips while I looked down on the kitchen floor at twenty wood samples, granite chunks lying near my feet. I've been showing up at warehouses, stoneyards, paying homage to materials.

"What goes under engineered hardwood to keep moisture from coming up?"

"How much does granite cost per square foot?"

A girl with a lot of tattoos and a ring in her lower lip pushed me toward engineered blackened walnut. I favored a cherry color that looked like sunshine coming down a chute. Wide planks. It has to be oversize in rooms this large. I'm learning to think "estate." It's a new language, uncharted land, a new country.

After dinner I walked around the neighborhood. Half a block away three teenage boys were skateboarding over a pipe in the road. Torn jeans falling off of their bony hips, one smiled, said "Hi" to the woman with long hair under the tweed hat. It was the secret masculine thrill I'd craved all day. They couldn't have known that I wanted to linger, tittering under the full moon at their high jumps.

Reluctantly, I took myself home. On the way I paused to take in a few winter wonderland front yards. In one a motorized reindeer looked right, left, in front of a fat Santa in a worn red velvet coat who waved from a sleigh bed piled high with shiny packages and grinning cartoon elves, reminding me that I'm a long way from the land of genuine white Christmases. But, hey, this...is Hollywood. Even front yards are "produced" here.

December 18, 2005 10:00 p.m.

I looked into the mirror. Behind me, Terrance stared back.

"So, how's it going?" he ventured, reaching for my hair and retreating at the same time. What was silky soft had grown dry, brittle. Being at "the front" was taking its toll.

"Okay. 'Pretty tired. I'm—it's all about dirt. I live in plaster dust."

"I see."

"I have hot water now. That's good."

"Are you eating?"

"I have these chicken things I microwave. They left a fridge. I have stuff."

"I see." His hands lifted more strands. He inhaled, picked up a comb, and set out to do the impossible; cut and color a pile of straw.

"Oh, ouch."

"Sorry, it's a little—"

"Tangled, I know."

I might as well have told him I was homeless, or living in the woods, or both. Two hours later, after two—count 'em, two—applications of conditioner, I was on my way. Terrance had worked his magic.

"Take this," he said, pulling cans of soup and vegetables, a box of crackers off of his shelf. "You need to eat! And condition, okay?"

December 19, 2005 4:55 p.m.

When I went across the street to get help, Stewart exploded in laughter.

"I watched you from my kitchen window and I said, 'She's an animal!'"

I'd pushed and leveraged that old fridge out of the shed. But when it fell in the driveway, I needed muscle. Sometimes a girl needs power tools. Son of a bitch, damn it, I needed men.

Enter Stewart and his lanky son, Trevor.

"You don't stop!" Stewart said as I led the way.

"I want this house," I explained, hearing myself snarl like a lioness.

"I can tell," Trevor agreed—ears back, wary. "I would never get between you and what you want. In fact, I'll help you get it!"

"That's it!" I thought. "I need to marry a teenager!"

The shed is clear now down to shabby floorboards, daylight shafting through holes in the roof. Roses in pots are now watered, soaked after much neglect. Oh yeah, I have been sick for over a month. I forgot. I feel like Rumpelstiltskin. That was some nap. The final treatment was to hose the driveway of dust, and hang the mammoth staghorn fern up on a hook outside the kitchen window. It took four tries and a lot of profanity to get that puppy up there.

Speaking of puppies, I'm asking the universe for a boxer pup in the spring. This place feels unprotected. We need dog energy.

December 20, 2005 7:15 a.m.

Ship's Log—severe storms last night. Interior, only, not a drop of water fell outside. How do you keep your body out of panic attacks? Breathe regularly even if your brain is telling you to run like hell. Talk out loud to yourself:

Say, "It's OK, honey, I'm right here." Say it again. "It's OK, honey, I'm right here."

Think only good thoughts. See only flowers, blooming. Smell only sweet, clean. Lavender helps. Breathe some more. When your brain says, "What about that flyer someone left on your door? The one that says the city's going to put a sewage treatment plant behind you, in Cow Field?" Say, "It's OK, honey, it's OK…"

I called Mrs. Dennison. She said she walked Cow Field with our city council members a few days ago, and overheard the mayor say to one of them, "They can't put a sewage treatment plant here. It's too toxic."

December 21, 2005 4:00 a.m.

Huge machines were eating, dragging all of the soil out of Cow Field. Loud, crashing, sounds of destruction became a cat moaning. I stood up to see a yellow tom running fast at the window in the living room.

Glass shattered. I bolted out of the door at the culprit—the yellow tom. He hissed, loud as a cougar.

Rocky's back in bed with me now. He knows that I'm under attack. There are things that I can see like that wild cat, and there's something even bigger after me—an idea that I was born into, cut my teeth on—a thing that wants me cornered, kept small, locked away, defeated.

Whatever it is that's brewing, it doesn't smell like coffee.

I've nicknamed the menace "Terrorist Cat." He's the one enemy I can see.

December 21, 2005 9:00 p.m.

"I live here. You can leave any packages," I reassured the UPS customer service lady.

"My report says, 'Vacant—do not deliver'."

"I know it looks bad, but I'm here! This is the second time they're telling me no one could possibly live here!"

Okay, so it's dark. Why spend money on lights? No question the place needs paint. But doesn't anyone notice a new roof? Don't they see six trashcans lined up, full, every week? There's work going on here. Lights and curtains? They're details, details! We're not quite there yet.

December 22, 2005 10:15 p.m.

Frosty knew. Frosty always knows.

"So, what?"

"I can't find—-I don't know where He is?"

"Who?"

"The Big Guy. The Chief."

"Oh, yeah," Frosty thought, staring down at my bare navel. "Can you handle that He knows where *you* are?"

"Yes."

"That'll work."

Magic, my familiar, my black cat, curious about who I was talking with, popped up, peering over the tub's edge. He sniffed Frosty's nose. "Big cat. Leopard. Wild beats! Cats hate me."

"Frosty, I came out of jail tonight and I cried."

"Shouldn't you be happy to get out of jail?"

"I was visiting friends who have to be there, and I came out and cried."

"Because you're free?"

"Because I'm free."

"And I always thought you were expensive!"

I walked past the joke.

"I can do anything, go anywhere, but I feel like I'm in prison because I still don't know if I'm 'enough.' Frosty," I choked, "Do you think God got me in here and then He dropped me?"

Enter Rocky, his plume of a grey tail interrupting.

"Two cats?"

The second curious onlooker joined Magic up on the side of the tub.

"Ah, another big cat. 'Snow leopard?"

I moved Frosty closer so that Rocky could sniff him. Rocky greeted politely, rubbing each side of Frosty's cheeks with his own. Then Frosty wiggled his carrot nose.

"See? Cats dig me! I have fur on my face now." Frosty took in all the walls—the exposed 2x4s, plaster mesh protruding, newspaper stuffed into plaster cracks. "It's gonna be real nice here. 'Real nice."

Then I kissed Frosty. I planted a real one on the wet puppet's face. He fell backward from the thrill, collected himself and stood up. I squeezed him to get more water out. It was cold, left over from yesterday's bath.

"Cold pee?" He joked, looking down at himself. "That's unusual!"

CHAPTER SEVEN

The Boxer

I AM HOUSE

I am house
I am home

How much is that doggie
The lost found
Discard no one
Was here to guard

I could not defend
A house cannot say
Get away stop tearing
Me apart

Bring that dog home
Tell him to
Keep them
Away

They came over the fence
Threw pieces into my deep
Place where water was a
House cannot scream

January 8, 2006 almost midnight

He nickered to me in his Barry White voice the second I stepped out of the car. Tyson looks like his old self again. The vet lanced an abscessed tooth, didn't have to pull it. No wonder he couldn't chew. He's back up to his old weight again. No more ribs. Close to thirty years old now the stallion can chill, and watch his "women" in the pasture across from him, wear a trough in the sand from patrolling. Mares move around a lot. You have to keep an eye on them.

All the horses looked better. There were a few tons of hay up on pallets, a shed full of bags of feed and grain. I spent a lot of time with a white Hanoverian mare named Jewel. She whinnied to me in her Dolly Parton voice. The other two mares in her corral pick on her. They left her alone when I went in. Jewel is the kind of horse who likes to rest her head against your chest like a big dog. She would have no problem sleeping in my bedroom on a nice stack of straw in the corner.

Under a tent of aqua sky swept clean of clouds, my horse and I celebrated my birthday. Great birthday—I got to be with my pony. What girl wouldn't want that?

"I'm working on bringing you home," I promised the black horse while I curried, combed, pulled his mane, finished with a soft polishing brush, and a damp rag until his coat shined and I could almost see the sunset in the gleam.

"I'm working on it."

January 16, 2006 11:30 p.m. Martin Luther King Day

Was it a deer? A head shot up, ears alert. A dog? A boxer? For real?

I parked, got out of my car for a closer look.

"Are you hungry?"

At forty feet I counted every bone. Eyes flashing in a warning, he showed fangs. One cropped ear flipped back and forth, listening. Cars flew behind me as I walked across four lanes. Why was it that no one else could see a purebred boxer lying in the grass outside a cement plant? Was I the only one? Maybe no one else was supposed to see him? Was he invisible to everyone—but me?

Legs folded, the feral dog took me in as I left three handfuls of dry cat food near him, crossed back across the street to watch what he would do.

The right rear leg hung limp as a rag as he stood and devoured the first two mounds. He collapsed before he could stagger over to the third.

I crossed again, slower this time, loose leash in my left hand.

"Who did this to you?"

This time he rolled on his back surrendering a white chest like a flag, growling at the same time.

"He's mentally ill," I thought. "He's frightened. And he's asking for help."

"Here's the deal." I laid it all out like I was talking to another human who I might have found in the same way. "I can come back here, tomorrow. I can check on you, but hey, what do you say, 'Wanna blow this joint?"

I watched my left hand like I had no association with as it slipped a noose over his head and pull it taut.

"Let's boogie!"

Question: How do you get a wild, starving three-legged animal that looks like he's ready to bite your arm off, up into a back seat? Answer: You tie the leash to the headrest on the passenger side, leave the rear passenger door open, and run back into the office you just worked at to see if you can find a few men crazy enough to lift him.

But a funny thing happened as the receptionist and I were watching. The boxer looked up at the seat, down at the floor, and made a decision. With his powerful front end, he pulled himself up on the seat and fell over onto his side.

"He's in! Thanks!" I exploded out the door with a yell as I ran out, slamming the car door. Talk about "closure!"

"Let's get you to a doctor," I said to the new face with the black muzzle in the rear view.

Miraculously, in the car he became tame. When we came home, he limped up the driveway on my left, sniffing the debris. We stopped at the fence in front of the pool. He took the place in like a security guard, first day on the job. Then *I* got a good look at the yard. Something was different. Had I moved those chairs? That wood? What was missing?

Edith called to me on our walk to the front yard.

"Boxer? Nice." She crowed, stretching her neck our way.

"I just found him."

"Bad accident? Someone hit him?"

"We're going to see a specialist tomorrow."

"Good. You need a dog. Kids broke into your yard today. My horses spooked. It was three-thirty. I looked over the fence. There were three guys throwing stuff into the bottom of the pool. They were skateboarding on the shallow end."

"In the pool?"

I said, "What're you doing?"

They said, "Hey, it's vacant! Who cares?"

January 17, 2006 10:00 p.m.

The back of my knees cramped in fear when I stared up at the x-rays—like when I'm too high, on an edge, afraid I'll fall. My dog's pelvis was shattered, wrapped around a femur ball that should have been solid, not split almost in two.

"I think he was hit by a truck. He's been out on the street, starving for weeks, maybe months? I can cut the ball out and in a few weeks he'll be fine," Dr. High said, settling on the floor, cradling my bony dog. "But, maybe, let's see if he can heal on his own? What's his name?"

"Sarge," I said.

"Sarge? He looks like a 'Sarge.'" Leave him with me for five days. I can give him stronger pain meds than you can."

'Next stop? Back home to Riverview to meet Officer Wimbly and Officer Gerard. They lingered in the driveway and didn't seem to be in any hurry to leave.

"How many times have you been vandalized?" Officer Wimbly asked. He had curly red hair shaved close to the scalp, a blue shirt pulled tight over layers of muscle and a bulletproof vest. He reminded me of a pit bull.

"They came back two times—Every day after school. I wait my whole life to live in this place and then people tear it up!"

"It's a lot of work," Officer Gerard added, taking in the termite ravaged gates, peeling paint. "You live here by yourself?" He was tan with a wavy handful of black hair cascading down over his forehead.

"No, I don't live here alone. I—I have a dog."

Officer Wimbly shifted his weight. "Your neighbor, Edith, identified the kids."

"I want to go to the principal of their school."

"And if you do, he doesn't have to do anything."

"I need to do something!"

"You did. You called us."

"This is a lot to do by yourself," Officer Gerard commiserated. "Hey, it looks vacant?"

"I know it looks vacant. I can't receive packages here. Why not trash a vacant house? Why not throw furniture and lumber into the pool, spray paint the walls? Why not? Nobody lives here!"

"Can I level with you?" Officer Wimbly confided, stepping six inches closer. "It's gonna be hard to stop these kids from coming in unless you get water back into that pool. They're living out a film they watch. Trust me, we'll do our job, but, hey, think about it."

Their squad car immediately pulled up next to three curious skateboarders who had maerialized in front of Stewart's house. Hands over their guns, the two men closed in, wilting the boys on the curb like shamed dogs.

I think it's time to fill that pool all the way again. With what? Water? How about fish?

January 22, 2006 11:00 p.m.

Dr. High's helper, Jose, presented a new dog. Sleek, little stump tail wiggling, Sargie leaned against my side, smiling wide at each person who appeared from the back of the hospital to say "goodbye."

"I can't believe how good he looks!" I said. "Thank you so much!" When I saw the bill's total, I reached for another tissue.

"Actors and Others for Animals paid one-half," the receptionist explained. "Dr. High neutered, gave shots for nothing."

"Enjoy your dog," said a masculine voice behind me. "Take good care of him." My vet grinned as he knelt down, his arm around Sarge, holding up a vial of pills. "Give him half of one of these, morning and night. Keep him restricted on a leash. In two months, look out, you're going to need obedience school!"

Today all that Sargie needed was a boost to get up onto the back seat.

"Paws up!" I coached.

He set his front feet on the seat and I lifted under his waist. Back home in the driveway, when I turned into the service porch where I had his bed and blankets, he pulled me out toward the fence we'd stopped at on our first night, where we'd overlooked the pool. Sarge remembered. He was already on the job, in a routine.

Pass on the gun. My guard dog is home.

CHAPTER EIGHT

My Walden[2]

2. *Walden: or Life in the Woods*, by Henry D. Thoreau, August 9, 1854.

I AM HOUSE

I am house
I am home

The rains
Cannot soak through
She gave me roof a new
Life proud beams strong

Bring on the storms
Try to hurt me tempest
I defy
I dare you

Whip me with
Branches
Go ahead I
Will cover

Her held up in
The backroom
Warm feet on
Cold stone

February 2, 2006 11:10 p.m.

Sebastian showed up unannounced.

"You need to get out of the front house so we can finish everything—floors included, by Saturday."

"I haven't even taken a bath yet."

"Don't take a bath this morning. We're here to get this going."

Today the troops flooded in on foot. I'm in a new "cave" tonight—the cobwebbed backroom with broken French windows and slanted ceiling. I'm up for the second time, trying to sleep on my lumpy temporary "bed," a sofa that my neighbors discarded in an alley. Tonight I threw the last things from my bedroom out on the new round porch (the rotunda), saying, "I'll move that later." Under a mountain of blankets, I'm listening to a fresh sound—water sheeting off of a new roof.

The rains have begun.

Anyone who wants to have this, to do this, has to wade through a night like tonight. The storm is the least of it. Trying to thaw from the cold after my second hot bath of the night, crossing that great hall of a living room, there was my mother the way I remember her, standing at the counter, like she did at the last house. I looked at her but she did not see me—My mother silhouetted in blue light, pouring another bottle of beer into a glass.

No God, no friends, frozen in loneliness, searching in a bottle for both, one after another, the empties lining the sink. This was her act of faith. Relief would be in the next drink. Or the one after that.

Strangled by loneliness, she called me incessantly after I'd escaped to the land of skyscrapers.

"You were crushing me, Momma, with your pain." I spoke to her ghost. "I know what your disease cost you. You didn't die from cancer in your brain. You died way before then, in the place where thoughts and hopes are born. You died encased in that house with the tall windows. You and daddy bought that big house hoping it would make everything perfect. It didn't cure alcoholism, Momma. It didn't fix anything."

Curled like a baby, writhing on a hardwood floor two thousand miles away in an apartment on 64th and Park Avenue in New York City, I felt her pain overtake like it was my own. I came to know that I could not save her. I couldn't take her desperate calls anymore, either. I had to divorce my parents, so I would stop drowning in their disease. I had to rise up and get off of that floor or I, too, would have been searching for relief in the same brown bottles.

Anyone who wants to have this has to wade through a night like tonight, seeing the past come to life like an apparition.

"Momma, I'm sorry I had to say, "Please don't call me anymore." I am so sorry."

I made that call to her with my feet dangling over the unknown, like I was on top of one of those skyscrapers. This was my leap—to tell my mother "My God, Momma, my God, I can't help you."

My mother didn't want help. Or she didn't think she deserved it? Repeatedly I'd tried to save her. I brought solutions, ideas, the Jaws of Life to cut her out of the wreck. Then she would crawl back in—to my father, to alcohol. My mother didn't want a fresh start—her own apartment, linen curtains, a literal new lease.

"We'll find you a cute place and we'll decorate it and put African violets on all the window sills and it will be so—"I'd say to her, each time she'd call to say she wanted to leave him, that she was dying there.

"Oh, Momma. What else could I have done? I could have, should have—"

Turning my back on the ghost, I implored the CEO, the Chief, The One Who I Cannot See, for support. "Will I ever call this 'home'?"

"This is the time when people go insane or they kill themselves," Wanda, a friend, told me this morning, not knowing that she was tossing a life preserver my way.

"Yes." I agreed, with tears building. By chance we'd met in a grocery store parking lot. 'By chance? "Yes, I see how someone going through this— the past rising—I see how they could end up in a psych ward. My mother did. I could see how someone would reach for a razor blade like she did—or buy a gun. That's what my family does. We think we can kill the problem."

Anyone who wants to have this, to do this, has to wade through a night like tonight. I'm in Grandma Gronski's cave, water seeping in under the doors, dripping off the roof. Yes, the floor is wet, but I have new shingles. I'll fix those leaking windows later. Rains mean new growth, cleansing. Winds are sweeping the old away. There would be spring. Summer will follow.

I wrote all of this with light from a single candle. Who knows where a lamp is?

February 3, 2006 11:00 p.m.

I had to pull over, right there. That ache that tells me I have to talk to Him, find Him, feel Him, had me stop right in front of Cow Horn Productions.

"I'm not doing well at all," I said. "Where do I start with Riverview when so much is unfinished? There's so much to do."

Head in my hands, I called out, "Mom! God! Anyone! Help me! It's too much! This house needs so much and I have so little!"

Eyes closed, I listened, hearing absolutely nothing. Then came a hint, a directive:

"*Cut the gardens.*"

"What gardens?"

"*Cut the gardens.*"

Was it His voice? 'My mother's?

When my eyes opened, I noticed workers in front of me trimming trees. Two men were chipping branches in the back of a truck. Pain transformed into idea—use the chips to layer over the gardens?

What gardens? Oh, the ones you're going to expose, dig out, the ones in front of your house, Kathy!

Oh, those gardens!

I stalked up to the two men in ear cups who were standing next to the truck.

"Could I have some chips?" I yelled over screeching gears.

The man on the right pulled a lever. Silence descended.

"How much do you need?"

"That much."

"A truckload?"

"A truckload."

"Where do you live?"

February 19, 2006 9:30 p.m.

I cut the front gardens today.

I threw clod after clod against the bricks. Rage, anger, pride, wonder and pain edged each other out of the way as dirt exploded, popping off of bricks, making smooth hills beneath. Why was I so angry? Who was the target?

The shovel wanted to smash faces that I couldn't see. No, they weren't faces or voices I was raging against. They were ideas; "Don't get too big. Don't stand too tall. Don't talk about what you've done. Let others do that. Don't reach too far. Don't, don't, don't. Stay small, stay—winter's coming. Keep those apples, potatoes in the cellar. Save. Survive. We have to make it to spring. We have to—"

The places I grew up in had low ceilings. The lives had short hopes.

"You have to have killer instinct," my father, high school football star who didn't make the cut in college, told me. "You have to have killer instinct, or you'll become a teacher."

My father became a teacher. I followed along, didn't make waves, graduated with a degree in education. Low ceilings made for drowning without rescue, inspirations aborted, never being born into the light of day.

"Don't dare—don't, don't. Don't even try—"

I threw another handful of soil against the wall. Sarge flinched next to me when he felt the force.

"No, Sargie, it's okay. It's okay. It's not you, Sargie. It's not you. I'm digging us out of the past. They wanted to bury me, Sargie. They wanted to bury me."

February 20, 2006 10:00 p.m.

"The river flooded here in 1927," an elderly, crackly voice sounded to my back. A hunchbacked white-haired woman with a short sassy haircut looked up at me and then back down to her lap from an ancient Oldsmobile caked in dust.

"It was before the homes were built, yours, mine—that's why we have this soil, why they call this the 'River bottom.' There are pictures of it in a deli over on Victory Boulevard."

"I'm Kathy," I introduced, walking to her car.

"I'm Florina," she smiled, reaching a bony hand out of the window. "You're doing wonders with this house."

"I'm 'wondering' what I'm doing with it—every day!"

"It was such a mess. We all hated to see a home this grand go down so far."

"Well, we're resurrecting each other!" I laughed. Yes, I did need to laugh.

"A woman designed your house. Post Depression. 'She

didn't live there long. I heard her family didn't want her to build it. 'Love that bay window."

"Figures it was a woman. Look at all that glass. Men build walls. Women build windows!"

"I have two horses—at the end of the street. They used to have a pony, here. Do you have horses?"

"No, I have a pool."

"I got rid of my pool. I wanted horses. Aren't you tired?"

"Exhausted. This soil is cement."

"This house is in love with you," She said, trying to lift her head against a spine that held her like a vise. About then Tony appeared out on his front porch. Florina noticed him and became another woman while I watched. She transformed into a girl, smoothing the hair on the back of her neck and smiling. Tony raised his hand. She raised hers.

As Florina drove off, a man in a baseball hat and a blonde woman pushing a baby in a stroller walked by.

"Don't give up the faith!" he yelled. "Don't give up! We bought a fixer, too. It almost killed us, but we made it. Don't give up. Keep digging!"

February 21, 2006 9:00 p.m.

Magic dug little holes right next to the big ones my shovel made. 'Third day of ground- breaking. I've never designed gardens this large. I drew a 45-degree line from the tip of the roof to the ground and took the edge to there. I'll have ten feet of garden in most parts. To me, it looks like "acreage." These gardens are the "apron" for the "dress" of the house. Didn't my mother say something about people never making their gardens wide enough?

Rocky barely left my side. We tumbled around together in the grass.

"I'm being stripped down to the foundation, just like my house," I told Wanda yesterday. No cable TV, heck, no TV at all! It's concrete slab—and me! But there are gardens, or at least there will be. "I'm in 'My Walden!'" I joked.

Then Wanda said something I wrote down right then and there:

"Somehow, we remember the music of the other place. And we're always listening for it."

March 2, 2006 8:30 p.m.

It was time to talk to the sponge.

"So?" he said, talking a dolphin dip under the suds, surfacing like a penguin on the isle of my stomach.

"I had a date tonight. With a neighbor."

"Right on! 'Lucky guy."

"He's eighty years old ."

"'Really lucky guy!"

"He put his hand on my leg."

"Oh, not-so-lucky guy."

"I said, 'You don't know me well enough to be doin' that!'"

"And then what?"

"Then we went to Bob's and looked at other old guys and old cars and talked to even older guys and some younger ones, too."

"Did he pay?"

"Of course! He's the guy! He eats mashed potatoes with brown gravy on them. We shared an apple pie à la mode."

"Apple pie à la mud?"

"Yeah, vanilla mud."

"You're smiling."

"Am I?"

Taking in the whale of a body he was on, Frosty declared, "Wow. You're proof that all you need to wear is a smile."

March 3, 2006 8:00 p.m.

Oh, man. The weirdest thing just happened. The folder I keep my notes in for the book about this house just fell off of the dresser onto the books below. My glasses fell, too.

And—nobody was touching them.

The cats were on the bed, ten feet away. They looked at the folder. I looked at the folder. I wasn't even close to it. I watched it happen like it was a movie. It wasn't near the edge. It was pushed—While I watched. Is someone or something trying to tell me something? Maybe I am supposed to tell this story? Would anyone really want to read story about a house?

March 5, 2006 9:00 p.m.

Tony pulled over on the wrong side of the street while I was digging.

"It looks much better," he said, elf grin showing.

Bent over, I let the shovel handle hold me up.

"Oh, Tony, tell me I'm not crazy. Tell me I can do this."

"You have such courage to do this."

"Courage and insanity hold hands."

"Of course," he tittered, laughing at my youth. "How 'bout we go to Bob's tomorrow and look at cars? 'My treat? I need mashed potatoes."

"Okay."

"Do you want to know the secret of life?"

I leaned closer, left ear eager.

"Sure. Lay it on me. Lay it on me. "(Because I'm strapped and I can't sell either one of those other houses because they're leased out and I can't pay for the plumbing here because I have no money left and I'm too tired to go to the real estate office and even feign professionalism. So I'm here, shovel in hand, risking, claiming, turning clod after clod, throwing them against bricks to save every piece of dust, because my hands have to touch it all so this place knows I mean business, or it won't become a yellow diamond!) "Yes, God help me; tell me, Tony, what *is* the secret of life?"

"Keep breathing."

CHAPTER NINE
Toxic

I AM HOUSE

I am house
I am home

She shivers in the
Cold my fire heart
Cannot beat
This too must be cut out

Better I have no breath
Years of choking
On the poison
Metal veins full

What did they bury
In the soil
Did they think
No one would find out

She trembles in the cold
Does not know
This is what saves
Her from the dust that kills

March 7, 2006 6:15 a.m.

"It's about money. It was always about money. It's always been about money. But no one talked about it. I knew it was about money when I was little. My Dad got a second job, and they never talked about it. There was that time when they fought and he left because there was only one can of peaches on the shelf. That was normal, to be down to one can of peaches. I didn't care. I liked peaches. But my mother cared. She wanted more. That was the only night my dad left and didn't come home. After he came back he took second jobs and worked after his regular job and on weekends. He was always tired. So the lesson was you have to work so hard that you can barely move and that was what you had to do to make it happen. You just sucked it up and got beat up doing a job, and there wasn't any other way."

Betty separated a piece of salmon from the fillet on her plate.

"Money is the biggest trip because of the way we think about it. If we can get you to look at money differently, your life will change. Rule Number One:" She said. "Pay yourself ten percent of every check."

I pulled a pen from my bag, opened a paper napkin, and began taking notes. Betty and Ron had eleven rental properties, enough income to take a cruise once a year.

"How do I keep ten percent when I need two hundred percent—which I'm not earning?"

"Start with five per cent."

I set the pen down. The way I saw it, this was already too much from too little. There was never enough.

"There's never enough," I told her.

Betty knew I wasn't sleeping. She knew I woke up every

few hours, wondering how I would make the mortgage payments. Every dollar had somewhere to go and it wasn't to me. Everyone else was getting paid, but not me.

"I make 7 K a month, and I feel like a pauper."

I sketched scenarios on the napkin—sell the first house, the Mother house; sell the second house, the pool house, sell both. Betty savored her grilled fish while my order of fish and chips grew cold.

Our waitress filled water glasses, often.

"I have three houses and no money," I said, shaking my head, laying the pen down. "Money is the biggest mind trip. 'More than sex!"

She leaned in. Reading her lips, I heard the words like a tattoo needle going into my brain. "If we can get you to look at money differently, your life will change."

"My fear is—I'm afraid I've failed—at everything."

"Not true. You are one of the bravest people I know. This—is growth. Right now it's costing you big bucks, but wait and see—"

I believed Betty because she's never lied to me. I believed her because she didn't want anything from me. Was I growing? Is this how trees feel when they're adding rings, reaching up taller, when their roots are growing deep? Did it hurt this much? Trees don't cry into napkins in restaurants.

"I want to feel like I deserve this house."

"Oh, honey," she reached over, squeezing my hand. "We're going to get you through this, we are. We might need a little help, but we'll do it."

I winced. "So, I guess I'm not selling anything today?"

"How do you feel when I say, 'Sell both rentals?'?"

"More free."

"Why is that?"

"Because then I can't go to one house and look over the fence and see they've chopped down the trees at the other. I'd be done with both."

"They're just stucco and wood to me. It's different for everyone. Ron went back and bought his mother's house. They're income to me. Aren't they making money now? Aren't they rented out?"

"Yes."

"Then maybe the houses aren't the problem. You're going to have to be very careful with your money," she warned. "Very careful. By the way, I have some friends who are very good with their money now, not that they always were. Why don't we give them a call? And, honey, I really think you need to keep writing. Don't let this money shit get in your way."

When the bill came, Betty paid $5 for her meal, which was more fish than my entire serving. My part was $ 9.95. That means I paid $5 extra for French fries and breading.

Betty and Ron own eleven rental houses.

Maybe next time I'll order the fillet.

March 8, 2006 11:00 p.m.

I cleaned off my desk and found a money order for $953 in my property tax folder. I forgot I'd slipped it in there a few months ago. I can pay the taxes on the Mother House ahead of time. 'Ahead of time? What's that? So when I take care of myself first, get things in order, money mysteriously shows up?

Exuberant, I went out to run in the rain. My legs felt strong like they used to before black mold and fever. I think I was excited because I met some of Betty's friends tonight. One was a woman named Rebecca, with a ferocious mane of red hair. Not her color. No roots.

"All you can do is all you can do," Rebecca reminded, "God has never let me down," she said, blinking through wet eyes. This confirmed my suspicion that she had a connection with Something—or Someone—Who was taking care of her and her money—*and her money*?

I believed her.

Her nails were done. She was going on a vacation that was all paid for—all cash, no credit cards.

"There's no God in credit," Rebecca scoffed. Eleven months before, she'd been homeless. *Homeless.* "You need to sleep, Kathy. People want to do business with people who feel good about themselves. And start writing all your numbers down, everything that goes out, comes in, even a quarter in a meter. Write them in a little notebook. We'll help you record them, use spreadsheets later."

Rebecca sleeps through the night. Rebecca isn't having panic attacks.

The plan was to jog to the corner and turn around but Sarge and I picked up speed past the rental stable at the end of the block. Horses were sleeping, standing, some were laying down, bellies round as hills. My feet kicked in, told me, "Relax, we'll do the work."

As I came around that corner under black skeleton trees glued to a wet grey flannel sky, I heard my words, what I'd confessed to Rebecca and my new friends. "Take away sex and manipulation, most of the lying and cheating, and what's left? Buying things?" We cracked up. It was a nice break from crying.

I ran hard, right into a connection with Him that made my eyes flood all the way down my face, my neck, and into my T-shirt. It kept coming, that feeling. Was this surrender?

But that's not all. After I ran, I drove over to the old neighborhood to take a look at my rentals. Peggy was outside, sitting on the steps of her porch.

I waved.

She waved back.

I pointed to Sarge in the back seat.

"You have a dog?" she stood up, taking a cautious step.

"Do you want to see him?"

We sat on the front porch, side by side, like, well, like we used to, while the clouds left and the sun made everything right that had been wrong. As Sargie ate snacks at our feet, I knew

God was doing this for me. It was as good as the ol' days when I'd breathe in the alyssum in Peggy's garden every year and feel that it was spring. I came home after that, "boxed" with my dog on the lawn while the sun kept shining like it wasn't done; would never set. And the moon was just going to have to wait.

March 9, 2006 9:15 p.m.

Mrs. Dennison came out of her house looking grim and determined. We greeted from the street, met at her car.

"How's it going?" She asked.

I was glad to see her. She was sounding strong.

"I'm going to clean my kitchen," I chimed. "I swear!"

"You clean it, you own it!" she grinned, dropping a package in on the passenger side. "I have to return theses clothes to Macy's. Nothing's fitting these days. I'm a 'four' now. I used to be an 'eight.'"

"You look great."

"I have to talk to you," she said, her eyes flashing. "We have big trouble with Cow Field."

"The sewer?"

"No, mercury, lead. 'Worse than Erin Brockovich's. A few neighbors and I paid to have the soil tested. 'Big trouble. They went in with a bulldozer, down twelve feet for core samples in seven different places. 'Big trouble. Chromium six. Mercury. We're going to have a class action lawsuit. I'll notify you by Wednesday. If you're going to take out a loan on your place, do it now. We're suing the city and Cow Horn. You need to get your money out—"

I was gasping, trying to breathe.

"Have you used your furnace?"

"No, why?"

She grabbed my arm.

"Good. It's airborne. It's in all of our ducts. Listen to me—I want you to get all your money out."

"I don't know what you mean?"

"For the depreciation. Because after this gets out, we're not worth anything."

CHAPTER TEN

Old Fences

I AM HOUSE

I am house
I am home

I am vain
Born of a
Soul who wanted life
Grounded in beauty

It hurt to grow
Old from neglect
In younger days
I cut a clean shadow

Lawn like soldier's
Hair smooth stucco
Flowers surrounded
Like a wreath

I have gardens now
To frame my walls
So people will turn and
Stop like they used to

March 26, 2006 10:10 p.m.

Earlier in the day, hands submerged in work gloves, bent over 10,000 clumps of dirt in the front yard, I was thinking, "Jee, a hot dog sure would taste good right now." I told no one. It was a passing whim. Evidently thoughts do travel, because in about four minutes neighbor Tony came ambling down his hill cane in one hand, and a plastic bag in the other. As usual I had a shovel in mine.

I challenged him, faked being angry, an Irish way of bestowing affection. "What do you want?"

"I have grapefruits for you."

"Thank you." I peered inside at three orbs. "Ruby reds? From Texas?"

"No, from my son's, here."

My finger attacked, peeled, offering the fruit for his nose to test. He declined, hand up.

"No thanks. I'm going to Pink's to buy a hotdog. Do you wanna go?"

"Really?" I chuckled. "Oh, thanks, I have so much to do here. Would you buy me one?"

"Sure."

I wanted to say, "Could I have fries, too?" But feigning class and decorum, I kept silent.

An hour later, another plastic bag was mine. Tony pulled up curbside in a long, white Chrysler Imperial, arm out. I went to pick up my lunch like a car hop. Chocolate shake, two hotdogs with the works, French fries and onion rings.

Just like that.

April 1, 2006 8:00 p.m.

"If you clean it, you own it."

The puppy isn't mine until I wash him in the bathtub, get a new collar around his neck. The car isn't mine until I hose, dry, wax it. The kitchen isn't mine until I break out the soft scrub and Palmolive, bleach for backup, rubber gloves and bucket as accessories.

I couldn't take it anymore. It was time. Today my kitchen and I had our date with destiny. I'd helped myself by taking everything out the night before. If I prep, I get to the job. I pulled the microwave out. Piles of papers, old Christmas cards, slid into the recycling bin. The dish rack was re-homed to the living room.

Then I could really see filth. I'd noticed dirt before, but with everything out, oh dear. I let go of the fact that I'd been walking over that floor since I'd moved in six months ago, had only swept up forty years of wreckage, forging ahead.

"Come on, forget that work inside," a voice in my head lured. "You could garden today. Wouldn't that be more fun than scraping walls in this greasy kitchen? You waited half a year to get to it, what does it matter?"

Undeterred, I opened the first cabinet. Like a surgeon to an assistant, I slipped into rubber gloves, ordering, "Sponge, please." Every inch got scrubbed with the abrasive side, was rinsed, scrubbed, and rinsed again. Black water that flooded out into buckets was emptied onto the ivy in the front yard.

Tracks from years of storing certain pots and pans on certain shelves lifted. Worn paint told the story of routines, repeated. The cutting board was worn through—two holes, right, left, from forty years of chopping—better to drop food through? Occasionally I caught a glimpse of the 'tar pit' where the stove had covered the floor. I'd put that off for tomorrow.

"Best 'til last," as they say.

When the first wall of cabinets was done, I stepped back

to admire. The lower cabinets are turquoise blue, matching the counter tops. I hated the color a day ago, held color swatches next to that Formica, plotting escape from sea foam green. But with the cabinets clean and the odd shaped knobs scrubbed and shining, suddenly it didn't look too bad. Besides—it was mine.

Staffordshire dinner plates left graciously by the Connollys were stacked over clean paper towels. Two dozen wine goblets I always keep in a box, just for parties, came out next. I lined them into diagonals on the top shelf, and felt rich.

Lemon Pledge on the counters and backsplash was the final blessing. After two white serving platters met scrub brush and soap, I set them up in display at the rear. This—was the collar on the dog.

I met a woman once who had stared out of her kitchen window at an old, broken fence in her backyard for ten years. She hated the fence, the decrepit wood, the way it leaned. Every day, a few times a day, she glared at the eyesore. One day she finished the dishes, set the sponge down next to the sink, and without much thought walked out to the fence, and pulled. With a few tugs, it fell, section after section.

"It was so easy," she celebrated. "And I looked at it for ten years!"

'The final target? Why wait? I took aim at my "old fence," the black tar pit. Yes, I did spray a few times with Sally's bleach. Next assault? Armed with a razor blade, I went to my knees. With every major job, sooner or later I have to get down on my knees to finish. Grease and rodent dirt oozed up, swipe after swipe. Then I poured soft scrub directly on the monster. In a few minutes and a roll of paper towels, yellow linoleum was smiling up at me.

After I dumped that last water bucket on the grass, hesitating in the doorway, I had a feeling that holds hands with awe, is best friends with the question, "Who would have thought?" Who would have thought that this old kitchen could look this good? Has it grown? I swear it's bigger.

"Who would have thought that soap and vision could grow "normal" into "exotic"? I asked as I stepped outside—and watched two white herons fly between the moon and the earth like wild flamingos.

April 6, 2006 Easter Sunday

I have a frog! Hallelujah! Sargie and I were in out in the back yard tonight and I heard it—a mating call.

"Baroom!"

It was coming from the bottom of the almost empty pool where rains are quickly filling a new "lake."

"Baroom! Baroom!"

"It doesn't sound like he's getting much action!" I mentioned to my trusty dog as we crept up to the edge. "Now, how's he going to find a lady frog way down there?"

April 21, 2006 10:15 p.m.

Sarge started it. It's all his fault! I ran with him in Cow Field. I had a perfectly good depression percolating before I let him loose. But as soon as he He tore up the trail through the tall weeds, he had me laughing, knowing that he wouldn't have come even if I'd called. So I ran after him.

An old horse wrangler told me once if a horse comes running at you and you're on another horse, turn around and he'll go around you. Face him and you will collide. I called Sarge three times. When I heard him thundering toward me, I turned my back. He blew past, ears flattened like a racehorse.

"You're running!" I exclaimed. "Like the good ol' days, huh?"

We met up with two goofy looking guys leading white and black horses, both rescues, they said, from the rental stables. Out of the blue one of the strangers asked, "Are you okay with your father?"

"I don't know how to answer that."

"I mean, do you think he did the best with what he had?"

"Absolutely," I said. "He's a very sick man. He did what he could. "

"Good."

"Why?"

"Because you're done choosing men like him."

I thought, "Where is this coming from? This guy doesn't even know me!"

I'll never know why I had to run home and polish all twenty nails after that. It was probably ceremonial.

April 26, 2006 10:00 p.m.

"Hey, wanna play on my bark chips?" I invited, pointing to the pile of wood chunks heaped in my driveway. The two teenagers and Lola, the incredibly beautiful woman across the street smiled, and began walking across Riverview.

"Sure," the girl answered.

"Okay," the boy agreed.

But the children stood still, not knowing what to do when confronted with a literal mountain of opportunity.

"Just go!" I coached.

Those poor, raised-inside kids did not know the first thing about playing "King of the Mountain." But soon they were climbing up the hill, making the risky assumption that they were, in fact, both kings of the mountain.

"I'm Manor. O-R," the girl spelled on descent.

"My name is Quentin," the boy huffed. "I'm named after Quentin Tarantino."

"Oh." I said.

"He's some director."

"I see. Are you in the film industry?"

"No," he said. "I'm in grade school."

April 27, 2006 8:00 p.m.

She pulled up next to me on the wrong side of the street.

"What's shakin'?" she asked, bald head shining, her eyes shooting sparks.

"Not much. 'You?"

"I'm in a sexy car, looking for trouble!"

The cherry-red Porsche convertible was purring like a steed ready to bolt, and stretch its legs.

"You all dressed up and nowhere to go?"

Danielle Dennison threw her head back in a wild laugh.

"Everyone's out of the house, so I've got the buggy out, my "top" is down! Ha! How's it going with the house? Tell me."

Off went the engine.

"I haven't given up the ship. I barbecued yesterday and Stewart and his neighbor came running over when they saw smoke coming out of the driveway. They thought I'd had enough and decided to burn the place down! I know people think I'm crazy."

"Get used to it. They think I'm crazy, too. People are mad because I'm stirring this—pollution thing up."

"People need to get stirred up so something will happen. I mean—chromium six—mercury?"

"We're going to win. We're all going to win. How's the dog doing?"

"He's great. He's on the job, see?" She peered down at my boxer sitting purposefully on my left foot.

"He's protecting you."

"Yep."

"We all need someone to protect us," she said, turning the key, letting the engine roar. "I called the *Times* six weeks ago, talked to a reporter—nothing."

"I know. They won't go up against Cow Horn. Have you talked to a lawyer?"

"I heard sheets rustling, Cow Horn's voice in the background, when I spoke with the receptionist!"

"Oh, that Russian guy? "I scoffed. "He's not returning my call either."

"He's not returning anyone's call since the second report came out, the one—"

"From the city? The 'its-low-level-go-ahead-and-play-there' *That* one?"

"Yeah, that one." Danielle shook her head." It's going to make the Love Canal look like a picnic in the park. This—has gone on for decades."

"The engineer from your testing place told me to grow tomatoes in pots. Not in the ground. He sounded scared." Then it was my turn to shift gears. "So, Mrs. Dennison, 'ye have a full tank of gas? 'Headin' for the border are ye?"

"Call me Danielle," she scolded, checking the gauge. "Almost a full tank. Hey, by the way, use the D and G behind your house—those mounds? It's not dirt. It's pre-digested granite for horse stalls. I ordered it, didn't need it for mine. You're going to ride that black into victory!"

"How'd you know my horse is black?"

"Lucky guess? Now I' m going to go—stir up some trouble!" The wild woman confirmed, gunning the engine, laughing like a defiant teenager in Daddy's stolen wheels.

"You go, girl!" I cheered as she pulled away, driving straight into a burning yellow sun that was melting like hot wax all over Cow Field.

CHAPTER ELEVEN

Chocolate Cake

I AM HOUSE

I am house
I am home

When the ground
Breathes my walls
Know to bend
My roof follows

Houses live on soil
Not on stilts
We are true children
Of the earth we know

The dust raged
In the field
How hard the
Earth fought

Choked for decades
On the poison it could
Only swallow so much and
Then the wind had to take over

May 12, 2006 9:00 p.m.

I don't think it's particularly nice to be saying not great things about a person while you're eating their food at their memorial. Certain neighbors whose names shall remain unmentioned sat at one of those wide round tables under tumbling crimson bougainvillea, and knife in hand, proceeded to carve Danielle Dennison out as a "gold digger" who wanted to capitalize on her cancer with a lawsuit.

(Oh, really? Have another helping of potato salad. Go for the ham while you're at it. Everyone's getting up for seconds, why should you be any different?)

"By the way, have you tried the chocolate cake?" I presented, rising. "There're at least ten to choose from. I baked one myself. It's on a blue plate. "Nice weather for a funeral, don't you agree?" Was my parting statement as I sought refuge at the bar, waiting for a young man with a yellow-ribbon garter on his arm to serve my club soda with lime.

There I met a tight lipped Austrian woman who introduced herself as a childhood friend of Danielle's. Everyone does grief differently. Her version was brittle, sharp as glass.

"Men couldn't keep up with her," she said, stirring her martini with an impaled olive on a red pick.

"I know," I agreed. "Do not get between Danielle and something she wanted!"

The woman, not being Irish, did not laugh.

I forged on, trying to lighten the moment.

"I heard she jack-hammered the kitchen floor open one day to get at a leaking pipe!"

With deadly seriousness she spat, "There are people here who did not like her. They are talking about her, about the lawsuit. Did you know the people two doors down? That woman died of breast cancer. Her husband got cancer. Now there son rents the house out, the two-story, you know? There are people here talking about her, and Larry."

Across the patio, Larry Dennison stood thronged by other men, their shirtsleeves rolled, ties loosened. Most clasped beer bottles. Thanks to cancer, Larry was down to one kidney. Before that, he had never been sick a day in his life.

"All along here, there are people—"

"I know. I've heard," I said, thinking it was about time for another soda.

"Are you—an enemy?" she confronted. "Are you enemy or friend?"

"I'm new here. Danielle was always kind to me."

Squinting, she veered in even closer, rattling her sabre.

"There are enemies all around us. They are sitting—"

"It really is a very nice day," I acknowledged, my eyes narrowing, spy-to-spy. "Have you tried the chocolate cake?"

May 13, 2006 9:00 p.m.

The woman had to hold tight on the reins. Her foaming-at-the-mouth Shire was not happy. His rider was taking too long with other humans, focused on conversation, and not him. He pawed the ground, trying to make his point. Bearer of bad news, she wore a black helmet with a sun visor that made her look like a policeman—or Darth Vader. Making stops all along Riverview, talking to neighbors, mine was literally the last house on the block—where I was, of course, digging.

"I'm Rachel Ramirez."

"Hello," I nodded, withholding salute.

"What Mrs. Dennison said might be true." Rachel spouted from her very high horse. "Fifty-six times more chromium than the government allows."

"I go there every night with my dog."

"Don't."

In that second, I hated the messenger—because I hated the message. I wanted to spear her with my shovel, put her out of *my* misery. Did she have an agenda?

"Hundreds of people and animals have died, along here." She said.

Where did Rachael get her figures? Anyone can spout a number. I didn't ask. I was struck, dumb, in front of a character who I would have cast easily in a World War II film—on the side of the Germans. Here was the Gestapo's answer to Nurse Ratchett.

"We'll have a class action lawsuit. I got some lawyer pal so it won't cost us anything. You're part of it because your property backs to it. They have to dig twenty feet down, take out all the dirty soil, seal it, fill it with clean. It's a huge process."

(Not to mention the publicity. Cow Horn Productions, the company that made a name for itself by rocking your babies to sleep, did not want to be known as "serial killer.")

"Does that mean the trees have to go?" I asked.

"Would you rather have trees or chromium six? That's why no one has tilled the weeds under. When you disturb the dirt, it's airborne. We all have to have our ductwork checked."

"I can't use mine." I said, as I dropped the shovel and my hands found my hips. Talk about taking a stance. I was not to be moved.

Standing in her stirrups, waving her crop, she came in for the close.

"My plan is to have Cow Field fenced—so only residents around here can use it. We'll have keys, but no one else will be able to come in."

"Like a country club?" I blinked, swallowing my own sarcasm.

"Yes, like that. The homeowner's association here used to

be very powerful. We did what we wanted. We'll do it again. I am not alone in this. Other people want it, too."

Right about then I picked up my shovel and staked it—and my opinion—hard in the ground. "I guess this is why we have a democratic process."

Ms. Vader made her exit soon after that. She said her horse wanted to get back to his stall. I wished her well and had to dig another hour and a half before I could calm down.

May 14, 2006 8:00 p.m.

"I might want to be a part of that lawsuit," Diana offered, folding her napkin until it was the size of a postage stamp.

For fifteen years I'd vowed that I would be her neighbor—because Diana's daughter kept her horse in their backyard and I wanted a backyard just like hers.

"One day, I'm going to move in, blocks from you." I'd threaten every time I'd walk across the office to her desk. Then one day, I did. "Now I can run over to your house in my pajamas!" I confirmed, the day I signed off on Riverview. "I'm going to be two blocks away—for a long time!"

"I might want to sue." Diana repeated, eyes on the placemat.

"You want to be part of the lawsuit? 'Because of Gene?"

"He was there every day, every afternoon all those years while the kids were in school, coaching them on the horses. Everyone was in Cow Field back then. No one was thinking about cancer."

"How long has it been?"

"Two years."

"I can still hear his—he had a DJ's voice."

"He had a voice. People still talk about that.

"I'll get the lawyer's number. 'Some Russian guy."

"Our horse died, too. The vet couldn't explain it. "Said it had to do with his lungs?"

I swiped the check. "I'll get this."

"No, you won't."

"I had a good week. Hey, didn't I always say I was going to be your neighbor? Besides, your money's no good here! Wow, I'm really living here, after twenty years of searching!"

Diana raised her almost empty water glass in a toast.

"Welcome to the neighborhood."

May 15, 2006 10:00 p.m.

I submerged Frosty in the bath water. He fell backwards, sprang up to life. I pried his orange nose loose from his face.

"Thank you," he said, turning to show both sides. "Nice profile, huh? My carrot is a little shriveled," he giggled, checking out his own belly. "So," he began, head up, taking in the bombed out holes-in-the-walls-stuffed-with-newspaper décor. "Who won that war?"

"I guess—I did?"

"Well, at least the battlefield is quiet." Then the sponge stared me down, waiting me out. "What are you worried about?"

"Money? This month, I—I'm tanking, Frosty. I'm thinking what's the point? I'm out of gas."

"He's got all the money. He owns all the real estate. He knows all the people. Go to Him. Then get some sleep."

"But I keep thinking—"

"Let Him do the thinking."

"Why?"

"Because you think small! It's all they knew to teach you. He's thinking big for you."

"Frosty, I'm lonely for Him. I—ache. I can't find God in this—house."

"Why don't you close your eyes and go to His house? Just see what you see? Why don't you have a blind date with God?"

Opened to: If *only I knew where to find Him, if only I could go to His dwelling!*

CHAPTER TWELVE

Blind Date

I AM HOUSE

I am house
I am home

Lay quiet
I tell her
Let me hold
The rain away

You
Have done
Enough for
Today I will speak

To Spirit for you
The One who makes
Green to grow splits
Seeds and hearts wide open

Souls into bodies
I will let Him know you
Cannot find Him no matter
How hard you look in all my corners

May 16, 2006 10:00 p.m. meditation

It was a white house. Two mammoth Cypress trees anchored double front doors. The place felt like money—old money. I knocked, circle drive behind me. I could hear waves crashing on sand. The air was better at His house. The doors opened and there He was—tall, lean, striding towards me in a rescue. I fell against His chest.

"Oh, God."

"I know," He said. "I know."

We stayed like that, standing on cool white marble that was somehow warming my bare feet at the same time.

"Come," He ushered me in with a strong yet gentle arm against the small of my back.

Together on a worn leather sofa in a paneled den off of the living room, we faced a wall of windows that overlooked endless ocean. Every room had this view. It figured that here you would be able to see forever.

"I—I'm scared."

He listened, right arm thrown back casually over the sofa. I noticed a carved desk in front of us. A single white piece of paper lay next to a silver pen. No phone. A large glass globe floated one golden angel's trumpet flower, about the size of a dinner plate. It honeyed the entire house, coating it like syrup.

"I thought it was the perfect house," I confessed. "It's exactly what I asked You for, dared You for, when I was under Live Oak, remember?"

He nodded, intent, head down.

"I married the son-of-a-bitch house and now I'm wondering what I ever saw in it! And this Cow Field pollution—it's a mess. But I have frogs—about twenty of them came in the pool after the rains."

"Every princess should have a frog in her pond. It oughta be the law."

I peeled my shoulders off of the ceiling. A deep calm began to blanket me. So this is grace? This is what it feels like to have a truly rich Daddy? I'd catered in mansions, studied the daughters, wives of wealthy men. Who would have thought? *I'm* a little rich girl, protected? I had no idea.

"I'm tired. I've been working so hard. I feel like the house isn't over drinking. Will it ever recover? Is it too far gone to save? I set the coconuts, smudged, prayed for the dark to go out, for light to come in. But I feel like I'm still in my parents' house and I'm finding all those empty beer bottles from the night before, lined up along the sink, and I have to rinse them, drop them back in the case, so it won't smell like a bar, so alcohol won't—kill us."

A white handkerchief came out of His back pocket. He shook it open.

I wiped my eyes, blew my nose. The linen wafted faintly of cornstarch and citrus.

Everything smelled good here.

Then I let it out.

"I guess—bad as it is—I don't think I deserve that house?"

He blinked in a knowing way, choosing His next words carefully.

"I have more that I want to give you. Don't worry about the storage fees! I'm keeping everything on hold."

"And I think I should do more."

"*I'm* doing more."

"Oh."

"All you have to do is write, dance, and ride your pony."

"Write, dance, and ride my pony?"

"And rest. My Baby is tired."

Then He kissed my forehead, and led me across gleaming hardwood into the living room. A grey Wiemaraner dog ran up to greet us, and leaned against my leg.

"She thinks she's supposed to guard you."

"What's her name?"

"Angel."

I looked up at Him while I pet Angel's back.

"What should I do about the house?"

"Are you doing everything I asked?"

"I'm showing up, being of service, doing my best."

Years before, He'd come to me in a meditation on a white Andalusian stallion in battered armor, disrobing, showing me His bare chest to let me know that He, too, was vulnerable in our relationship. He'd appeared in a rowboat on a lakeshore in another meditation, a rock-n-roll kind of guy, dark, sexy, with long brown hair. One pull of the oars and we were halfway across the lake. (When you have that kind of power, you get across water, quick). But every time He'd appeared, His presence, the core, was the same. And I never had to share Him with anyone. I am always His entire focus. Maybe that's why the Name translates to 'I AM?'"

Captured in His grin, infected with His warmth, I asked, "Why couldn't I find You after I moved into that house?"

"You had to learn—that you have 'direct access.' Visit more." It was a stern, loving order.

"But you have so many—"

He half scowled. "I built this place, your place, for you and Me to live in. Now, go swim! I'll join you for lunch."

Angel led me out to a cabana next to the pool, her tail slowly wagging. The first item of clothing I set down on the lounge was the handkerchief. Three embroidered letters caught my eye; I smiled to read "G.O.D."

May 17, 2006 9:30 a.m.

I didn't know why there were so many dead dragonflies in the pond. Yesterday morning, there they were, floating, still. Dragonflies I see over water are dangerous, accurate fighter pilots. That's after they've lived as grubs in the muck, underwater for a year, emerging out of old brown cases, resurrected, unrecognizable as their former selves. Why have these come here to die?

This morning I got my answer. It wasn't adults, returning. It was the young who were dying. Wings outstretched, partially folded, a dragonfly was struggling on the surface. I lifted it out with a stick, set in on a dry step of the pool. But it needed something to crawl up on. I moved it to a tall weed. There it clung, exhausted but determined.

Others not as lucky had given up. All along the pool's edge, a few inches above the water, empty shells where someone once lived were clinging to plaster. I knelt down close to examine one. A tiny slit on the top told the whole story. Whatever lived inside had become too big, had no choice but to crawl out—and fly.

"I would love to see them take flight," I said to Sarge. "It's probably too sacred a thing for us mere mortals?"

May 18, 2006 10:00 p.m.

So hot. So damn hot. This is no week to start hot flashing.

"Is it hot or is it me?"

Came home at eight o'clock and the place was a barbecue. It's against my rules to let cats out after dark. We have coyotes here. But tonight, they flew out. Even with doors and windows open, attic fan churning, the house was an inferno.

"That's it!" I decided. "I'm out of here! I'm—by January first when the tenants' lease is up on the pool house, I'm gone. S.O.L.D. It's been nice. 'Sure thought it would work."

But then, I always leave—the man, the job, my parents, and now, a house?

"Gotta go, can't fix this. Sorry. Bye."

"Manageable." The word appears like a running teletype on the stomach of a blimp, floating over all usual thoughts.

"Manageable." You might want to try something more, well, "manageable?"

To pack or unpack, that is the question? Whether 'tis nobler in the mind to suffer the slings and arrows of outrageous fears, or to take arms against a sea of payments and by selling, end them?

To liquidate, to surrender? Ah, but in that escrow, what regrets may come?

I came close to collapsing a few times today over anything, nothing, over being lost on streets I've driven for twenty years. I'm easily shaken, emptied, worn thin. I risked saying "No" graciously to a couple of requests. But I did say "Yes" to the urge to go over to the Mother House, my first house, and walk around those lush gardens. I took some seaweed out of the pond in the backyard, bought it here, and threw it in a tub of water. It was my last exasperated act of the day. I was done.

"There. There's my pond." I said, running a hose until it overflowed. Something needed to be filled around here. I'm dry. Everything's dry. I froze here in the winter. Now, six months later, it's like living on the sun.

Why did all those dragonflies die? There are fewer frogs now. I don't know where they came from or where they're going? The minnows I released to eat the mosquito larvae in the pool aren't to be seen, either.

I wanted this place so badly, and now all I can do is wander around aimlessly, sweating, pleading for an answer to the question—

"Should I stay?"

I haven't removed a single box from Butch's collection stacked in the den.

A few nights ago June asked, "So, are we moving you in or moving you out?"

"Frankly, my dear," I said. "I don't give a damn."

June 18, 2006 Father's Day almost midnight

The curtain went up on a phone message from Tony. He read the article that I wrote for the Star about Amelia Earhart's house. His take was, "You should quit your real estate job and do your writing!"

Later, on his front porch sipping root beer floats, I confessed, "I wrote two novels and I need 10 K to publish the first—" when my cell phone went off. It was Wanda, telling me a friend's book just got picked up for the entire back page review in *O*.

"So, I guess it's a doable thing?" I laughed. "Interesting that I was just talking about books and publishing when I get that call? It could happen, huh?"

Tony winked, digging into his tall float glass with a long handled spoon. "Propitious."

"I didn't know you knew big words."

"I don't. Just that one."

We finished our drinks on his steps, lingering in a day tasting of Dad's root beer and thick, cold vanilla-bean ice cream. Tony's porch isn't big and grand with wicker chairs and ferns. It has barely room enough for two people to sit side-by-side and look down at the Chinese elm, his old fir tree—and my house.

"Your bedroom windows are just tall enough," he mused, closing in on the last of the ice cream. Tony knew I wasn't big on clothes—or draperies. Those casement windows—I was pretty sure—come up to my shoulders.

"Maybe letting go of this home is the way to go," I said, spearing the last of the iceberg at the bottom of my glass. "Society says, 'The more the better.' But maybe—"

"Are you worth more today than when you bought them?"

"Heck, yeah."

"Then you're making money while we're sitting here."

"But—"

"Do you have more money coming in that going out?"

"Barely."

"Then you're doing okay."

"I'm homesick, Tony," I told him, looking down at melting cream so I wouldn't have to see his face, and so he wouldn't see my tears. "I need to come home. The only problem, I'm not quite sure where home is?"

"I'm trying to help you feel more like home."

It was no use trying to pour the last of the can of root beer into his glass. His trembling freckled hand forced the contents back to my glass.

He mentioned something about thinking of me all day.

"Oh, Tony, you're not going to get weird on me, are you? You're supposed to be my 'father figure.'"

"I'll be your grandfather."

"That'll work. Then we have to talk about horses. Gramps always wanted a horse. One with a lotta chrome—like a car!"

This brings me to the last page of this notebook. I'm writing on the hard inside back cover because all the pages are used up. My new one is at the office-supply store, wrapped in plastic, waiting for me. One day soon I hope that a book that I wrote will be waiting for people.

End of this journal.

CHAPTER THIRTEEN

Kitty Boy

I AM HOUSE

I am house
I am home

A kitten plays in my
Rooms now I
Had other cats a
Little dog

A pony in the
Yard long tail
Thick mane I know
What hay smells like

Sweet and rich if houses
Could eat they would
Bite into green alfalfa sleep
Legs folded head down like foals

A kitten
Gallops in my
Halls tonight and
Thousands of nights ago

June 19, 2006 9:30 p.m.

"Unhand me, you heathen!" warned the sponge.

Kitty Boy had Frosty in his mouth by the back of his neck, was dragging him into the laundry basket like a leopard taking an antelope up a tree. "Don't just sit there!" the snowman called. "Save me!"

I collected the sponge from the cub, slipped a sock over my hand, and offered fresh meat for attack—my own flesh.

"Where did you get that animal?" the sponge asked, assembling himself on my stomach, the island of refuge in a sea of bubbles.

"He found me. I heard screaming from some bushes, pulled the branches back, and as soon as he saw me, he ran straight at me, yowling. He's only four weeks old, is my guess."

"No wonder his mother left him!" Frosty jeered.

"I think he rescued me! Wait! Listen! Kitty Boy's lapping milk out of a dish for the first time!"

"Ah, he 'took'," the sponge nodded, taking a peek over the edge. "Like a plant taking root."

"Yes, he 'took.' No more two a.m. feedings with an eyedropper! 'Music to my ears," I said, closing my eyes, resting my head against white porcelain. "That yellow tom that used to live here? The one who broke the window—with the big, round head? Check out that kitten's face. I think he's the father. I called that tom "Terrorist cat." Frosty, he's the only cat I would have shot. And now here I am, in love with is son. Life is so weird. Listen to that cat drink. No more two a.m. feedings. I can't believe it."

June 20, 2006 3:55 a.m.

Kitty Boy wrapped around my neck like a fur boa, calm and trusting. It wasn't a far drive to the pet shop. But one look at the metal cages where they hold the kittens for adoption, and I felt my eyes growing wet. Michelle, the manager, big and broad, approached, wearing a sweet face that doesn't often see makeup. Odds are she has more than one cat at home.

"If you have any doubt, don't give him to us. Because if you want him back and he's gone—"

"I don't know. I have two already. "

"He's cute. 'Part Siamese—the crossed eyes. They'll figure it out," she said. "I'd use a spray bottle with water in it if they fight, but eventually you're gonna have to let them work things out."

It was going to be so neat, so clean. Drop the kitten off; go on with the day, one more errand done. Then I got it. He was one of the "troops of angels" sent to save me. Kitty Boy needed me. He gave me: mission. In the process, I couldn't sink into doubt. I was busy making sure he was okay. 'Those two a.m. feedings? They were the antidote for my three a.m. panic attacks.

Besides, the damn cat makes me laugh.

Tonight I introduced Kitty Boy to humility and powerlessness. If he was going to have a life outside of the bathroom where I'd kept him sequestered, he was going to have to meet the big boys—Magic and Rocky. Kitty Boy crouched in his crate while Magic dominated, jumping on top, growling, punching the gate until the metal door rattled. Rocky stayed resigned, deliberating on the sidelines, white paws folded against his chest.

When we were back in the bath behind closed doors, and I was deep in the tub, Kitty Boy stepped from the edge over foaming water to my shoulder, licking, and drinking water off of my face. He doesn't seem to mind soap. I would have missed that moment if I'd left him with Michelle. I'd be here, knowing that my kitten was half a mile away behind bars in a pet shop window. I would have missed him leaping off the tub onto the vanity, four feet away, from a standstill—proof that if he were human, he'd be Olympic material.

June 21, 2006 10:00 p.m.

I buried St. Joseph tonight, twice. I dug fast after dark with the claw end of a hammer so none of my former neighbors would see me and ask questions. I didn't have a shovel. Brokers all over the country are burying little St. Joseph statues in front yards of houses that aren't selling. Supposedly, St. Joseph takes care of wayward realtors—and their properties. There's a St. Joe in front of the Mother House and just for good measure, at the pool house next door. What do I do now? If the first one sells, it sells. Right now, I have no clue. I'm trying to do what I'm doing and ignore the feeling that whatever I'm doing isn't enough.

Saint Joe hit the dirt—head down—wrapped in a note listing all of the things I want help with: mortgages, even painting Riverview. He's got tools. He's well connected. He can help. Mom would only pray to Saint Joseph.

"God's too busy," she always said. "I pray to Saint Joe."

Saint Joe probably got a kick out of me digging with a hammer.

June 24, 2006 10:00 p.m. meditation

I didn't know He had a second story. I made a right to an upper-level porch out onto a roof patio. His back was to me. He was surrounded, focused on huge clear maps of the world that showed dark areas which, as soon as I walked in, disappeared into thin air. His focus went directly on me. With warmth and directness, He reassured me that He was taking care of all my affairs—All my affairs. Evidently, God can multitask—keep an eye on the Middle East, Africa—and me.

I could feel the unspoken weight of global concerns linger behind His eyes as He led me to a telescope overlooking the ocean. Swiveling it to face land, encouraging me to look through it, I spied on a couple, a man and a woman, kissing in the front seat of a red vintage T-bird convertible. He watched as I pivoted the telescope back out over the ocean.

"You'll have that, too," He said, turning the idea and the telescope—back on me. "If you want it?"

I took Him in, the man in the expensive suede shoes, cool linen shirt, trousers. The Chief knows how to dress. But it wasn't about the clothes. He was cool—Like He invented "cool." Like He invented, well, everything.

"When you're ready," He smiled, with a wry grin. "So, hey, would you fly with Me?""

"Fly?"

"I know. It's weird, but 'wanna fly? We don't need a plane. We can do it—ourselves!"

"I have no idea what You are talking about."

"Um, just put your arms around Me, here," He demonstrated, stepping in front of me, wrapping my arms around Him in a hug. "Just hold on and—"

"Oh! You might drop me."

"I've heard you say that before."

"You're right. I'm always afraid—You'll drop me. "

He looked down at the tiles at His feet like He wanted to memorize each one.

"I know. "He said. "Can you keep a secret?'

"Okay, I guess."

"It's impossible for Me to drop you. We are not separate. I committed to you before time began. I'm—invested in you."

With that, I did wrap my arms around His back and we lifted up! But He knew I was scared, so He came right back down.

"Ready? Try again?"

"I guess so." Third try, off we went, skimming over waves,

me on His back, flat out, almost touching a whale's back as it surfaced, traveling over a pod of dolphins, circling, then landing back where we started—like nothing strange had happened.

"Like—You just—fly?"

He looked down at His feet, then out at the horizon while He organized His thoughts. "It's strange for Me to fly, too."

"Really?"

"It's cool, but—it's not the flying that's odd—it's trusting that I can do it—that's the big deal, I guess."

"Trusting Yourself? You? And You—like—You just fly! You don't like have a cape or anything!"

"Oh, yeah, a cape. Maybe I should get a cape?"

Opened to: A*ssuredly I say to you, today you shall be with me in Paradise.*

CHAPTER FOURTEEN

Flying Dragons

I AM HOUSE

I am house
I am home

The winds are wild
Daughters in search of
Their Father
The One who breathes

Life into all
Houses are not
Blind and
Dumb behind paint

We know
Who grew trees
To make us tall stone
To ground us to earth

We whisper to the
Winds you must
Be quiet only when
You rest can you hear Him

June 26, 2006 10:30 p.m.

I crossed the street, stumbled over to Tony and Stewart. "I—I think I'm going to have to sell Riverview. I can't do these payments. I can't. I—"

"Can't you sell your other houses and stay?" Tony posed, glass of wine in hand.

"I've got one 'on the block.' The other one is rented. No one's buying that one, either. It was all going to be so easy—rent them out, live happily ever after."

"I wish I'd bought rental property," Stewart coughed, downing the last of his Santa Barbara red. "With all the money I made, I should have apartment buildings!"

Tony faced us both. "It's stuff. It's—you gotta say, 'Am I making more than is going out?'"

Stewart and I exchanged looks. He frowned in concern.

"I don't want you to go, Kathy. We have to figure out a way. Couldn't you grow catfish in your pond? Sell them?"

I said nothing. Maybe Stewart had a point. Was what I needed already here?

"Tony," I asked, "How much do they charge for catfish?"

"Ah," he said, "That would be sliding scale."

June 27, 2006 11:00 p.m.

"When I was growing up I heard too many women groan, 'I wish I would have, I wish I would have, I wish I would have.' I thought, "If I can get on premises, I can make it happen. If I can just get in that house—'"

Betty disagreed. "No, it has to make sense."

Ceremoniously we slid little pieces of paper with my name and Riverview's into a crystal box for the universe to handle.

We wiped our faces, often. Was I saying goodbye to my house? Do dreams bleed red when they die? Do they soak the ground in rivers? Do they mix with tears?

The humans were gone when I moved into Riverview, but there was a lot of blood left on the floor from visions, sacrificed. Was I supposed to leave my dreams there, too? Was it my turn, now, to walk from that place—To abandon the block of white carrara marble? Say it was flawed?

"I've been wanting to have this conversation with you for a long time. "She dared. "It's—this house is making you sick. You can't keep going into debt. Sometimes it's the dark forces in me that make me go out of control. It's my navel that I need to contemplate," she purred, in a tone that could warm a pot of tea, smooth sheets, plant a flower, caress a hand. This time it was my hand. We sat very close, thigh-to-thigh. "I wish you could hold up and write for a year."

"I can't go through another winter with no heat or air and holes in the walls. The first house isn't selling. The second barely covers its mortgage. With no rental income, I've got about three months' reserve to feed the troops, and then it's time to slaughter the horses—and eat them."

July 3, 2006 11:00 p.m.

Could it be? Barely a quarter of an inch long, it was jetting through the weeds in that little tub of water. A month ago, totally depressed, out of hope, didn't I bring some seaweed from the koi pond at the Mother house back here in a plastic bag and throw it in there saying, "Here's my pond?" I hadn't paid much attention after that.

Stooping low, I saw more movement—more baby fish—a second, a third.

But I never put fish in that container. Put this in italics: *I never put fish in there.*

I spent a good bit of time looking down at them, seeing living creatures. Even this small, I could tell they weren't minnows. Their heads were too big. Some were shadowed in colors—subtle orange, black. These were koi babies. How did this happen?

Then an idea took hold. "There must have been eggs on those weeds?" But…it can't be. Those weeds were out of water, dry for a long time.

Didn't He supply loaves, fishes, food for multitudes, vast amounts out of nothing?

"What would you have Me do for you?" the Great Healer asked people, over and over. So when I said, "Hey, this is my pond," I guess—I was pronouncing it a done deal? Could it be that simple? Say what I want Him to do for me? Ask, and the fish will appear?

It defied logic. Just-when-I-think-I'm-crazy-for-buying-this-house a miracle happens, a pitch, right over home plate. Koi—out of nowhere.

It's always darkest before the spawn.

July 5, 2006 10:00 p.m.

So that was it. 'Second man in a week sent to ask the same questions. He knew my name. Just like the other man did.

"Do you want to sell?"

"No! Do you see a 'For Sale' sign?"

Maybe he knew I was tax delinquent? Soon he was going to know something else—that when I'm scared, I get angry, and when I'm angry, I'm big trouble.

"Have a good evening," I growled, Sarge clinging to my side, growling like a lion. Subtext? Well, you know the subtext: "And the horse you rode in on!"

Dog and I trotted down the driveway, away from the not very well dressed man in the wrinkled shiny black suit. Other subtext: “Take yourself and that fin on your back and get the fuck off my lawn.”

But he wasn’t done.

Farther up Riverview his car slid up next to us.

We did an abrupt about face.

He found the accelerator and burned off.

July 7, 2006 11:00 p.m.

If I hadn’t brought a plate of barbecue ribs over to Lynn’s house, if I hadn’t walked across my lawn and then his, I never would have found out. The plot thickens. Mrs. Dennison gave Lynn a copy of the report from the core samples. He taught me how to read it. The words were as dry as the soil in Cow Field:

The summary said high levels of chromium 6 and mercury were consistently found to depths of 12": Remediation recommended.

Right about dessert time, Lynn nudged himself away from the table and told me the reason I hadn’t seen his partner, Richard, for a while.

“A month ago, he died.”

“What?”

“He went in for a biopsy, a simple biopsy on his liver and he bled to death on the operating table.”

I didn’t know what to say, what to do. It seemed like yesterday that I’d seen Richard striding up the walk.

“He was fifty-two,” Lynn told me, dry eyed. “There was a time when he was the best dancer on Broadway. That was him, on the billboard over Times Square, doing the splits, six feet in the air—” His eyes were traveling far away, had to fight to get back in focus with me, the live person sitting across from him. “He was fifty-two. I’m … I think I’m in shock. It hasn’t sunk in yet.”

“Of course you’re still in shock!”

"It's like he's on a trip. I keep thinking he'll be home any day now."

I was about to ask why he hadn't said anything and then I remembered, everyone does grief differently. Some do it silently—and alone.

His dogs felt the change in the room. They gathered around him, three tails wagging.

"Dogs know," I said. "They all know."

"My partner died of liver failure, there's a sore on my leg that won't heal. Four of my prize Lipizzaner horses died from hoof sores. I tried to keep them alive for too long. They were always healthy before I moved here. It all started three years ago when I came. No explanation." He took a breath, like he'd been running too fast. "And my lymph glands are swollen and sore. I'm thinking of moving. I don't have family to take care of me when I'm dead or half-dead!"

"I just had lunch with a girlfriend. Her husband died of cancer two years ago. He was in the Field every day with their son, growing up. She told me her son was just diagnosed with leukemia—and that Russian lawyer? The one who's not returning anyone's calls? He returned hers, grilled her vehemently about why did she want to know what disclosures she should use for her real estate transactions—regarding the Cow Horn issue?

He backed her into a corner with, 'How long have you been practicing real estate? What makes this important?'"

"He's been bought off."

"Of course. He won't be the last."

"Lynn," I said, staring out into the living room past his collection of saddles, photos, ribbons from horse shows. "This is serious. People don't know. They keep going over there with their children and ponies."

"I know," he said. "There's no publicity. No warning."

"I want to call the *L.A. Times.* Danielle Dennison did, and they didn't do anything, but maybe—"

"Be careful," he warned. "If you identify Cow Horn and they're not at fault, they'll sue you for libel."

"I hope I'm wrong. I hope everything is just 'coincidence.' I hope we can eat mud pies out of Cow Field. But, Lynn, people need to know."

July 9, 2006 8:30 p.m.

It's the best show in Hollywood—and it's free! Here's what you do; Sit on the edge of the shallow side of the pool just after the sun goes down. Let your feet dangle. Ask your dog to sit on your right side. Hold your arm over his back. And wait. And wait. Because you know they'll come. They always show up.

The entire clan was here tonight. I hope they eat their weight in mosquitos. They fly so close to Edith's fence that I'm sure they'll crash, and then they veer down into the pool canyon, swooping, almost hitting the steep sides. I cringe at how amazing they are, defying odds. I revel to hear the soft rush of their bat wings as they fly past.

I am eight or twelve or ten again. Maybe this is another reason that He brought me to this place, why I have water back in a pool? So frogs would sing. So dragonflies would lay eggs. So fish would breed. So mosquitos would hatch. So bats would fly. So I would learn that even if you start to fill it, they will come.

July 10, 2006 9:00 p.m.

The hole dug itself. I cut sod away in chunks the night before, knowing where I wanted her. I went thirty-six inches deep without any effort. Even the soil seemed to say, 'Yes, let's have her here. We need a tree—here."

I ran a hose, filled it. "I never plant a tree in a dry hole," a tree man taught me. He fills his three times with water before he sinks a root ball. I only had time to fill once before Joey, Tony's unofficial 'adopted' son, and I hit the road in Tony's Toyota half-ton. Our goal? Secure the Jacaranda.

"How much for this tree?" Was my question for Jacqueline two days ago when she parted branches of pepper and sycamore saplings, opened space for me to see the bending, angular trunk. She said something in Spanish to her male partner. He lowered his newspaper and nodded.

"Three hundred dollars," she quoted. "But for joo, two hundred."

"Really?"

"Sure. Joo are a good customer."

I wanted a Jacaranda big time, even though it made no financial sense to be tree shopping this week. I needed every cent to make that mortgage payment—every penny. But my *soul* needed feminine, leafy, lavender flowers cooling the front of my home—to balance the sturdy, no-nonsense masculine Olive on the other side.

It took five of us to lift the twenty-four inch box up into the truck bed. I was on the end of the "push." My shovel severed the taproot, the umbilical cord, her "reach" to the sand underneath. This girl had outgrown her old world. She was ready for a move. But changes cost. She left a core part of her old self back in that crowded nursery.

Joey laid a four-by-four at the curb, making less of a "step" for the truck to back up onto the lawn. We "walked" her to the end of the truck's bed. Then I slit three bags of planting compost, added them into the 'soup' while the hose ran full speed. He asked why I tossed twenty-five cow bones in as well?

"One day a woman showed me a bone she'd had in a spider plant's pot. The roots had eaten through the bone in tunnels. Plants want calcium and phosphorus. I'm giving her plenty—because I won't be down there, again!"

Joey measured the depths of the root ball with the handle of his shovel. We opted to fill in more dirt so the tree would "sit" above the lawn with a trough around her root ball. Then we hacked pieces off of the box like we were freeing someone who'd been imprisoned.

It didn't take much to her slide down into place. He used his post hole digger to pivot the trunk the way I wanted her to face. I tried to explain why her 'arm' had to reach across the house, bringing the sight line around from the Olive, then back to her.

"It's harmony. A big circle."

They say you can measure the energy of anything as changing when someone looks at it. I've adored her at least thirty times since she came here to bless and protect this house. I can see her fluffy blooms and leaves when I stand in the living room. I 'm studying the tips of her branches from my bed. She's growing from me seeing her, helping me to say, "Here's proof. I live here."

The only casualty was a branch that broke off in my hands as I pulled twigs apart to "open" the tree. I chastised myself for a hand too hard, too tired. There was a fleeting thought about slipping a message into a bottle and dropping it down there with her roots. But what would I have said? "It's July tenth, 2006, and I'm planting my dream tree in my dream yard of my dream house. These are uncertain times, but today the only thing I know is my soul wanted this tree, and now she's here."

A yellow swallowtail butterfly is lingering on one of her blooms. I wrote this entry while it rested, then fluttered off.

She's here. I can go on to other things. She's home. The Jacaranda is in.

July 11, 2006 5:00 a.m.

I didn't want to be up in the dark. Why was I being pulled out of bed? What was so important in the backyard? In the breath of early light I looked down at the pond, and I couldn't believe the sight—hundreds of them. As it dawned I saw the first, then others—dragonflies—up and down the steep sides of the pool, standing on old carcasses, wings outstretched; waiting like airplanes for takeoff.

One struggled in the water. I ran for a net, laid the creature on the diving board. A second couldn't pull its other wing out of the case. I lifted that wing out, slowly, carefully. A third had its wings stuck together. I brought it up with the net; let it rest on the diving board. Soon, both wings outstretched, it too, waited.

For what?

It happened while I watched. At the same moment, like dancers on cue, all the dragons took flight, swooping, dipping. In twos and twenties and hundreds, abdomens curled, hanging, they moved together in a slow cloud rising onto the morning sky. They circled almost aimlessly, like they were hearing music that I could not.

Then, together, up toward the west, congealing into a cloud of forms, sensing the same direction, they took off.

Gone.

Opened to: *Did I not say to you that if you would believe you would see the glory of God*?

CHAPTER FIFTEEN

Shotgun

I AM HOUSE

I am house
I am home

She does not
Know that we
See the others who
Walk through our walls

Souls who
Linger over
Ours under blankets
Or when they hold a shovel

The one who
Bore her is here
Bandage on one
Wrist a mark of courage

She knits next to
The bed when mine
Sleeps I hear her say I
Love you Baby Girl

November 25, 2006 Naples, Florida 6:45 a.m.

I started at noon, finished at five. Auntie Maureen walked in when things were not quite back in order. The lanai had everything back in place, was hosed, but kitchen and garage had my trademark—newspapers and drop clothes, everywhere.

"You're creating!" she announced.

And I thought she'd be upset.

The second coat of tung oil went on the Amish rocker as she played an Ella Fitzgerald Christmas album, loud, and began to prepare dinner. The sun was collapsing like a deflated balloon, bathing the scene.

"This…is love. This…is family," I thought, as half a bottle of varnish soaked into bent willow. "Does it get any better than this?"

Garage door open, children peered in as they slid past on skateboards. A little girl on pink rollerblades smiled and waved.

My aunt and I took pictures of each other at the table I'd set with sunflowers and green and white striped leaves from the garden. We figure we'll splice the two photos together so we can both be in the picture.

The menu? Chicken breast marinated in Turkish spices (collected from one of her trips), broccoli and cauliflower with Parmesan cheese and garlic, coleslaw, salad with crumbled feta.

More delicious were her stories about exploring the world: Turkey, Greece, and Venice.

"I have a deep need to be in a place where I don't speak the language or where I don't know how I'll spend the night."

When my uncle Jim was alive, when he sat in the chair that the Amish carpenter made, she had no idea that she would travel the world. Disaster, his death, made her different, gave her a new title: Adventurer.

"We're sixteen, mother-daughter, friends, aunt-niece," she explained to a coworker this week about me. Lying on her bed tonight, watching TV, she wanted to know if I was ever with someone who wouldn't take "No" for an answer.

At first I told her about the drunken man who I stopped in a parking lot by pointing my finger into his throat. Then I remembered another.

"I said "No" twice, and still let him the third time. Because—I guess—I went back to that place where I had to do what my father said or he might kill me."

The curtain went down on us in front of the fire in the chimenea, stars glittering through the pool cage, reflecting on the water. My aunt has made her cottage by the lake. It's what we do in our family—find a lake and make a home on the shore. For me it's a pool that became a pond.

I have to fly home today. Tonight, I'll tell my kitties and my dog how much I missed them. That sore throat and exhaustion I arrived with? It's almost gone. It was warmer, softer, better here. I actually sat on a sofa, every day. How strange.

The old rocker was my reminder that who I am is best felt when I have a brush in one hand and a shovel in the other. One more time I'm leaving a silk dress, going back to wear burlap. And I'm not looking forward to it.

November 25, 2006 in the air 9:00 p.m.

I'm sitting next to Nick. His baseball hat is tilted sideways.

"I'm disappointed in this book," My fellow traveler told me, holding up the white dust jacket as evidence.

"Did you read the back cover?" I asked, thinking about by own (future) books.

"No."

"You bought it off the front cover?"

"Yes."

"What were your expectations?"

"I thought it would have something new about growing your wealth. It wasn't—it didn't have any new ideas."

"You're over eighteen. Start buying your own real estate."

"I'm nineteen."

"You don't need parental consent. You just need to qualify for a loan or get investors. The money I invested in my real estate license is the best two hundred dollars I ever spent. I bought my first building before I graduated from college."

"I know good areas to invest in," he said, drumming the book's cover with his fingers. "I can see them—the places that are turning."

I handed him my card.

"In case you ever need a boost, later. But I don't think you will! I think you'll be just fine!"

In D Concourse on that last layover I noticed many books lined on shelves waiting for buyers. In an airport, almost everyone's waiting for something. If pregnant women feel flutters in their stomachs, then authors feel tingles as well. In front of that display while I waited for change, I felt a surge that I can't describe. What moved in my gut told me what was missing—a book by me.

And I was the only one who knew it wasn't there.

November 30, 2006 3:35 a.m.

This part feels like throwing up. I don't want to get this out. Am I my mother, missing the second house, the one she made perfect? Did she sink like this? Was she going down like I am? It wasn't long after we moved into the big house, the third, when she sought out a razor blade. Oh my God, she was fifty-three like I am.

Why do I keep fantasizing about selling Riverview and moving back into my second house?

The toilet overflowed again, today. My house is sick. The day left tire tracks on me. I'm trapped in the land beyond fatigue. When I ran into Nancy, a girl I barely knew, it leaked out—how black it is.

"Oh, you're in your dream house?" she spouted, digging in her purse for cigarettes and a lighter. "I would fuck that up! I always fuck everything up! I would be all—trying to do it perfect. For me, what you're in, that's a guaranteed crash and burn!"

"I picked up a re-fi check today. It's been a year. I can do heat and air now, maybe even paint the place. And all I feel is burned out, hollow. It was supposed to be better now."

Wasn't it getting better? I felt safe in Florida. Now I'm back, and it looks even worse. Too big. Too much. Too cold. I can't go back across that desert again. I know what Lawrence[3] felt like. It will kill me. I…can't.

I ordered heat and central air today. One phone call, like I was ordering a pizza. When you don't want to come home at night because your place is as cold as a meat locker, when jackets are mandatory, it's time to make a barn into a home and trust that there will be enough money to pay the gas bill.

My new creed:

There is enough time.
There is enough money.
God is supplying my every need.

My God, I don't want to write this. This is the part—I opened the journal again. I don't—it hurts. I don't want to say this. I don't want to write this.

Tonight I asked a neighbor how much a shotgun costs? And it wasn't because I was going pheasant hunting.

I heard myself say it and it wasn't me and I was sort of next to myself and we were in their front yard talking about shooting

---

3. *Lawrence of Arabia*, 1962, David Lean, director.

skeet and it was my voice but it was real cool and metallic and I was watching me ask him so casual and I couldn't get back in my body to stop the words.

"How much does a 410 shotgun cost?"

Oh, God.

Oh, my God.

December 3, 2006 9:00 p.m.

"I'm not happy we're both struggling," I told Teddy as she drove us way up to the top of Mulholland. We parked, got out, and looked out at a view that crowned Hollywood and the San Fernando Valley. She'd had a 'vibe' today, thought it might be a good idea to chat in person.

I told her about the gun.

"I went down on the floor after that and I promised my cats I would never leave them." I said, watching cars steaming up the 101 freeway. "I got out of bed twice that night on my knees, saying, 'God, help me' because it was bad. It got better in Florida and when I came home it didn't feel like home and I was trapped and lost and nowhere was safe and do you think—is this how my mother felt when she reached for a blade?"

Teddy stepped closer. We were almost forehead-to-forehead.

"My friend, you took on the biggest fixer any of us will ever see. You worked on it while you did your regular job. You didn't give up. I don't know anyone—listen to me—people try and kill themselves after it gets better and then it takes a turn, and it goes worse."

"Today I was dancing at the studio and I heard myself laugh. How can it be that extreme? The next day, I'm laughing?"

Teddy spent some time digging her toe in the sand.

"Is taking dance lessons what makes you happy?"

"Yes."

"What else?"

"Gardening, being with friends, writing, being with my horse."

"Isn't it time the horse came home?"

"I've been thinking about that."

December 4, 2006 11:00 p.m. meditation

I went to Dad's house. He opened the door, brought me right over to His desk. "What do you need?"

"I need a fence. I need a fence my dog can't get out of."

Pen met paper. A check found my palm.

"And?"

"Taxes, paint, windows."

More checks joined the first in my open hand.

"How about sanity?" God asked causally, like we might as well add that to the list.

"I—"

I collapsed. He knew it was coming. He caught me.

"My sweet girl. Let Me do this for you. Let Me do all of this for you." He lifted my chin. "Didn't I take care of Kitty Boy? Didn't he go to your best friend?"

"It was so easy."

"See? I don't make bad deals."

Then He knelt. God got down on both knees before me.

"Let me take care of you. Let Me. I *live* to take care of you. Ignore those dark voices. They are not Me. All you have to do is write, and ride your pony. I'll do the rest."

Opened to: *Ask, and you will receive, that your joy may be full.*

CHAPTER SIXTEEN

Bionic House

I AM HOUSE

I am house
I am home

He cut deep
Down to my oh no do not
Do this I said if you
Go into my

Spine beyond to soil
Buried seventy
Years
Ago

Waiting for
Sunlight decades
Eroding seasons it
Gets to the point when

Even a house does not care
If it dies someone else has to
Because there was no half way not
Anymore

December 6, 2006 10:00 p.m.

"What do you think?"

"What do you think?"

"No, really," Stewart prodded. "I want to know."

We were outside the bay window on his lawn crunching on sycamore leaves, arms folded, taking in the stag. The skeleton family of Halloween had been replaced by a Tom turkey and a giant knife and fork, and now that staging had made way for the most magnificent animal, a genuine white tail buck, ears up, staring at us through brown glass eyes.

Tonight Stewart had tied a string of old-fashioned Christmas lights through his antlers.

I winced. "N.G. No. Nada. You know, you should do the windows for Bloomingdale's in New York?"

"I'm really good, aren't I?"

"Yeah!"

I felt honored to be inner sanctum, a part of a director's "direction."

"So," he posed, "What should I do with this deer?"

"Maybe a wreath around his neck like a winning racehorse?"

Quietly, an idea lit on us both. Stewart spoke first.

"Maybe I don't need to do anything to the deer?"

"I guess—just put up with perfection?"

Stewart vanished inside, stripped the lights, and adjusted one of the spots over the perfect animal's face.

"There," he said when he came out, like he was ready to yell, "Action!" "It's good now, don't you think?"

December 7, 2006 11:00 p.m.

"I have to show you something," Lucio cautioned.

When your plumber meets you at your car as soon as you come home from work, you know it's serious. "Take it easy," he warned, readying the patient for bad news. "Take it easy," he repeated, like he wanted to take my hand as we walked together into the living room, and then stopped, abruptly, in the kitchen.

"It's gone from worse to worse!" I wheezed, looking down into a trench that ran the entire length of the room, through the service porch with a three-foot-high pile of soil, accompanying. "Oh, my. How long will it be like this?"

"Three days," my plumber answered. "I have to lay, new, recover, then we pour cement, seal it. It's—it has to slant down one inch per foot, for drainage, that's why it's lower the closer it gets to the outside."

"I'll call Forest Lawn Cemetery. We could bring in a lot of bodies."

Lucio looked at me. I looked at Lucio. Then we both stared down into the hole, at earth, upturned, that hadn't seen the light of day for almost seventy years. On cue Magic appeared, straddling the top of the fresh heap, squatting.

"Have at it, Magie," I said to my cat. "Go for it."

December 8, 2006 8:40 p.m.

A seventeen month old baby girl taught me a lesson today. Her name is Amber. She's a client's daughter. Wise, with beautiful, mystical dark eyes, she cried when her mom came home and didn't go to her, first.

"We've been really busy and she's had a lot of different babysitters this month," Her mother explained. "She cries a lot. She's cried for the past three days. See? Her eyes are bulging and puffed up."

Every time she put the baby down, Amber started to wail.

I know how Amber feels.

"Whenever I have a panic attack," a friend told me, "it's because I'm not taking care of a little someone inside."

Oh, maybe I need to stop berating myself, asking "What's wrong with me?" and say instead, "How can I take care of little Kathy?" Maybe I need to stop judging myself for taking this giant leap into the unknown, and start seeing how remarkable it is that I came through last year intact? Not to mention last month or my childhood. By my own power, even with hope, I don't think so. The green lights have to come from Him.

They literally did. Traffic parted like the Red Sea after I left Amber's family. I made all the lights on my way to the grocery store. Rounding the last aisle, I saw Opal, one of the friends Betty introduced me to. Opal is struggling to keep her apartment building.

"Opal, think of it in the scale of the world: We're single women who own multiple properties! I have to remember, it's not mine, anyway. I'm managing my Father's estate."

Her jaw fell open. I could see her bottom teeth, plainly.

"The way you said that—'I'm managing my Father's estate…'"

"Are you guys in line?" a fellow shopper leaning over his cart handle, asked from behind us.

"No, we're just talking. We better move our carts!" I giggled in apology.

Opal confided, "It's been so painful, thinking, 'How can I keep this building? I just cried yesterday… I just cried."

"I know. Me, too." Then I told her about little Amber. "I need to take care of me," I said. "—before I take care of houses."

"It's getting better. I have a good manager who is fixing up the units. I'm getting two hundred more on rents now. Other people on the street are starting to fix up their buildings."

"What's your last name?"

"Robinson."

"They're keeping up with the Robinsons!"

She laughed. Opal, who doesn't smile much, threw her head back and let loose.

"So that's what she looks like happy," I thought.

"Being an entrepreneur is tough," I said. "We go ahead, take the hits first. My tenants have furnaces. I don't. A friend asked, 'When are you going to have a housewarming party?' I said, 'When I have heat!' "

December 9, 2006 9:50 p.m.

There's technique for having a "honey bucket" in the bathroom when your toilet is out of order. First off, you need a bucket with no cracks or leaks. I cannot emphasize this enough. A tall bucket is preferable—less squatting. Oh, and extra padding/partial wrapping of your terry cloth robe under your seat—not too far under your seat—makes the experience more desirable.

Then there's the scent issue. I recommend aggressive applications of Palmolive soap to counter balance.

Disposal? A deep hole, dug in advance, somewhere in the yard is the plan. It may be the front yard, so your dog cannot revisit the site.

There you have it. So when you're out front, dumping the contents in a hole next to the tall plants and your neighbor, Scarlett, comes by and wants to chat, just say you're "recycling," which, in fact, you are.

Scarlett was on her way up the street to check out the movie filming that was going on. The night was black as coal, and evening shoots are always dramatic. She said that she was bored and there was a cute cop who she wanted to check out. Did I want to come along?

I put my pail down and off we went to be groupies. She was right. The policeman was impressive. And of course, he knew it.

He focused on Scarlett right away.

"Do you have a boyfriend?"

We found his brazen behavior abhorrent, so we had no choice but to stay, mesmerized.

"Yes, I do." Scarlett said.

I broke the moment. "We were hoping for two cups of hot chocolate from Craft Services?"

"Can't help you with that," he said. "I'm here to save your life."

Oh, dear. He had broad shoulders and eyelashes so long that we could see them in the dark. He did not, however, help us get invited to the big white tent fifty yards away, where attendants in green aprons were setting warm chocolate chip cookies out in wicker baskets.

"Oh well, we tried," I said, drenched in the seduction of brown sugar and cinnamon. On our walk back up the street with a motorcycle cop escort, we learned that our city's finest work for time and a half anytime they're on a shoot.

"Beats waitressing," I said.

Mr. Handsome took us all the way to our houses. I introduced him to Tony and Joey, who looked up from under the hood of Tony's half-ton pickup and waved.

"Do *you* have a boyfriend?" the officer asked me as I started up my walk.

"No, but I have a plumber, and at the moment, that's a lot more important."

December 10, 2006 9:00 p.m.

Stewart's deer watched me through the living room window from across the street. He was the only one who saw a woman on her lawn, writing on a single piece of paper under a half-moon. I scratched the message out, put it in a bottle, winked at that moon, and tightened the cap. Then I went back inside, laid it in under the pipe that Lucio and his band of merry men will be covering tomorrow.

My left hand took charge of the pen, told my right hand to take a break. The printing came out like a child's.

My name is Kathy O'Brien. I am remodeling this house.

I can't believe I get to live here. I wake up and it feels like I'm still dreaming.

But it's like a nightmare some days. I feel like I'm living in the woods, and in the city.

The Elephant Man said his head was so big because it was so full of dreams.[4]

I think God drove my car here, two times, because He wanted to prove to me that I'll need a house this big so none of my dreams will get left out. Thanks for reading my message.

Sincerely,

K. O.

December 10, 2006

December 11, 2006 9:30 p.m.

I saved big time, at the salvage yard. Windows and doors exactly to my measurements flew out at me, calling, "Buy me!" The major prize was a set of sliding patio doors with two side lights that matched exactly—all in double-paned glass—for those haunted back rooms. And a double-paned glass door to

4. *The Elephant Man*, the play, by Bernard Pomerance.

match—for my bedroom. Why pay full price for new? Five thousand dollars' worth of windows cost six fifty.

Everything I touched was right. My carpenters' tape felt like a magic wand. Everything I laid it on was perfect, to spec, right on.

But I didn't stop there. Lowe's was the next destination, where I ordered a vanity for the guest bath, took the matching mirror/medicine cabinet home with me, trunk open.

There's more! Lucio's pal, Juan, filled in the trench. The message in the bottle and a lot of dirt went down, buried under concrete. My whole house smells like a new driveway. If a new "roof" signifies a fresh start, new plumbing is abdominal. Across the board—all the boards—this is becoming the bionic house.

CHAPTER SEVENTEEN
'Twas the Night before Christmas

I AM HOUSE

I am house
I am home

When
Pines drop
Cones is the
Time for my door
To wear branches

Needles sharp from
The forest where sound
Falls to the ground like
Snow she wraps packages

In brown paper stacks
Them for others under the
Balsam talks to the ones she
Loves far away in cold who cannot

See my
Face
Scarlet
With pride

December 20, 2006 midnight

"That was a nice ten-minute nap you had," Tony said when I woke up. We were near the end of Griffith Park's Festival of Lights on a slow conveyor, sunroof open, rolling between other cars to see "Christmas," to get inside of the holiday, be closer to snowmen, giant candy canes, thousands of waving elves, and carolers.

I sat up, alarmed. "I don't know how long it was. I was asleep!"

"You look peaceful when you sleep."

I was embarrassed. "I don't like anyone to see me sleeping. Did I drool?"

"You hungry?"

"I'm always hungry."

"I love a woman who can eat."

The guys holding vigil with their cars at Bob's liked Tony's red Santa hat trimmed in genuine fake ermine. The white beard was a closer. They treated him like the elder statesman he is, sharing stories, answering questions about cars, eager to display engines cleaner than any machine has a right to be. I asked a man next to his Olds Cutlass if I could sit in the passenger seat?

"Sure," he said. "Have a look."

It was the dashboard that helped me feel twenty again—round dials—the slant of the wheel. My soldier boy, the one who wore the Green Beret, had that car. No one around me knew that I was breathing next to a man who I was still thinking about thirty years later.

On the way in, a gull-winged Mercedes Roadster pulled our focus from the Oldsmobile, kept us inspecting for a while.

"How much is it worth?" Tony asked the owner in a way that told all of us he already knew the answer.

"Two fifty."

Tony nodded.

"I think I'd rather have real estate," I laughed, as we filed through the crowd at the door, zeroing in on two stools at the counter.

Tony ordered the prime rib and I asked for liver and onions. His chocolate shake came first. He didn't know why the disobedient spoon kept jumping out of his hand, slipping from his fingers. I poured the canister into a glass, tapped a little into a glass for me. It's the law: chocolate must be shared.

"So, who had the Olds Cutlass? 'Your dad?" He asked, swiveling on the stool next to mine, dropping his cane.

"A guy. High school. College." I said, retrieving the stick, planting it between us under the counter.

"High school. College—too?"

"Yeah."

"Why didn't you marry him?

Folding a napkin, unfolding it, folding it again, I thought out loud. "I don't know, I guess—because I was moving too fast."

"If you married him, you never would have moved in across the street."

"Correct. I'd be living in Paradise, Wisconsin, wondering when my children would have children."

"You would have been a good mother," he told me, his shaking hand chasing the spoon.

"I didn't think so." I contradicted, pouring the last of the malt from the sweating aluminum canister into his glass. "We pass on what we get, don't we? Were you a good father?"

"I don't think so," Tony said, Santa eyes twinkling at a girl and a guy walking by us, holding hands, wearing matching red earmuffs.

"Did you hit your kids?" I asked, chewing on a hangnail.

"No. I wasn't home much. When you're not home, your kids drink. Accidents happen."

Tony did pretty well cutting his prime rib. I poured excessive amounts of A-1 sauce on my plate. We dug in like lumberjacks.

"How's the liver?" he asked as I cleared gristle to the side of my plate.

I shook my head. "These people have no respect for organ meat."

"My rib was dry—too. We should stick to the burgers."

"—And the mashed potatoes."

"Does he still live there?"

"Who?"

"The Cutlass guy."

"Yes."

"Does he come here?"

"No, I go back there."

"When?"

"Every ten years—Whether I need it or not!"

"What happened last time?"

"I proposed."

"Was he moving too fast?"

"Maybe."

"I'd slow down for you."

"Thanks, Tony."

"Here, finish," he urged, sliding the bowl doused in gravy towards me. "I can't eat all of this."

"See that parking lot? 'Behind the fence?" He gestured on the way home, pulling the LeBaron up to a driveway, flashing lights onto a commercial garage. "That was my machine shop. I stayed there thirty years."

A block from home we stopped alongside a house surrounded by tall cacti, a stone's throw from us.

"This belongs to a woman I almost married."

"I always wonder about people who plant cacti around their house. It's bad feng shui. I guess if you married her, I wouldn't know you now, would I? Is she your 'Cutlass Guy'?"

Dodging the question, Tony pulled onto the wrong side of the road, curbside, to drop me off. "You must have taken your pills today?"

"What pills are those?"

"Pretty pills."

Christmas Eve, 2006 11:00 p.m.

We were all there—Tony, on a low stool near the fire, his guestroom tenant, Julia, on the armchair to his left. A couple, Chris and Serena, who live a few doors down had brought their teenage boy, Peter. Their older son, Mark, was absent. Stewart was busy filling the cheese and cracker tray, and slicing summer sausage. I liked the hard salami. I visited the tray often.

No one was decked in what they usually wear. Instead of jeans and t-shirts, red, green, and black velvet had emerged out of closets, groggy from mothballs, and twelve months of storage. Nat King Cole was singing merrily along with Bing. Stewart is big into setting 'mood.'

Tony was in his usual black sweats, topped off with a sea-foam green sweater and Santa hat. Julia trailed a long cotton summer mermaid gown with aqua flowers, plunging neckline. She didn't mind spilling out, tipping over the food tray. Tony didn't seem to mind, either. Julia is a free spirit, put some miles on in the '60s, is my guess, in soft gauze dresses, barefoot, with black eyeliner, long hair tumbling, when everything was truly free and nobody paid for anything.

"One of zee cats retreated to zee bushes," Serena complained, smoothing her red silk taffeta skirt. "Mark doesn't feed zee wet cat food. He says it's 'gross.' Zee cats are so happy we are home and opening cans for zem. Zey are delirious!" her French accent lingered in the air like perfume. "I don't think what people say is true. I think cats do need people, not like every minute, but to know that you are around."

"Like teenagers?" I lobbed, hard, over the net, swallowing

one of the cheese crackers whole. Subtext: "I heard your son, Mark, is one of the boys who paid homage to my backyard?"

Serena is refined. Chris looks like a truck driver. Maybe he should be driving cross-country, window open, arm out, stogie permanently jutting out of his cheek, Willie Nelson blaring. Odd couple. Never home. Seldom together. Always on the road. Stewart confided in me that he feeds Mark often, along with other sons from empty homes that look darn opulent from the outside.

She's usually away on corporate business trips to Paris or London or Rome. They have Peter secured in a boarding school outside of Paris. Chris has been starting a new business in Mississippi. They leave Mark home alone with another teen.

When someone, not I, brought up the subject of vandalism, Chris said, "Children have a right to self-expression."

I ceased breathing, felt my eyes meet Stewart's, and look away.

"Peter wants to come back home where it's easy," Serena added, shifting gears, nudging her son in his very thin ribcage.

"Let's try this," Stewart, our host, proposed, gripping the stem of his wineglass with his fist. "Don't you want to be *with* your son?" He said it like he was a megaphone, and she was hard of hearing—or deaf.

"I am with him a lot these days. I've been stationed en Paris!"

Young Peter, perched and sinking on the couch next to her, was book-ended on the other side by his father. This was a lot of bodily contact for this family, to be sure. Peter wasn't eating much. I saw the child, the toddler, in his fifteen-year-old body. I saw through the thick front he wore, knew his anxiety, caught scent of their loneliness, felt a chill from the frozen abyss that they live in, each staked out on their own rock ledge.

(Ma'am, Sir, how much did you sell your children for? A hundred grand? Half a mill? A promotion? If your sons died tomorrow, would both of you wished that you had done it differently? Would you have wanted to be home more? In hotels less?)

Suddenly it became necessary to migrate to the other side of the immense coffee table, and serve Tony some crackers with soft cheese spread. His hands, too weak to corral a green olive on a relish tray, welcomed a red-pepper garnish.

“Cheese and crackers are nice,” he accepted.

Raising my glass to the group, I submitted that we had our own “Santa” in the midst, cleverly disguised as a “normal” person. That led Stewart to tell the tale of buying the fat Santa suit one day, and Tony wearing it to a party like he’d wear anything else—on the Fourth of July.

“I grew a long beard, then, too!” the old man smiled, breaking into a raspy cough.

I often wonder—are Tony’s bags packed? It’s in the way he connects, the way his eyes are seeing something on the horizon that mine can’t.

A year ago I was lying here deciding not to die. Tonight, it just turned Christmas, 2006. What a difference a year makes. Four seasons, twelve moons.

Behind us in the bay window under a single light, the stag, our sentinel, was listening, ears up, eyes watching, emerald garland wrapped in his antlers. Stewart decided that on Christmas Eve, a little bling was not a bad thing.

T’was the night before Christmas, and soon Riverview will have new paint.

CHAPTER EIGHTEEN

Fire

I AM HOUSE

I am house
I am home

Men grunted like
Beasts to set my
Posts raise beams
Claim the slab

On brown black
Soil rich I was eager
As a tree to
Be planted

Fresh birthed I said this
Will work right here
Right now
Bring nails

Now outside in
I am made new
The only fear is
Fire

January 2, 2007 9:00 p.m. meditation

He was putting in the living room into a glass laid on its side. He tested the ball with the club, tapped, hit, bingo, in.

God looked over at me sitting on a bench, and leaned on the club's handle. "People are going to want to be okay the way you're okay."

I blinked. "I can't—that's beyond my comprehension."

"Some people, dark forces who used to be close to Me, are going to try and pull you off course. They're going to lie to you, tell you you're in danger. Stay close to Me—and, hey, shop some more bargains for the house, make it nice for yourself." Reaching in His pocket, dropping another ball on the floor, His question was, "Do you like all your workers?"

"Yes."

"There's going to be one—one who isn't worthy to be there."

"Worthy? People should be "worthy" to be around me? I never thought of it being an honor to be on my team?"

He measured the next putt, tapped. The ball moved with determination, dodging the glass, kept going on self-will until it hit the wall, bounded off, rolling to a belligerent stop behind a chair.

"You missed one?"

I couldn't believe it. How could God be so—human?

"Keep it quiet," He hushed, almost bashful. "Golf's a tough game."

January 8, 2007 8:30 p.m.

Sebastian came up the walk beaten and humble. Two years ago he didn't have enough men for his jobs. Today he didn't have enough jobs for his men.

"Where are you?" he'd asked a few hours before on a phone call. "Are you at home?"

"I'm driving."

"I'm at your house."

I guess he waited for me. I didn't blame him for coming to pick up what I owe him. Did he know I had re-fi money now? Is it an annual scent that goes out, like a pheromone?

"I'm not calling because I want my money. I'm calling you because your house needs to be painted."

"Sebastian! I still owe you nine thousand dollars!" I blurted as we met on the lawn. It hurts to not pay my people!"

"You're not the only one. Can I walk around? Give you an estimate?"

"You bought the big house!" he closed, tour finished, at the street. "I told you you would. And we are going to paint it."

I had to stand there and breathe while I felt another door swing wide open.

"You guys can be here five days a week—no Saturdays or Sundays. I'll go crazy if we do that. And I'm already a little nuts."

"You bought the big house," he nodded again, stamping the day like a package to be shipped. "And we are going to paint it."

This is what happened today on my birthday, my grandmother's birthday, and Elvis' birthday. There you have it. Damn it, Riverview just signed up for a facelift. Why not? After all, this is Hollywood.

January 9, 2007 7:00 a.m.

Reggie, one of the heating/air guys, is sleeping outside in his truck. I understand. I sleep in my car often. I take naps even a half block away. There's no way I can chill out in a house with three men pounding on sheet metal up in the attic.

The troops are back. We're surging ahead, claiming the next part of the kingdom.

"I'm so proud of you!" Betty crowed. "Isn't it weird that when you were ready to give it up, that's when it got better? I get to keep things when I'm ready to let them go!"

"Betty, I have to say something."

Then I told her about the shotgun.

"I—have a book—" she stammered, telling me something that I knew she told no one else about. "It's—it tells you how to do it. I got it because if someone says I had Alzheimer's and I wanted to know—in case I decided—you can borrow it if you want—but I want you to make me one promise—"

"That I'll bring it back?"

Then I waded into the swamp, the awful truth.

"I thought I was such burden to everyone, to you, this year. When I came back from Florida, it all looked—I felt like a failure. It was too much for me to do—I felt like I'd disappointed you and everyone else. I couldn't face—"

"You are my shining star! I tell everyone how far you've come, especially the way you handle money. I want you to promise me—if you ever decide—that you will come to my door so I can hug you and say 'goodbye?' I would feel terrible if I couldn't do that."

So I mopped my face, made that promise, wondering how many people take their own lives on misperceptions—right before it turns.

January 10, 2007 11:00 p.m.

Wow, my room is warm. I walked in after my bath, and it's—for the first time the room isn't cold. The bricks at the back of the fireplace are throwing off heat. Coals from Tony's logs are glowing red and white. This was my first fire in the master-bedroom fireplace. I feel like I'm in a castle—straight out of Camelot!

Riverview is becoming a home. I can feel a heartbeat. If someone told me there could be this much order in the midst of chaos, that tea candles flickering around that old bathtub could make gashes in half-destroyed walls beautiful, I never would have believed them. Do I have to learn to love the scarred, the unlovable, before I have permission to transform it?

"Light that fire!" Tony cheered. "Take some of my logs. Don't wait for a boyfriend to do it!"

Today Tony came across the street, rocking uneasily. No cane. To my surprise, he lowered himself to the ground, joined my picnic on the lawn as I was finishing a bowl of chili. He came bearing gifts—grapefruit. I tore into it, offering two sections.

"I only want one."

"What? Why? "I probed. "Ya tryin' to quit?"

"I only eat them after five."

He said Julia gave him one vicodin and now his hips, knees, barely bothered him.

"Bone on bone, no cartilage left," he said, rubbing his legs. Today nothing was slowing Tony Manicetti. He was borderline immortal.

Edith walked by about then leading her leopard grey stallion, who was carrying both her young nephew and his friend. We joked about her horse wanting a raise for "double duty."

"He wants to retire!" she yelled back.

"What happened to your knees, Tony? Soccer?"

"Trapeze. I held five, six people hanging from my knees."

I flinched. "Holy shit!"

"I did that for ten years."

"You're a gymnast?"

"We did well. People liked us. We went all over."

"When was that—before the machine shop?"

"Way before."

"There was a white egret in your tree, outside your bedroom window yesterday," I mentioned, offering another section of fruit. "—And a falcon, right above it. They stayed like that for an hour."

January 12, 2007 10:00 p.m.

She was on her side, back to the door when I walked in.

"Teddy?"

"Kathy."

I came around to face her. Arms were in white. Her head was wrapped in a puffy ski mask. Feet were encased in bandages, socks.

"You look pretty," she said.

"Thanks. You can see me?" It wasn't Teddy's face. Eyes were slits in gauze holes. One eye opened, the other fought a swollen lid. "I mean it. I'm glad you can see me."

She lifted her lip again, said nothing.

"Your lips look good." I commented." 'Amazing. 'Radical skin peel. 'Hungry?"

I fed her through a hole in the bandage. It's not easy to do anything when you're wrapped up like the Mummy. She moved her face, raised her lip in a snarl to move the crispy skin across her nose and cheeks.

"Cadaver skin," the nurse told me. "The skin on my arms is pig."

Spoonful by spoonful, pudding landed on a pink tongue in a gruesome face that I used to know as my friend's. I made the mistake of trying to spoon the juice as well. It ran down her lower lip. She winced, arms pumping up and down.

"Oh! Wipe it! Get it! Quick!"

I dabbed again and again. "I am so sorry."

"Here," she pushed a box of tissues toward me. "Here, to the right, do it!"

"I am so sorry!"

After that we employed a straw, one of those bent like a rain gutter.

"Come on, let's get you out of this place." I whispered. "What do you say?'

The head turned. Both eyes focused on me.

"Fire sucks," she said. "Fix your furnace. I should have fixed mine."

"You're going to get better," I said, hoping she couldn't read my other thought, which was, "I hope you won't die from this."

"So, I guess a manicure is out?" She posed, offering two mittened hands.

"How are those veins?"

"Lost in translation."

"Feel like a facial?"

"Ahhh…."

"Can we interest you in a chemical peel?"

I headed off into the bright day; smooth skinned, bandage free, pain free, feeling the cool breeze on my arms, face and neck. Why didn't Teddy wake up sooner? She's the lightest sleeper I know. I was grateful that my fire stayed in the fireplace after I went to sleep, that I never did use that old furnace. Teddy used hers and she fell asleep, 'came to' in her backyard, when it was almost too late.

January 17, 2007 8:00 p.m.

I got this urge to go out in a robe and slippers and start the fire. Every morning now I make sure the painters come into a yard with heat. This is the coldest winter in decades. I have two rules in my house: One is no one is cold, and the second, no one is hungry. Too bad I don't follow them myself.

I lit a match on a newspaper in the Weber and it caught fast—and so did my robe.

"My God!"

Patches of red flames were shooting up the front, over my legs, I swatted—then I heard a crackling behind me. Fire was flaring up my back! I stomped, shaking, realized that I was naked. I guess I dropped the robe.

An hour later, Sebastian's men and I were warming ourselves around the same barbecue. Scrap two-by-fours burn well. Flames were shooting sparks high into the frigid morning air. One of the men had only a t-shirt on. The rest of us, Sebastian included, wore jackets and sweaters.

"Where's your jacket?" I asked the man.

He shrugged.

"Doesn't he pay you? Get a sweater!"

Same shrug. It's a common San Salvadoran answer.

"Do you want a sweatshirt?"

His eyes didn't argue.

I returned with two sweatshirts. He layered them, ready for the cold. I left a smiling man, a few smiling men waving their hands.

When I came home I couldn't find the barbecue. It had been moved next to the house—right next to the house. I opened the lid. Live red coals glared at me from a bed of smoldering ash—twelve inches from the house's wall.

Then I was hot. Then *I* was livid.

Fire is a little too close for comfort these days. 'Teddy, me, and now—my house? I flew into mental ultimatums. No matter how good the painting was—they could not—then I noticed that the ground was wet. It had rained today. I walked a little farther and found my two sweatshirts, balled up, soaked.

He worked in the rain. The man stayed on, wet and cold in the rain. *That's* why he had the fire next to him.

"Sebastian?" I said on my contractor's voice mail. "Please meet me here tomorrow, 6:45 a.m.. We have something to discuss."

January 18, 2007 10:00 p.m.

All the painters gathered around the fire at 7:00 a.m., like I asked. Sebastian translated. I started out by saying how grateful I was for their help and how it made me have tears—because I appreciated them.

I talked about the fire. I mentioned how my own clothes caught on fire. Then I spelled out what Sebastian had told me to say:

"If I come home and the barbecue has been moved, I will ask you all to leave."

One by one, I shook each of their hands. The one who wore my sweatshirts told me he was sorry. Today he was wearing a jacket.

When we walked out to Sebastian's truck, I had a warning.

"If I ever find these men working in the rain without raincoats, I will send them home."

When I returned today, the guys had sanded a lot of the rafters down to the wood—as fresh as new pink skin.

January 21, 2007 9:00 p.m.

A single flake of old red skin fell off of Teddy's arm into the hospital sheet. Bandages are gone except for the foot with the case of the missing toes, which was wrapped in a purple sock. Her eyes were flashing around the room, plotting escape. In ten days, she'll have to chart an exit plan—for real—no matter what. Unfortunately there's a lot of demand for beds in a burn unit.

I offered a chocolate shake; precious contraband. She grabbed it like a monkey with fast fingers.

"They scrub my arms once a day to take all the skin off. It's torture. I'm into skin pain, but not that much!"

"So, 'getting any 'action?'" I asked my gay friend, as if we were sharing national security secrets.

"Yeah, there was a really pretty nurse—"

She had finished the yogurt on her tray so I was cleaning up the cottage cheese and fruit.

"If you're not going to eat your food, I'll visit more."

"I blew up at a therapist today," Teddy snorted, creasing the sheet with her right hand, unfolding it with her left. "She got way too personal. Name? Address? Way too personal. I sent her right the hell out of here!"

While she hobbled to the bathroom, as I was mentioning to her that "ornery" makes for faster healing, two petite Filipino nurses whisked in, wanting to help her in the bathroom. They started all their words with little "b's." Terry declined their offer.

They signed off with—Berry well den. You have a berry good day."

"Whatever happened to that guy? The military guy? Back home?" Teddy asked, perching on the corner of the bed.

"You're getting way too personal."

"Tough. I need distraction. What? What happened?"

"I just gave his army shirt away. Last week. I donated it to a thrift shop. Every time I wore it, I felt all this—weight."

"Like you felt like the fucking Statue of Liberty? Arm up?"

"A torch? Yeah, like that. A few years ago, I was dying over him. Now I only do that over real estate."

"I'm not dying over anyone now," she said. "I've had trial by fire."

January 24, 2007 8:00 a.m.

It was barely dawning when I ran out front to the street in my robe and slippers. I was not on fire. The house was not on fire. But I was scared. I stood in the middle of the street looking up at my house newly transformed by paint. We'd swatched, tried patches, but Sherman Williams' "Blonde" was the color that had claimed possession.

Was I wrong?

Yesterday Stewart thought I was wrong. He exploded.

"Another yellow house? There are three of them in a row! What about sage green? Pale grey? Does it have to be *yellow*?"

"It's not yellow, Stewart. It's gold, 1940s gold. Think post-Depression."

Not the pale, pasty hues of the 1990s; or the stark, dreary whites of the 1970s. "Blonde" was my color. But at six am, clad only in pajamas, holding a fan of color samples in my hand, I knew I'd made a mistake—and a "repaint" was more money than I had.

Along came a jogger, a tall fit woman in blue sweats.

"Excuse me," I asked. "Do you like the color of that house?"

"Yes, yes, I do," she said, catching breath.

"Good, because I couldn't sleep. I thought it is all wrong, that I made a—"

"I love it. It's very World War II or something. What year is the home?"

"1939."

"Perfect. I like it. And I'm an interior designer. I know color."

"I can't thank you enough!" I was so grateful, I wanted to hug her. So I did. The perfect stranger and I embraced right there.

Just when I needed an expert's opinion, she showed up.

Interesting? "Blonde" it is. But in Hollywood, what other color would it be?

CHAPTER NINETEEN

The Fall

I AM HOUSE

I am house
I am home

She did not
See the bent one
Stop the big man
Cross the street

She does not know
He sent the stranger away
Before his hand was on
My door

The white beard watched
Every day kept his
Stick close
Speared

The one
Who said he was her
Father told him he was not
Invited

June 18, 2007 5:15 a.m.

Can't sleep. Woke up scared. Not about money. About Cow Field. Yesterday I took a nap in my car at the end of the street in front of Danielle's house because workmen were here. It was warm outside. I left the windows halfway down. I think I slept for an hour. When I woke up my throat was burning. A few hundred yards away, a woman was lunging a horse. Clouds of dust were drifting my way.

"The dirt is angry," I said, forcing myself to swallow the burn.

I don't know what to do. I called the *L.A. Times* and they never returned my call. The last lawyer left the case and another bellied up to take his place. Lawyers are repelled from this issue or fattened, push themselves from the table.

Tonight in the dark before I went to bed, I walked down to the end of our street to the cul-de-sac, overlooking acres of tall grass that look, well, normal. What do you do when you think everything you worked for might be covered in something toxic? When you wonder if it's safe to breathe?

Opened to: *But the Lord is faithful, who will establish you and guard you from the evil one.*

June 19, 2007 8:00 p.m.

The sore throat is staying on like an unwelcome guest. Hot tea and honey are of no avail. Maybe I'm just coming down with something? A wild screaming raccoon dispute had me up, checking out the side yard at 5:00 a.m. Later, walking with Sarge, we met an adolescent raven. Everywhere my dog and I went, the bird flew alongside us, landing in trees, on the fence, unafraid, trying to get our focus.

The bird is letting me know that we live on the edge of wilderness here.

Overhead, the stars aligned like an arrow at a 45-degree angle onto my house.

"Are my planets 'lining up?" I asked.

It went like this—star, crescent moon, Venus, then my home, in a chain.

Speaking of Venus, this is the first month without a reminder that I am, in fact, female.

June 20, 2007 6:12 p.m. meditation

He was in tennis whites, had *Gulliver's Travels* under one arm, a tennis racket under the other. He knew I wasn't up for small talk. I started with this question:

"'Should I move?"

Changing the tempo, He placed the book and his racket on the table, dug his hands into both pockets.

"Are you doing everything I asked?"

"Yes."

"And you're living in a nice place?"

"Yes."

"Are you using your tools?"

"Not my shovel, lately."

"Then break it out. Do you have gas in the tank?"

"Yes."

"Do you have food?"

"Yes, but—should I move?"

"Are you moving—today?"

"No."

"Go to work. Make time to dance. Have fun! I have you covered. I've got a deadly serve!"

Ah, yes. He never misses—(unless it's golf).

"You play against Me, and—'God help you!'" He laughed, grabbing the racket, scooping me up in His arm, helping me along to the patio. "Exercise. Enjoy the day. I've got a lot of nice things waiting for you. Don't you want to travel? Gulliver did. He met a lot of new people. Don't you want to wake up in a strange place? Have breakfast at a café in Dublin? Watch the sun set over the Coliseum? "

I looked at Him. He knew what I was thinking, why I was there.

"I can't even think about traveling. 'This Cow Field thing. I swallowed it. It tastes like—it burns. Should I stay or go?"

Both of His hands found my arms. For a second, I thought He was going to ask me to dance.

"The only thing—the only thing I want you to think about is—I only want you to think about you!" Then He wrapped me in those arms. "I made you." He whispered into my ear. "You are safe."

"Oh," I gulped, wiping my eyes with the back of my hand until the white handkerchief came to my rescue, neatly folded.

"Come," He said. It was an invitation to stand at the patio's edge. "Let Me take care of everything. 'Everything."

Don't you know—as soon as He pulled me towards Him, lightning crackled? 'Opening act of a big show. On the horizon, charcoal grey clouds were assembling like a herd of bison.

"Storm's coming," He smiled, like He was surprised by the great event. Pulling me closer. "Don't worry. That business with the field—I'm on it. I have people on it. I'm not big on injustice. I can settle any score. "

I had to hear Him say it again.

"Am I safe? Should I move? Is this a bad deal?"

He reminded me, "I don't make bad deals."

June 21, 2007 10:00 p.m.

"I'm ashamed, Betty. There's always a stain on his pants, and an odor. It's hard to go in public with him."

"He's not into Depends?"

"Literally."

"It's hard."

"It's hard." Then I felt awkward. I wasn't thinking about how hard it was for Tony. "It has to be tough for him. It's happening to him, not me. What can I do?"

"Nothing. If you don't want to go in public with him, see him on the lawn."

"I just remembered. Vicks."

"Vicks?"

"We put Vicks on stallions' noses if we don't want them to smell mares. I could put some under my nose. Damn. I don't go—I haven't gone into his house. I know what I'm going to see there. I don't have time to clean two houses! This is—what did Bette Davis say? 'Getting old ain't for sissies.' Now I really feel bad. I was only thinking about me! I blew him off, Friday, when he wanted to go to Bob's, said I was working. Then I had to go somewhere so he wouldn't see my car! He stinks! Betty, why does life always come down to piss and shit?"

"I hate it when people become human." she said.

June 22, 2007 9:00 p.m.

He ordered mashed potatoes with brown gravy, and a chocolate shake. He said I could have his salad, as much of the shake as I wanted. I ordered the Cobb, two bleu-cheese dressings on the side. I offered my crackers.

"No thanks, I'm trying to quit." He disdained, waving a shaky hand in the air. "So, how much are you worth now?"

I took him in, slowly, rocking back and forth on the stool, deliberating, inching the chocolate shake closer to him.

"I'm priceless."

"On paper."

"Let's see—" I pulled a napkin over, uncapped a pen from my bag, scribbled a figure.

"Beats being homeless."

"Beats being homeless. But there's a lot of paper on those houses."

"Is there more coming in than going out?"

"Barely."

"Then you're golden."

"No, you're golden," I countered, dripping the last of the milk shake into his glass. "Can I put a head on this for you?"

"Did it ever cross your mind that I like spending time with you?"

"Frankly, no."

"Then I have to put a big 'X' on your forehead so it can cross your mind! By the way, is that a new perfume?"

"Oh, it's Vicks. I thought I was catching a cold."

I invited Tony to take the long trek up the driveway when we came back. I needed a witness to see the old black-mold bathroom, gutted, with a gash open to the outside, no walls, a raw pit in the dirt floor. The entire room was in ruins, dug out, sledge-hammered—except for the shower wall with glass block.

"I kept what I wanted, the rest had to go. Look! No more black walls! We tore them right the hell out!" I preened. "It's a mess! I love this!"

Wavering on uneven knees, leaning on the cane and what was left of a wall, Tony pronounced, "You're an idealist." And then he made his exit.

June 24, 2007 11:00 p.m.

This time we crossed Riverside Drive to Marie's. Bob's was too crowded. You can always get a booth at Marie's. 'Tony's call. I don't think he wanted to sit on a stool tonight. I had the potato cheese soup. He ordered clam chowder and a turkey burger. I cut the sandwich in halves for him.

"Thank you," he said, pausing to let his vibrating hands

pick up the bread. He stopped, mid-bite, setting it down on the plate. Something was in the air. Maybe it was my fingers drumming the table. I stopped, pulled my hands onto my lap.

"So, what do *you* want?" He asked, trying to lighten the moment.

"I'm okay."

"Liar."

"I'm—"

"Come on. Have at it."

"I'm—pissed!"

"That's more like it."

"My father won't leave me alone. My father has never left me alone."

Tony nodded. The food could wait. Everything would wait.

"He called me, left a message on my office phone. He tried to get my number from my aunt, but she wouldn't give it to him. She doesn't want anything to do with him, either. So he found it off the net or somewhere. Anyway, he said, 'Gloria and I are coming to—' and then I deleted it. I told him, I've been very clear. I told him—in writing—I want nothing to do with him." I balled my napkin, threw it, overhand, hard, past Tony's right ear, against the back of the booth.

He didn't flinch.

"Narcissistic son of a bitch! Fuck him! He's never heard me. He can't hear me. I have this funny feeling I'm going to come home from work and he'll be sitting in my living room, saying, "Isn't it nice that I dropped in?" Like he'll think it's charming and how could I refuse him—if he drives all the way across the country? Tony, I fucking hate my father!"

I threw a napkin, and another. Tony slid the tray of sugars and sweeteners my way. I pulled packets out, crushed them, hurled. "I fucking hate my father!" Standing, I attacked. "He can't hear me! He has never heard me! There was no safe place in that house. You couldn't lock a door, he'd come in and get you— you couldn't outrun him—he'd run you down, beat—fucking monster. FUCK. HIM. FUCK. HIM. FUCK—" Clutching my knife, I stabbed the placemat. "I want to kill my father!"

The waitress showed up looking startled.

"Is everything—can I bring you anything?"

"Some more sugar?" Tony suggested, raising the empty container. "We seem to be running low."

Eying the knife, she picked up the dish, made a military turn on her heels.

"If he showed up, you'd call the police, right?"

"Absolutely. I've rehearsed it in my mind. Son of a bitch, damn it, the doors are all open for workmen. I can't lock anything."

"What does he drive?"

"I don't know. A rental? He probably wouldn't drive cross-country."

"What does he look like?"

"Big guy. A cross between Hoss Cartwright and Gerald Ford."

"You need an Orange Julius."

"What? What's an Orange Julius?"

"I'll get you one sometime. What else do you want?"

"I want to bring my horse home. And I want you to live forever."

"Piece of cake."

"I was thinking pie. After all, it's Marie's?"

"I mean, 'piece of pie!"

I laughed so loud then that the whole restaurant turned around. Some of the patrons started to laugh, too, and they didn't know why?

"You take your pills today?"

"What pills are those?"

"Pretty pills," we chimed together.

On the drive home, when we were about a minute away from Bob's, he posed, "When I'm gone, how do you want me to talk to you?"

"Long-distance? Tony! Why are we talking about this? You're going to live forever, aren't you? You're here, today!"

"Tell me."

"Lightning? Headlights? Thun—"

Bam! Something cracked, hit hard, fell under the truck with a bang.

"That was my alternator!" He blurted, looking in the rear view.

"Now what? Shouldn't we stop and pick it up?"

"We can't stop now."

"What do we do?"

"We find water, quick!"

"Let's go to my rental. The tenants are gone. It's close. Make a left on Hollywood Way."

In the driveway of the Mother House, in total darkness, Tony opened the hood, was filling the radiator when Louis, a neighbor, came up on us with his sheepdog.

"Kathy, are you okay?" was what Louis said. What he wanted to say was, "What are you doing in the dark with a pickup truck and a man who looks like Kris Kringle?"

"We're okay, Louie, thanks. We ran out of water."

As soon as the radiator filled, we were off.

"This should get us home," Tony said, sitting up very straight behind the wheel.

"You're an exciting date." I remarked.

"Not as exciting as you."

"Next time, let's take the Le Baron?"

"As soon as I get a muffler on it. I'm waiting for parts."

June 26, 2007 11:30 p.m.

He was flat-out mean to the waitress. She was the cutest girl, probably sixteen, with a perfect blonde ponytail and frosty pink lip gloss. He was flat-out rude to her. She answered his question about the options on the menu and then, when she was going to suggest something else, he cut her off.

"I didn't ask you about that!" he snapped.

Her ears did something. I watched her take two steps back while she stood absolutely still. She barely spoke after that. Food was delivered with a polite, distant, Marie Callender's smile.

What was going on with Tony?

It took all I had to say nothing, to not apologize for the dog that bit, to not take her aside, say, "I'm really sorry. He's not usually like this—"

What was going on with Tony? Why was he mad at a girl? For being alive?

He didn't drive us straight home. We pulled up next to the same cyclone fence, chained with a giant padlock where we'd stopped weeks before.

"That was my machine shop. I had that for over twenty years."

I said nothing.

Next stop was a tiny storefront on Magnolia Boulevard across from the senior center that read, "Nathan's Photography."

"That's my friend's shop. And there's my Imperial." Our headlights lit up the chrome grill of a sled of a car. "That's mine. The best car ever made. Chrysler Imperial. Makes Caddies blush. I have too many cars. Nath lets me keep it here."

Stop after that, two blocks from ours, was the 'cacti house.'

"She rents it out now. She moved to the desert."

"Oh, yeah, the Cactus Lady. She should live in the desert. I guess you finally 'got the point?'"

He made a right, raised a limp left hand at a tree in the parkway.

"That's where my son died."

"Excuse me?"

"My son. I got a call one night, ten o'clock. He hit that tree. Not a good night."

"I'm sorry, Tony."

"Me, too."

When he slid the stick into park in front of my house, Tony patted the back of my hand on the front seat.

"Thank you."

"I'm sorry, Tony."

"Me, too. Twenty years ago—tonight."

June 30, 2007 10:00 p.m.

"What do *you* want?" I growled from the doorway.

"You." The man in the hospital bed answered.

"It took me forty-five fucking minutes to find you! 'Fucking place is a maze."

Tony made a sad face.

"You're not in Room 1616 anymore, in case you haven't noticed! Six nurses had to give me directions," I complained, resting on the edge of the mattress.

He stretched out his hand. Mine held his. The bed began to vibrate.

"Is that the bed, or are you just happy to see me?"

Tony's legs looked shrunken and thin under the cotton blanket, like someone had transplanted a child's limbs onto a man. Joey told me he'd lost weight—Since the fall.

"You can swim anytime," his voice cracked.

"I don't want to bother Julia."

He frowned. "Use the pool!"

"She wouldn't care, would she? It's been so hot."

He shook his head.

"Go in through the side gate."

"Sure."

"Okay. It's getting hot. Too hot for June," I agreed, taking in the covered tray on the side of the cabinet. "Are you eating?"

"I'm waiting for Johnnie and Lorraine to feed me."

"Oh, your son?"

"And his wife. They went out for dinner."

"You want to show them how well you're doing?"

The nod, the half-wink.

I moved in a little closer, encasing his right hand in my left.

"Tony, I want you to know—I don't want you for your real estate. I have enough of my own."

That was when two people appeared at the foot of the bed, looking suspiciously at me. I introduced myself, faked shock, concern in Tony's direction.

"Now they've found us together! They know the rumors are true!" Rising, I offered my hand. "My name is Kathy. You must be Lorraine and Johnnie—"

In a second we were sharing in their story of being high school sweethearts, losing track of, and then finding each other twenty-five years later. They sported the grins of people who had landed on their feet smack dab in the middle of a happy ending.

"One more day and we have to go back to Utah," Johnnie, mirror image of Tony, said, holding an arm around his girl.

"Dinner?" Lorraine asked Tony, coming to the other side of the bed.

Tony sighed.

"Too tired?"

He nodded.

A few more stories flitted around the room. The day, the heat, how good Tony's house looked. And wasn't it a plus that there were all those trees to keep it in the shade? Then they were off leaving me and an old man in a room alone together.

"You should paint your gate the same color as the shutters." Tony said.

"I'm replacing it, Tony. It's falling apart. I want some nice carved gates, wrought iron. I haven't seen them yet, but God'll take me to them. What the hell, He brought me to the house. Now *I'm* waiting for parts!"

Tony answered with his "of course" wink.

"I want you to get better, Tony. Not for me, for Joey. He's a mess. He's like this—" I worked my hands together like a squirrel, fidgeting. "He can fix anything with those hands, but he can't fix this." I fanned my palms over Tony's chest. "He can't fix you."

He sighed again, blinking at the woman walking round his hospital room..

"I asked Joey, 'Are you sleeping?' His eyes were so black. But today he was on his bike riding around." I raised my hands, high, imitating Joey driving his motorcycle. "He doesn't know what to do. He loves you."

Tony's lips shaped the words, "I love him, too."

"I know you do. He's your other son. He's like your own blood. Tony, I didn't want you to think I—I wanted to come as soon as I heard, but it's been ten and twelve hour days. I have five things going into escrow. One guy called, said, 'List my house, and let's go get me another one!'"

He grinned the "why should it be any other way?" smile, like he had an inside track on how it was all going to be delivered. "It changed for you."

"Yes, it did."

"Five escrows?"

"I'm sorry, Tony," I apologized. "Who found you? Joey?"

"Julia. I was on the floor for a day and a half. I couldn't get up."

I turned away. "I feel so bad! I was right across the street and I didn't know! What the—What's the matter with me? I should be more psychic!"

"I'd rather you be 'psychic' than 'Kike-ic.'"

I had to lean in close, to have him repeat. Then I got it. He was talking about Edith.

"I'm actually a little Jewish," I chastised, one eyebrow arched.

Tony didn't buy it.

"Loebenthal. My great-grandfather."

We were trying valiantly to change the subject, to make a joke, to dig in, anywhere, to water soil that was too dry, hard. It was absurd, this being fed by a tube, life gelled to a soft place on a hospital bed.

"I didn't have anything to eat from Wednesday until Friday."

"Tony—"

"And it was so cold."

"Oh, God!" I blinked, closing my eyes like I was in a movie theatre, avoiding the screen "I can't believe you were right there and I didn't know! No, now you gotta come home!"

He took a breath. "I'm going to a convalescent home."

"For a while?"

"Uh-huh. On Victory and Coldwater."

"Are you okay with that?"

He nodded. "How's the house coming?"

"Two bathrooms almost done and a third on the way."

"And five escrows."

"Tony, I gotta go. I haven't eaten dinner, and I can't eat yours!"

He turned a stiff neck in the direction of the nutrient bag hanging on a pole. "We could share?"

"No, thanks. It looks like something I used to feed baby pigeons."

His face wrinkled in distaste. "Well, you can't taste it."

"Vanilla shake?" I joked.

"Yeah, it—"

"It looks like a vanilla shake. I'd rather have one from Bob's. I wanted to bring you one, chocolate, but they say you can't swallow. Do you want a little sip of water?"

Tony shook his head, slowly. Talking was taking a lot of energy.

I wrapped my hands on the bars around his bed like I wanted to tear them down. "I always want to break the rules."

"Me, too," he said, across a field of resolve.

"Do you want me to turn these headlights off?"

He motioned past the blue fluorescent lights near his bed. I fumbled, unable to find the switch.

"I'll get a nurse." I gave him a peck on his cheek.

"Do you know me well enough to be doin' that?'

"I love you, Tony."

"I'm proud of you," he winked, like he and God knew something that I didn't.

Almost to the elevator, I made a U-turn back to the nurses' station and asked about Tony's lights coming off so he could sleep. Then I tracked to his room to retrieve the Godiva chocolates I'd left on his table. I retraced my steps through ten miles of corridors, following shiny blue stars on the wall until I was back in the room where I found a miniature smiling man with pink tubes running out of his nose and his arm looking like a cheap imitation of an elephant.

"If you're not going to eat the chocolates, I will." I announced.

We stared at each other for a while.

"I see God in you, Tony. I think I moved in across the street from—God."

Then I patted his hand.

When I was crossing Buena Vista, I knew people in cars could tell where I'd just been. People walk differently after they've been to the hospital. Even if nothing bad has happened.

Standing by my pond looking down at the fish, a mourning cloak butterfly fluttered over, landing on my right arm. I got a really good look at it. A line of sapphire—blue dots went along the golden edge, brown melting into purple. Part of one wing was missing. It's not easy to fly around that fragile.

But there's more.

The butterfly stayed for a long time, circling over Edith's stable, coming back to my other arm. Finally it left, having changed me with a profound sense of everything being perfectly timed.

It's not every day you get knighted by a butterfly.

CHAPTER TWENTY

The Countdown

I AM HOUSE

I am house
I am home

I saw him fall
The Spanish knew
His house watched the
One on my left we
Heard him call out

But houses
Can say nothing only
Wait and hope our soft ones
Will listen with bigger ears

We hear with roofs
See through windows
Our hearts beat hot or cold
Feet planted on the soil

Houses can only wait
While leaves drop
And branches grow to cover
So birds will have more places

July 1, 2007 3:00 a.m.

A few other religious gardeners and I were at Home Depot paying homage to plants when I felt her. I was there on a mission—to find the last additions to the "welcome" pot at the front door, the graceful terra cotta with curving handles that Stewart had brought back from Mexico years ago for Tony. Last week when he set it out on the curb, I adopted it. It's going to send a message to all that I do, in fact, live here.

"Mom?" I asked, pushing my cart past geraniums, sunny pungent marigolds. "I need one more plant. What do you think?" Almost immediately, I saw them—her favorites—Moss Rose.

"Ah, she is here." Maybe I wasn't imagining her warm exotic scent, like she was alive, real, and standing next to me?

"But Mom, they only have flats of Moss Rose." I chatted, like we used to when we were out shopping. "We need a six-pack."

Pushing my cart another ten feet, I saw some. "Ah, they do have six packs!"

My eyes caught a prime set with strong plants ready to bloom, a large peach flower, budding in the corner. No wilting plants to be seen.

"Look for the plants ready to bloom, thick stems, not the ones blooming or already spent," she'd say.

I took her advice. With the moss rose and a few others bagged, I was out the door when the feelings impaled me. I had to grasp the handle of the cart to hold myself up from the blow to my gut.

"I miss you so much," I told her. "I miss my mother."

Fresh earth, green leaves reaching up, working together, our hands deep in soil, she'd direct; "Dig deeper, honey, over here. Make it easy for those roots."

Her words came streaming back, making me eight or nine again as the slanting afternoon light caught the top of buildings, underscoring the sense that I am a woman, alone, a daughter, orphaned, not walking with her mother.

"You should be here. You should be in my living room watching HGTV, knitting your next sweater." Choking on the acid reality, I heard my own despair. "It was too soon. You died too soon. But you left every time you reached for a glass. You sat right there and—and you were gone. Only the shell of you stayed, Mommy. And I never knew when you'd come back."

I rolled the length of the parking lot past men loading four-by-eight sheets of plywood into open pick-up beds, and a young man pushing an older man in a wheelchair toward a white van. I was jealous of that man. He had his father with him. It made me want to be with my mother even more. I set my plants on the backseat, hadn't driven far on San Fernando when I was bombarded with longing.

"Goddamn alcoholism!" I cursed, over and over. Other drivers went around as I drove too long with my turn signal on, vacant, distracted. Finally, I parked.

"Momma!" The plea came up from the deep, a place beyond normal reach. "Goddamn alcoholism. It—destroyed us. Oh, God, Momma. Goddamn alcoholism. You gave me your best. I know you did. You taught me how to make a house a home. I couldn't be doing this—I wouldn't be in Riverview without you. Are you there, Mom? Are you here with me?"

Maybe feelings are the armor, the gate that opens the drawbridge to a new life? Home with Sarge next to me, we filled that pot. The open mouth devoured soil. The healing moment, first to settle, free of its plastic pot, was ivy, for truth, then geranium for endurance, next, red miniature rose for love, and for my mother, for all eternity, six sturdy peach-faced Moss Rose.

Another layer of planting mix on top, a few waterings to soak, and the community was ready. Only one other woman knew what was really in that arrangement. Spilling out if it was my life and her legacy—all that my mother taught me before the disease of alcoholism closed in on her. She was there—nurturing, guiding, supporting, encouraging. When the sweet smell of the dirt came back up to meet me, I knew I was done. And somehow I knew that I wasn't alone.

"I want to keep this house, Momma." I prayed under the porch light. "Can you help me? I don't want to have to sell Riverview to someone with more money than me."

A minute ago under the stars I walked out to check on the pot. Even in amber light, I could see that the plants are growing, that they've stretched. They're home. They're not going anywhere.

July 2, 2007 8:00 a.m. meditation

"Why did You take my mother so soon?"

He bowed His head.

"She was only fifty-six! She was supposed to be here with me—planting flowers. Why the—why did You take my Momma?" I was cracking down the middle, falling apart in front of Him. "Oh, God, why?"

Maybe there are moments when even God doesn't know what to do. I felt Him close in on me. I could sense His breathing like He was taking in enough breath for two.

"I. Hate. You." I broke away, screaming, pointing. "I—if You can do anything—why? I—hate—"

Then I wasn't the only one crying.

"Sometimes," He ventured, squeezing words, "Sometimes—it's the best I can do under the circumstances."

I was inconsolable. "If I can't go to You—"

He walked to a crystal lamp, yanked the cord out of the wall, and presented it. I took it, questioning, panting. He nodded.

I threw the thing on the floor. It smashed, sending glass everywhere. Then He walked to His desk, picked up a glass globe filled with calla lilies. I smashed that, too. Water, glass, shattered. A platter resting on a table came next.

"I. AM. VERY. ANGRY."

"I hope so." He said. "It's about time."

"She's gone. Twenty years. She's fucking gone!" I sank into the sofa and wept for days. I felt Him settle next to me. "I'm lost. Or something?"

"When your heart is breaking, so is Mine." I heard Him say.

I couldn't even talk. We were there forever. The handkerchief was offered. I hesitated then accepted.

"Is it—ever—going to stop hurting?"

"Seeds of pain grow joy," He promised, riveted on the ocean.

"I find that hard to believe."

"That would be appropriate."

Then I was in His arms, close enough to feel His heart beat.

"This...being alive is hard."

"Science fiction, huh? Try wiring a soul to a body? You need to know—your mother moved the notebook—the day when the folder came off of the table?"

"Oh, that day? That was my mother?"

"She was trying to tell you that the book is important—that you have to tell the story, hers, yours. If you don't, it won't be told."

"No wonder she drank. No wonder she was jealous of me. I got everything she didn't. She was smart, she could do anything, but she didn't think she deserved anything. She thought poor. She felt defeated. No wonder she saw me as a threat. She knew I wouldn't fit in that small life, forever. She knew I'd have to leave. She raised me to be big and all the time she knew she'd have to stay small. I feel like this pain wants to kill me."

"I'll help you make it part of your genius." He promised. "I'll help you build a cathedral out of faith."

Opened to: *An inheritance incorruptible and undefiled that does not fade away.*

July 2, 2007 8:00 p.m.

And then there's that raven, cat-food eater, bird with no fear of people, and less fear of dogs, the animal who zeroes in on me like I'm fresh meat every time I go outside.

"Where is your family?" I grilled the black bird with steely bright eyes.

Lynn approached, pointing, "We have another 'creature.'"

"The raven?"

"The raven."

"I just fed him half a can of cat food. Every time I take Sarge for a walk, he calls to me."

"Well, he's got dog food and water over here." He motioned to a table near his back door. " For three weeks I've been feeding him, ever since he fell out of the nest."

Zooming out of one of Lynn's trees, the raven swooped down to the fence, focused on us both, ruffling shiny new black feathers.

"Come here, Jasper," Lynn called.

The bird resisted. Ravens are big into defiance.

"I make Sarge 'sit' every time the bird comes over to our yard. The bird wants to play with him."

"He plays with my dogs. Maybe he thinks he *is* a dog? I put a sticker on the back patio door so he won't fly at it, break his neck. Should I get a cage for him to spend the night?"

I shrugged. "He's got to learn to be a bird."

"I had a crow growing up. I called him Jasper."

"You named him 'Jasper'?"

"Caw! Caw!" The bird joined in, hopping closer to us on a lower branch, then to the ground where he began digging with his beak for worms.

"He trashed my desk and all my papers." Lynn spouted. "Grabbed my little dog by the tail and wouldn't let go!"

July 3, 2007 3:30 a.m.

The rhythm of Trevor's skateboard hitting the curb changed the day, drumming an insistent march, a force wanting flight yet resigned to earth.

Tony called me today. He left a message that he was back home, and I should come over, saying something about an Orange Julius. Where do I get an Orange Julius? When I was scaling the hill to his door, I continued to ask, "What is an Orange Julius, anyway?"

Lorraine suggested I wait in the dining room.

"We're trying to get Tony back into bed" She said, wiping her hands on a towel. "Oh, Tony wants you to have half of the Orange Julius in the fridge. We didn't know where to get one and Trevor said he did."

The drink met my hand sweating and cold. I poured half in a glass, and was met by a delicious bite of fresh orange juice calmed by vanilla ice cream.

In a room layered with ragged carpet remnants, held together with, of course, gaffer's tape, I met the other Tony. He smiled out at me from a photo taken decades before I was born—tousled hair, tan, nude from the waist up, arms and shoulders rippling, white shorts clinging tight to perfection. Shy and warm, he was squinting into the brightness of the future. Here was the man—at twenty or twenty-five—a god, a man, a lover, brimming with dreams, immortal—before his bones gave up from being pulled too far apart, from hanging upside down on a trapeze, swinging fifty feet, one hundred feet above, for all to see.

So *this* is the man who sat next to me on a stool? Not the white-haired grandpa with the cane, legs collapsing, joints betraying. This is the man who joined me on the lawn, introduced me to other silver-haired men in cafes—Nathan, Byron, Matthew, who sported worn shirts, and bantered in gentle jokes.

"Did you hear the one—So there was this priest, he walks into a bar—"

Now it was about living the day, each day, valiantly.

This is the man who mused about what it would have been like to marry the woman across the street?

"Marry me? I don't think so. Been there, burned the t-shirt!"

"We would have had fun. We would have been good together."

I held the photo of the young man, picked up the others. There was Tony half a century later, bent, bearded, Santa Claus hat, crimson trimmed with white.

I never did get to see him last night. I let myself out after dark, overhearing three people straining to get a man back into his bed. Standing in the middle of Riverview, I was addressing a dozen stars, praying for my greatest and highest good, when Lorraine came down the hill to join me.

"We thought he wasn't going to make it through the night last night. He didn't sleep. We didn't sleep! We'd get up every few hours to see if—" Her hand rested over her chest, "to see if he was breathing. But then, this morning, he said, "I want some tomato soup. Can we get some tomato soup?" He spent three hours outside by the pool. He did a one-eighty. He had a big day."

Lorraine went back up the hill and down came Gloria, Tony's daughter. She explained why I had an Orange Julius today.

"When I was little," she held her hand thigh-high, "I didn't see much of him, but when I did, I'd say, 'Daddy, let's go down to the Boulebard!' The place was on Hollywood Boulevard. So we'd go down to the 'boulebard' to the stand, and get us an Orange Julius. This morning, I didn't know where to go to get one anymore, so I asked Trevor."

Today, Gloria had an Orange Julius with her dad. Lorraine

got to see her father-in-law bright, and awake. And I got to see Tony Manicetti the way he still sees himself—glowing, and invincible, while across the way Trevor's skateboard cracked on asphalt, hard as a hammer.

July 5, 2007 9:00 p.m.

This morning two black Mercedes pulled up in front of Tony's house. One, a diesel, sounded like a semi truck.

"You should leave it running!" I yelled to Sam, one of Tony's pals, as he escorted a stout man carrying a black briefcase up the steps. I'd met Sam a few times. He warms the red bricks on Tony's porch, often. Like Tony, he's married to cars. That Benz is his drug of choice. Marine Corps crew cut, Sam always wears the same uniform—black vest with a million pockets, like he's ready to go on safari—black pants, black tennis shoes. He waved back at me, guiding the other man in the pinstriped suit through the front door. Sam was a man with many things on his mind. His best friend, Tony, was dying, and there was a lot to get in order.

Tonight when I brought a plate of ribs and baked potatoes over to Lorraine, we sat at the top of the hill in the Adirondack chairs next to Tony's wood pile. She spoke about him not being able to keep food down for three weeks.

"It runs out of him. The doctor says one to two weeks, at the most."

"He's shutting down," I said, remembering my cat, Princess, at nineteen, almost twenty, weeks before she passed, the clear-eyed, shrinking frame, her "What's happening to me?" stare.

We lingered up on that knoll. Lorraine passed on the ribs, inhaled dessert—a homemade sundae, heaping with chocolate chips.

"Sometimes I eat chocolate chips right out of the bag," she confessed.

"I don't have a problem with that."

Earlier, during my short stay on the edge of Tony's bed, I teased him. "You look good without a shirt."

He answered with the usual half-wink.

We visited for about five minutes. No tubes anywhere. Just Tony, à la carte, uncovered from the waist up, quietly staring out at the world.

"You really do look good without a shirt."

He waved me in, closer.

"Joey's getting the house." Then he whispered. "Listen to me. You're the one who got away!"

I glanced at him.

"Not the Cutlass guy. *You're* the one who got away."

July 6, 2007 11:00 p.m.

Joey let me see him cry tonight. Joey, who isn't into public displays, who disappears, travels under the sidewalk, let salt water track down his face. I knelt next to Tony's little black trash can, looking up into his pain. I handed him a cup of grapefruit juice. He'd been attacking the lawn, the ivy, blindly, for hours. Something had to pay for this agony—all of it.

"I'm buying you a drink," I said, offering the glass.

"What is it?"

"Grapefruit. 'Straight up."

He leaned against Tony's brick wall. Everyone leans on Tony's bricks.

Gloria came out, hugged and kissed me and told me how loving I was. Then she addressed Joey. "He doesn't look that bad. He's not clammy. His teeth aren't staying tight on his gums so they slip down and look funny and his eyes are a little glazed from the morphine but it's not that bad. You can go in there now. It's okay."

After Gloria got into her car, and made a U-turn on Riverview, I told Joey that Tony had called me over today, how I'd held his head so he could sip the chocolate shake I brought.

"Contraband! From Bob's!" I told Tony, as I handed it to him clandestinely, like we were two addicts about to do drugs together.

"Where's our Joey?" I'd asked.

"He's outside," Tony mused, wrapping each word in understanding and love. He knew Joey was trying to come to grips with the idea of death.

"They say he's only got a few days," Joey's red eyes blazed.

"Maybe," I said, idly twisting the stem on an ivy leaf. "Whatever you do, it's—Do you want me to go in with you?"

"No, I'll be okay."

Back in my own kitchen I got to my knees, forehead on the rug.

"I'm praying for my greatest and highest good. I'm praying for Joey's greatest and highest good. I'm praying for Tony's greatest and highest good. I'm lifting the situation up—to You, Lord."

I have comfort knowing that Tony is still alive over there, hovering somewhere between Heaven and Earth.

CHAPTER TWENTY-ONE

Burying Tony

I AM HOUSE

I am house
I am home

He came out
Fast like a
Bird through
My wall

No one knew
But the houses he
Watched her sleep saw
The one who sits next to her

He smiled to be
Young not in the old
Body anymore he wanted to
Touch her say good bye

The mother smiled
Raised her hand said
Thank you for
Being my daughter's friend

July 7, 2007 8:15 a.m.

I woke up at four and saw something or someone, a man silhouetted in my bedroom doorway. Half asleep, more dreaming than awake, I went back to sleep. I think I heard the falcon scream once.

Then a branch cracked—and fell.

July 7, 2007 10:45 p.m.

When I heard Joey's voice, I knew.

"Some time in the morning, early." He said. "He was such a good guy."

"I know."

"I don't know what I'm going to do."

"Well, I'll stay close to you."

That was twelve hours ago. Tonight I stretched out with one leg up over Tony's wall, and had a peach sundae with fruit from Florina's little tree. Wandering, circling, sighing all day, I'd forgotten my keys at least twice. Over there on his spotty lawn, something eased. A breeze picked up.

Behind me, Tony's house stood quiet. All relatives have loaded into vehicles with looks of relief. The day before they reminded me of scavenger birds, wings folded over their backs, waiting for the beast to drop.

"Where were these sons of bitches all the years he lived here? Were *they* cooking him dinner?" Stewart growled, finishing another glass of merlot out on the street. "They didn't come because they didn't like the way he kept the house? Were they ever here to help him clean it? Fuck these people! I have no use for them! They're trash and they don't care about him. Didn't care about him. Joey cared. He was here every day. I fed Tony more dinners than I can count. What the fuck?"

A different lamp resides in Tony's living room now, not the stained glass one I'm used to seeing. The clan of four chairs on the lawn is fresh out of humans.

The inevitable inevitably happened.

Joey wasn't sure if it was 7 a.m. or earlier. Wasn't it this morning at four or five—when I saw a shadow in my doorway? Could it have been Tony, confirming his suspicion that Kathy O'Brien does, in fact, sleep in the nude?

July 9, 2007 8:10 a.m.

Tony died two days, four hours, and ten minutes ago. It's like he's on a road trip. All of his cars are still parked out front. I hope he's even happier than the day I came home to find him and Joey glowing, side-by-side out on the porch, both wearing the same face—complete and total bliss, overshadowed only by reckless abandon.

"We went to Jay's today," Tony explained. "We looked at all his cars."

Evidently still too moved, Joey couldn't speak. Holding a cold can of root beer, manning a wide grin was all he could handle. Seeing the eighth wonder had done him in.

"Whose cars?" I came up closer. I didn't want to miss a word.

"Jay Leno's. I know the guy who keeps the warehouse. He gave us the tour. We were there for two hours."

Joey nodded, mute.

"Truly, you have just come back from Mecca. How many are there?"

Two speechless men eyed each other with a "how`-can-you-say-how-many-gallons-there-are-in-the-ocean" glance.

"At least two hundred." Tony decided.

"And he can go by there, any time of the day or night, and

drive one—any one!" Joey added, finding the strength to form words.

Today those children of Tony's, who I wanted to hate two days ago, are asking all of us individually about our schedules so that they can try to accommodate everyone. They called Stewart first.

There is talk of all of us meeting at Bob's on Friday.

July 14, 2007 4:40 a.m.

"Tony's going to help me find a parking place," I decided. Sure enough, two big spots on Riverside Drive, a half block from Bob's appeared—on a Friday night? 'Damn close to a miracle.

"Do you come here often?" I asked a man in a satin Road Kings jacket, who was arranging something in a cherry-red Ford's trunk. It wasn't a line. I really wanted to know.

"Yes," he stood up, eyes alert. Maybe he was hoping it was a line?

I told him why I was there.

"What did he look like? What kind of car did he drive?"

Neon from Bob's signs was becoming molten, dripping off of hoods, chrome fenders, reflecting in each window as I drifted from one vehicle to the next—without my anchor—without Tony.

"You could always do a poster to tell everyone he passed with the announcement: 'No more parts available?'"

Next, I asked a line of men in folding chairs if they knew Tony Manicetti.

"Was he a member of the Road Kings?" a man in a Dodgers hat asked.

"What kind of cars?" Another man asked.

"Old! He looked like Santa Claus," I said, scanning the crowd for the man with white hair. "Old."

When I saw all the people lined up on stools at the counter

I balked, wondering if coming was the right decision? Walled in a booth with Sam and Stewart, ordering mashed potatoes with brown gravy, I relaxed. As we dipped ceremonial forks, I tasted, swallowed.

"I see why he liked this." I decided.

"He blew the tree out," Sam sputtered, reminding us that the big sycamore branch fell at the same time Tony passed.

"Wasn't it the same day he died?" I asked. "It was such a long time ago."

"The same day," Stewart confirmed. "Took Joey five hours to cut it up. Where is Joey?"

I shrugged. "He said he'd be here."

"Maybe he's not ready for 'Prime Time?'" was Stewart's idea.

Sam agreed. "He'll show up. Maybe he's out there, talkin' with Tony, lookin' at cars? My 'Benz didn't want to start today," he chuckled. "In honor of Tony! He blew that tree out. He blasted out of the room, fast start, 'Gotta go!' and bam, tore that tree up!" Sam laughed, going for his third forkful of potatoes.

"Came out like a rocket!" Stewart said.

"It's all—these days—it's dense," I said, mixing more gravy into the mash. "And here it is—Friday the thirteenth."

"Well, he's got more firewood now," Sam laughed. "That house was so cold. He never turned the heat on."

"You could feel the cold coming up, through the floor," Stewart reminisced. "He loved his little heater. If he kept it right in front of him—"

We lingered in the parking lot, checking out a few cars.

"This—is 'America'," I said, absorbing the crowd. "You know, no matter how many weeds I pulled tonight, I couldn't bring him back."

"The falcon landed in front of me and stayed there for a long time today," Stewart said, right before he veered left, signing off. He was on his way to Mo's, across the street. They serve alcohol there. Stewart needed a drink.

"He's around," Sam confirmed, unzipping one of his pockets, searching deep in another for his keys. "Lorraine told me they all agreed that he broke down on the way up to Heaven, but then he got it running and made it the rest of the way."

"How old was Tony?"

"Eighty-five," Sam and Stewart answered in unison.

"But he lied about his age," Stewart explained, backing farther away. "He said he was eighty-three. Hey, this is Hollywood!"

When I was almost to my car, I saw a dark figure in a hooded sweatshirt leaning against it. I stopped. Then the figure raised a hand and waved.

"Hey," he said, slipping out of the hood. "It's me, Joey."

"Joey! What the—? You scared me! You look like the damn Grim Reaper! Where were you?"

"I...couldn't come in." Joey looked down, shuffling his work boots.

My hand went to his arm. "It's okay. It's hard. It's hard for everyone."

We glanced over at the festival of cars, the lights, people milling.

"I hope they have car shows in Heaven." He said.

July 16, 2007 10:00 p.m.

The black dress was not up for apologies. It didn't care what others' opinions were. It carried me up the center aisle, falling seriously on my hips, dipping low in front. The dress wasn't up for excuses or explanations about how I came to fall for a man thirty years older than me. The dress—was taking no prisoners. Besides, Tony would have liked it. Tony would have liked it—a lot.

I didn't expect to sing in front of one hundred people in a

church at Forest Lawn today. It just kind of happened. At the podium the first verse of *You Made Me Love You* rolled out. I had no speech prepared.

"I'm a newcomer to the 'I Love Tony Club,'" I opened, as light from the stained glass windows gilded every person in saffron. "I only knew him about a year. I thought I'd be nice to him because he had tools and he knew how to fix things, and I had an old house. What I didn't know was that the tools I needed weren't in his garage."

By invitation of the family we all reconvened at the Tennis Club's dining room down the street. Someone who lives very close, who of course, shall remain nameless, remarked over a heaping plate of finger sandwiches that Anthony Manicetti was a womanizer who had slept with more women in this city than she could mention.

"Evidently, not *you*," trotted through my mind, as I noticed Scarlett, eyes down, glued on her plate of curly pasta.

"He was always nice to me," I tossed, overhand. "And much more talented in bed than I expected."

Everyone stopped chewing.

"Just kidding," I said, rising. "Seconds, anyone?"

"Oh, God," the neighbor choked. "For a minute, I thought you were serious!"

Back at the main buffet table, the Preacher, who had gone on quite a bit about "earning" a good life afterwards, droning on about what a good guy Tony was—in a canned speech that I could tell he'd delivered at least two hundred times before—materialized next to me, asking how long I knew Tony—and where did I live? I didn't trust this man any farther than I could throw him. Sometimes you smell a cheater and the whole room needs airing out. About a second later, his slim, tan, (and I'm sure, second or third) wife sidled up next to me, flashing a mouthful of Chiclets, telling me how happy they were and how she got to travel with him—all the time.

"Leash that dog!" was what I wanted to say, but instead, you guessed it, out it came;

"Have you tried the chocolate cake?"

Scarlett was the only person who stayed at Tony's house until almost dark. She hovered alone outside of his bedroom window, arms dangling at her sides, moving back and forth like they didn't know if they should stay on her body or not.

I found solace in the old shed. I went back there to talk with Gramps, to ask him to pour Tony a drink or something over there. Magic surprised me, jumped through the open side window, was walking across the dirt floor, when out of nowhere Jasper flew up in front of me, landing on my shoulder. The surprise was to rest my head against his chest while the raven gently tugged on my hair, to not feel him pull away.

"He's so warm." I thought, expecting a purr. Then the bird lit on my head. It's hard to be sad when you have a raven smack dab on you, like a hat. I mean, really? On top of your head?

July 17, 2007 midnight

"I had to ask myself what my impression of death is. I mean, no one knows, but there are gifted people like you who know things, who channel. I get to go on my own idea. I think my grandmother will be there. She knows just how I like my tea—with a little milk. She'll have a cup of tea waiting for me, and if I can tell you I'm okay, I will."

I was inching toward the edge of Betty's pool, listening, drawn to where she moved, both of my hands clasping tile. Exhausted from treading water, I was sick of hovering over this faceless, nameless fear.

"I used to be afraid of dying. I'm not now," Betty said, looking up at the flat azure sky. "Maybe none of us want to make that leap, but I'm not afraid of being there."

I'd started out talking about Tony, how empty it feels—all the cars gone, except for the Imperial.

"I mean this in the highest way. He got to me like an animal does. I had no defenses. I wonder if he fell on purpose, if he knew it was hard to be around him—If he wanted to 'make an exit?'"

"When my dad died, my mother shut the door on me. I wasn't allowed to go see him. When my mother died, my sister shut me out of that funeral. I was twenty-five. Center stage, my behavior was excellent. But I could have really gotten drunk over that, stayed drunk over it! Thank God, I didn't. Everyone puts their own signature on grief. That's how we treated death in our house. Later, I had to let those feelings run rampant."

"Feelings? I don't want to have these feelings! It's crowded in here! I have to get things in order, my animals, what if I—"

I could only stare down into the blue water. It was too hard to lift my head.

Betty chattered a little more about something, I can't remember what. Her words trickled softly like the water lapping at the edge.

Then I said, "I need to go to the mountain and grieve my own mortality."

Betty heard me. She almost collapsed in relief. Her head fell forward. She let out a sigh. A cool hand met my shoulder.

I was heading toward shallow water. I had hit bottom. It wasn't as deep as I thought.

"That's it. That's what's been bothering me. Death."

"Be careful," she warned, "With this concept, when you work with other women. Let them come to this realization themselves. Otherwise, they'll resent you."

"I would just like—*evidence,* I guess, that we go on," I explained, gripping hard, like some current might carry me away. "I would just like to see, to have—I don't know—proof."

Opened to: *And I will raise him up at the last day.*

July 18, 2007 5:30 a.m.

We all ended up at Tony's again tonight. I went over to see Joey when I heard his truck pull up. He was focused on excavating the whole front patio next to the porch, looking for a lost sprinkler head. Scarlett crossed over from Edith's a few minutes later, began presiding.

"There used to be a table here, remember? People sat all around it. When was that? How many years ago was it?"

Joey wasn't much for conversation. Clasping a shovel, he dug with determination.

"This pipe has to be here, somewhere." He muttered.

It bothered me that the lawn was depleted. Other projects called to me from my own house—hosing off my driveway, transplanting those flowers that were root bound. I was ready to attack all of that until my stomach told me to go get a wheelbarrow and start to dig out extra dirt and take it across the street.

Because we had to bury Tony.

Soon Scarlett held a shovel, too. She used it more as a pointer.

"Remember when we… remember when… I told him he should go, travel, have fun. He should have been going somewhere, but he never did."

"Maybe he was having fun?" I said, dumping a load of dirt on a bare place near the wall.

"There used to be a table here," Scarlett said, pointing, touching soil with the tip of the blade. "The hose used to catch it, remember?"

I was covering grass, raking, smashing clods, stomping, when a cowbird flew onto the bricks.

"That's a cowbird, isn't it?" Scarlett said.

We watched the bird who, obviously, wished I'd vacate the fresh soil for her inspection. The cowbird was picking her way through leaves, each step a clear chirp. She was our muse, the music, our clarity.

"Don't they lay eggs in other people's nests?" Scarlett asked.

"Could a song this sweet have another side to it?" I asked myself.

The bird stayed, fertile in her search, while we, like her, unearthed bits and pieces, passed memories, palm-to-palm, heart-to-heart, wrapped and unwrapped.

"Do you know, "Scarlett reminisced, "He had a house in Palm Springs? He kept six cars there."

I can hear the cowbird singing again, the first call of the morning, louder, more insistent. It ribbons the air, rising, like the light blue sky behind Tony's elm and pine.

On and on she goes in chain links of song.

August 1, 2007 11:00 p.m.

I leaned against the front fender of the car, looking over at my house, missing him. The thing about death is it's so final. Days wash together like watercolors on wet paper. I don't have Tony to run things by now. I'm an athlete without a coach.

Closing my eyes, I tried to see him.

"Tony, wherever you are, I hope it's really, really good. I hope it's a damn party over there. Keep an eye on me, Tony. I don't want to get into trouble."

Then I turned to take in his prize, the Great White Whale, last of its kind, stallion with no rider; the Chrysler Imperial.

And the headlights went on.

This got my attention.

I leashed Sarge, took a walk up Riverview. When we returned, the cars lights were off.

And I wondered if I'd imagined the whole thing.

CHAPTER TWENTY-TWO

Magic Carpets

I AM HOUSE

I am house
I am home

I couldn't give her
Much the one by her
Bed told me
We had little

We were going to do it
Different than our
Parents but the money
Didn't come never came

When she was small
I taught her how to
Make houses
Come back to life I

Thought if she
Knew how to paint
And plaster she
Would always have bread

August 5, 2007 10:55 p.m.

No bird. No Jasper hopping on the chairs around the picnic table, begging for peanut butter, cracking jokes, wanting to play tag with Sarge.

No bird.

No raven.

Third day.

Black bird gone, vanished.

It was my idea to band him.

"Lynn, why did I think a yellow leg band was necessary? Maybe the same thing that set him apart made him a target? He changed my life. It was like—making friends with the wild side."

"He makes me laugh." Lynn said.

Tonight except for the crickets, the backyard is quiet. I feel Jasper is trapped, trying to get home, not dead, but in deep trouble.

Opened to: *Then the Proconsul believed, when he saw what had been done.*

August 6, 2007 11:00 p.m.

Then *I* believed. I heard the screaming when I was on the floor doing my morning pushups. Insistent, shrill—I looked out, and there was Sarge, going after a black bird. I grabbed peanut butter, a knife, ran out.

"Jasper!"

"CAWWW!" he answered, wings out, mouth wide open. I made Sarge sit, fed Jasper peanut butter off of a knife. His feathers were ragged, white bird "chalk" under what was left of a tail. He ate like he was starving. Then he held his left leg up—and looked at me like he'd just come back from Hell.

Twice the size of the right, swollen, he could barely put weight on it. A closer look showed a wound torn through waxy skin.

I picked him up between my hands, brought him inside, set him in a cat's crate, called a coworker for the bird vet she uses, wrote the number on a card, taped it to the top of the carrier, and brought it to Lynn's front door. It took a lot of knocking, but I got him out of bed.

After work, there was a knock on my door. An angry Lynn stalked in carrying a small glass vile.

"Is he—"

"He's going to be okay. The vet had to operate. Here's what was in his leg—and his wing." He held up a test tube, two small copper beads rolling at the bottom.

"BB's?"

"BB's from a pellet gun. Some bastard shot him. Then I figure a dog attacked him when he fell."

"My God!"

"Some people should be shot!"

"But he's going to be okay?"

"He'll fly—But not for a long time. I have him in a parrot cage so he can heal. Damn bird used up a few of his nine lives."

"But he came home. Somehow he made it."

"He came back to his family."

August 23, 2007 7:00 a.m.

While it was still murky and dark, I slapped a metal tape on the floor. There I was, up at four a.m., when all good witches are conjuring.

"I'd like a rug," I told Him, measuring. "Nine by twelve would be nice. I can't afford Persian. Even a remnant would be okay, Lord. I need help 'warming' these rooms."

Then I popped into my Levi's, and Sarge and I headed off down Riverview. As Dawn sat up on her bed sheets, was combing clouds out of her hair, we walked a mile or two past arenas littered with sleeping horses.

Something is changing. I can feel it in the air—or is it just autumn? Magic's been "banking" off of the living room walls, skittering down the hall, arching his back like the true black Halloween cat that he is. Rocky cheers him on from the back of the sofa, making sounds like a coffeepot perking.

There's a large garden spider at home outside my bedroom window. Her web has a grey and white zipper down the middle. She's weaving her own rug. This is not an option for me.

August 23, 2007 11:00 p.m.

"I have a rug for you," Terrance, my hairdresser, fellow dumpster diver, announced. It was eight hours after I'd pulled out the tape measure—telling no one—and forgotten all about it.

"It's probably not Persian," I muttered, driving over the Cahuenga Pass, down into West Hollywood. "If it is, it'll be a piece of crap."

His old heavy garage door creaked open in protest as sunlight flooded the back of a fine hand knotted antique rug. Terrance has a "prep" carpet that he uses for decorating sets, his other job. I figured this rug was his.

"No, that's it. That's it. The Persian one!" He corrected when I went back upstairs to his apartment. "Some girl was carrying it to the curb, and I said, 'Do you want that?' and she said, "No," and I said, "Well, I do!" And then I called you."

I unrolled it on his driveway and could not speak. Bright crimson and navy, it sported vibrant patterns of little people in skirts opening their arms waving up at me in joy—or were they horses? Red fades in sun, fibers wear thin from traffic. This exquisite creation, born in the '20s or the '30s, had brilliant red pile that stood up, fresh and full. No animal stains. No dirt. No odor—Like it had been kept safe in a vault—for me.

I unrolled it on the living-room floor and felt a change. If clothes make the man, then carpets make the house. Then I watched with embarrassment at what I did next.

I had the nerve to pull that same metal tape out. I heard myself say, "Lord, I am so grateful for my Persian rug. I will tell everyone I know what You did for me—Now, what I would like—is a really big one for my bedroom! Hey, what do You say?"

August 24, 2007 11:00 p.m.

"I have a rug for you," Terrance, my hairdresser, fellow dumpster diver, announced. "Big. Nine by twelve. Chinese."

"Really?" Was this "Groundhog Day?" I hadn't said anything to anyone. In fact, I'd forgotten all about it. I grabbed work gloves, jumped in my car, and sped over to the West Side.

No kidding it was big. It took Terrance pushing, me pulling, to stuff the dead weight it in the backseat.

"One, two, three—" He panted.

"Push! Terrance! It's so big, I don't think I can…"

"One, two, three…come on, pull!"

"I can't ! It's too big—"

One final shove and we were done.

"Holy shit! If any of my neighbors heard us!" he laughed, slamming the car door with finality.

"Hey, if they did, they knew we were having a really good time!"

Pale ivory ground with a few scattered bouquets of camellias, green leaves in four corners, this carpet, the missing piece of the puzzle, fits almost wall-to-wall in my bedroom, the library. The flowers are faded 1930s shades—the same pale mustard of the outside walls, the exact rusty shade of the fireplace bricks.

"My neighbors sold all his antiques and didn't want to deal

with it." Terrance laughed. "Yesterday he asked, 'Do you want this rug?' 'No,' I said, 'but I know someone who might!'"

God must be in the living room with me. I guess He knows I'm His "material girl?" I can't deny it anymore. Now I know He hears me. I have evidence. His fingerprints are all over those rugs. I can feel Him—warm, breathing, and alive, on the sofa next to me. Like Someone I could dance with.

August 26, 2007 7:35 a.m. meditation

I didn't expect Him to be wearing a cutaway tuxedo, shiny patent leather shoes, starched white shirt, and a bow tie. His hair was slicked back, waves prominent at His crown. My God, God is handsome.

And He was waiting to dance with someone. Oh, me?

But I had no dress.

"Will you, would you dance with Me?" He invited.

In a blink, a white rhinestone ball gown fell around me. Long sleeves, close to my body like a leotard, it flowed like it was made of vapor. He lifted His arms, inviting. Here was the Partner I'd been longing for. The downbeat told me it was a waltz. He led—of course. I had never felt such power, unison. I stretched out far into His right arm to what felt like endless space.

On and on, we danced—half naturals, double reverses, running weaves that left the floor, so high that we hung in the air. When the song tapered to close, He turned me out, then back into Him, looking into my eyes, twirling me out again to face an imaginary crowd.

"I need you to be My partner," He confided. "Dance with Me. You want rugs? I'll bring you rugs. You want houses? I'll bring you houses. You want a man? I'll bring you a man."

It was the casual wrist throw of the all-powerful, the fearless.

"I'm afraid, I'm still afraid of dying." I blurted, sure that I was blowing the moment.

"Could it be, could it possibly be that you're afraid of living?" My Partner asked, whispering in my ear. "Death is a 'front.' I'll show you."

Opened to: *Whatever you ask the Father in My name He may give you.*

August 28, 2007 9:00 p.m.

I dragged all of my carpets onto the lawn today, spreading them out like pelts, including the two hundred pound Chinese. This was not easy. They almost covered the entire front yard. A brush, hose, Woolite, helped me delight in dirty water sheeting off.

Within minutes, an old BMW 7 Series pulled up. A dark man rolling a toothpick in his mouth stepped out and walked right up on the grass. With the toe of his shoe he turned over a corner of the Persian carpet that Terrance gave me, counting knots.

Pulling the toothpick out of his mouth, he asked, "Do you want to sell any of dese rugs?"

"I can't." I said. "They're magic."

CHAPTER TWENTY-THREE

The Crash

I AM HOUSE

I am house
I am home

It happened before
Like this people
Ran scared in terror
The Depression

Men leapt off of rooftops women
Wrung hands grew
Food in the yard
They vowed

To
Save
Their houses
At all costs

Souls starved then by
The millions when numbers
Ruled and many
Obeyed

January 6, 2008 10:10 p.m.

The black stallion was milling around in his corral but halted, ears up when I walked to the gate.

"Let's go." I said.

He let Mary halter him. David, the hauler, escorted him to the back of the van. I hugged John and Mary.

"Sixteen years." I announced over the roar of the wind.

"Seventeen." Mary corrected.

"Seventeen," I repeated. "A divorce, some deaths, hired, fired, buy something, loose something. That was quick!" My right hand found John's shoulder, my left, Mary's. I stood between them. "This is sad. I don't want to—"

"It's time," she took over, her hands on my arms like she was about to shake some sense into me. "You need him now. He needs you. It's time."

My horse did need me. Something had changed since I last saw him. His ribs were protruding again. I said nothing. Whatever the problem was we'd fix it soon, when we got him home. The terrible winds we fought on the drive up took pleasure in whipping us, tossing my horse's mane straight up in a Mohawk he loaded on the second try.

"I had a dream," Mary said over the gusts as Dave and John bolted the van's gate. "I ran out after I woke up in the freezing cold in my robe and slippers, you know when you wake up and say, 'Was that...was that real?' I ran out here, really, because in the dream he lay down and didn't get up." She looked up through the open bars of the trailer at the horse's big face, the glowing white star. "But there he was."

"That'll happen with me. He'll lie down and—"

"I don't like to haul at night," Dave mentioned when we made a slow rocking turn out of the ranch gates onto the dirt trail, passing Joshua trees reaching spiny arms out into our headlights. "But this is the only time I had."

"We're off road," I said, looking back at the trailer in the side-view. "Is he quiet?"

"He's not moving," Dave said, shifting the Cummings Diesel, glancing at the clock on the dash. "Figure it'll take three hours. I don't go over fifty-five when I'm hauling."

"You're the boss," I said, my back making friends with the seat. "This is your show."

January 9, 2008 9:30 p.m.

"He's very thin," Gloria appraised. "He can't chew hay pellets. We need to have a doctor look at his teeth. When was the last time you had them floated?"

"About a year ago?"

She held her right hand up, finger pointing at the barn ceiling. "I know. We'll put him on the "Flash Diet.""

"What's that?"

"Tizz Whiz, all the sweet feed he can eat, and alfalfa hay."

"He needs to put on two hundred and fifty pounds."

"You'll see," she said, walking across the aisle to an empty stall stacked with hay bales and plastic feed containers. She scooped molasses-heavy sweet feed into a bucket, added some pellets that looked like rabbit food. "Try this," she said. "Take a look at Flash."

I walked over to a chestnut Arabian stallion in the stall next to Tyson's who had a white face, four white "stockings," and round, full sides. No ribs here, thank you very much.

"Flash is how old?"

"Thirty."

"Damn, Tyson's twenty-nine. I want him to look that good! He did—six weeks ago. I don't know what happened."

"Teeth stuff can change a horse fast. Besides, it's winter."

"I don't have money for a vet," I confessed, doused in shame.

"I'll cover it. You can pay me back later."

Gloria was the only person in a five-mile radius who would take another stallion in her barn. No one else, none of the other trainers, wanted the liability. After I got Mary's call, the one where she said, "John has a growth on his lungs. We're liquidating the herd," I ran next door to Edith's.

"I don't have ten K to fill in the pool and make stables. Where can I board my stallion?"

"There's only one person who takes stallions. It's Gloria Hollingsworth. "I bought mine from her. She's three blocks away."

Gloria was petite, fit, tan, sported a baseball hat and a tiny docked ponytail.

"He's a stallion?" she repeated, a second after we shook hands. "Bring him in! I have lots of stallions. He can hang next to my old stallion," Flash.""

January 12, 2008 11:00 p.m.

"See that? At the bottom of the eye socket?" the vet, Dr. Walling, said as she held a scope against my droopy tranquilized horse's left eye. I didn't have to squint or use my glasses to see what looked like a large contact lens folded over, laying at the base of the eyeball.

"That's his retina." She told me. "It's been detached."

"How does this happen?"

"Impact? He hit a something. Who knows?"

Maybe that's what he was trying to tell me about the night of the wedding.

"Can you reconnect it?"

"No."

"So, he's blind on his left side?"

"Correct. And he's got cataracts growing on the right." She paused, letting me find my balance. "But for a horse his age—"

"We just had his teeth floated. He's digesting better. The problem is there aren't a lot of teeth left!"

"He's on the "Flash Diet!"" Gloria quipped. "He'll be running fences, yelling to mares, in no time at all!"

Gloria was right. When I went to see Tyson after work, as I led him out into a corral, the horse that had stumbled off a van a few days before dropped to the ground happily rolling, with all four feet in the air, then took off neighing in the direction of a mare two pens over. No kidding, he was thin. Yes, his gait was off. But softer food had begun to make a difference. He had energy. A dull coat had begun to shine.

"He's getting his dignity back," I confirmed, holding the top rail, stepping up for a better view. "Resurrection' is my horse's middle name."

January 14, 2008 8:00 a.m. meditation

"I'm so happy, I can't stand it. But none of it "pencils out!" I have no money!"

God listened as He picked up His 12-gauge shotgun, opening the barrel. He dropped shells in, closed it, walked to the patio's edge and called, "Pull!" Instantly, two clay pigeons jettisoned out over the ocean. He hit both, of course.

"Can I try?"

He was the picture of a sportsman, tweed jacket, suede patches. The gun found a home on a table as He hugged me.

"How's my girl?"

"How the heck am I going to pay board for a horse plus a mortgage?"

"Is your horse home?"

"Yes. My pony came home on my birthday!"

"Happy Birthday! He's doing better?"

"Yes! I'm so happy, I can't stand it. But none of it pencils out!"

He retrieved the rifle, held it out to me, sideways.

"Have a go?" He stood behind me, steadied my shoulder, called, "Pull!"

I missed both.

"You're trying too hard. Let the gun do the work," He said, loading more shells. That time when He yelled, "Pull!" I hit one. Clay shattered to dust. This made me very happy.

"Yay!"

"Better!" He smiled, relieving me of the weapon. "See? It's better when you know it's going to hit. "

"But I barely focused. And it—how did it happen?"

"That's what faith is. 'Knowing it's going to hit. It's that easy. That's why it's so hard! Good for you!"

"I don't get it. How did it—"

"Because you let go and you trusted!" He grinned, amused. "Just—*act* like it's going to hit. You don't have to know how! Let Me do it—Whatever it is. I can bring in the heavy lifting machines. That's My job. Try Me. See what happens? If I don't nail it, then it was a bad deal in the first place. Hey, go play with your pony. Enjoy him. It was time."

"But I have no money!"

"Has that ever stopped you from getting what you want?"

"Riverview's going on the block. Tomorrow 'sign's going up."

God paused, looking over the top of my head at something I couldn't see.

"Yeah, cut the grass, enjoy the gardens. Plant some stuff in the shade."

"Impatiens?"

"Why not? They're named after you!"

Opened to: *Where is your faith?*

January 18, 2008 10:00 p.m.

We didn't stay long at the second place. It wasn't as bad as the first one we looked at. That house had a gash sledge hammered into the kitchen wall big enough to drive a car through. All plumbing had been stripped. Some angry homeowners are taking the pipes with them. Rats hadn't even signed up to live there. Oddly, the listing broker had hung a lockbox on the front door's security gate. Really? We need a key when we can walk *through* the wall? We left that one shaking our heads. But it was the second one—

From the street, it looked like all the other houses.

"I haven't sent a crew in to clean yet," the listing agent mentioned when he gave me the combo code: 666. "Just look past all the stuff."

It was hard to look past all the stuff. Bowls of Cheerios dried in milk, a frying pan reeking of bacon grease had over taken the counters. Upstairs in the children's room, I held my breath. Was this a crime scene? Part of me was on the lookout for a body. All beds were intact with tousled blankets, pillows, sheets. The pink bedroom wafted of baby powder, had tiny shirts and dresses clinging to hangers at odd angles inside the closet. Stuffed animals, a zebra and a lion, lay side by side on dusty hardwood.

This house, like so many houses—

Scenes of families fleeing dust bowls, hanging off of old cars and trucks, clutching belongings, flooded in. Here was our plague—in my face—driven by greed, grounded in anonymity. Another family leaving in the night, running away from their only safe place, a home that they'd clung to it like a life raft for as long as they could—sinking, sinking…

It was happening across the country. One family at a time, millions were taking to the road. Too tired to fight, they were fleeing secretly, silently, and alone.

Was I next? Was Riverview going to look like this? Pangs of guilt and fear had me wondering if carpetbaggers felt the same shock after the Civil war, coming up on decimated places in the South that once were great, homes that had been burned to the ground?

"I guess they left quick, huh?" My buyer, Ralph, said in the backyard as he bent to pick up a deflated yellow and green plastic frog that once held water as a pool.

Last summer, children splashed here, laughed here. Last summer, before—

He dropped the toy on the ground. "How many square feet did you say this one is?"

January 30, 2008 10:00 p.m.

After I talked with the gas company and the Department of Water & Power, when I was leaving the Temporary Aid office with a check for $100 to pay the gas bill, anxiety the size of a boulder hammered my back.

I can't pay the mortgage. Even with tenants, here I go, under-earning again. I don't want to destroy my credit score. It was my stamp of approval in society.

"You got credit? You're in!"

I'm certified to buy houses on a signature. The game is on. Correction: The game *was* on? Now I'm walking towards a wall. It's solid rock. There's no way around it. Soon the entire world will know that I have no credit, no money—that Kathy O'Brien cannot pay.

I heard a story about a man who killed himself because he couldn't make the payments on his second house. I get him. I understand. The nightmares sweep over me often, annihilating hope. What was I thinking when I bought Riverview? What was I thinking? Didn't He co-sign it with me in the sky that night with the shooting star?

"You're not your credit score," Betty's friends tell me. Then they add, "There's no God in credit," and "We don't debt, one day at a time."

How do I not debt? I want to make my payments. The mortgage stockholders deserve their money. I'm willing to earn. Evidently, I don't know how?

Now there are no dance lessons. I can't afford to work with my teacher, Yonnie. There was luxury, years with him, training, competitions, and now there's sacrifice. I go to the dance studio only to practice by myself. Today Yonnie and I waved at each other across the ballroom as I buckled the straps of my high heels and he stepped into dance shoes. One time we happened to come together in the middle of the floor, two people dancing separately under a mirrored ball, so close that I could hear the man breathe.

Next stop, the barn. Eye-to-eye on opposite sides of the fence, my other partner, Tyson, and I, trotted back and forth so close that I could hear him breathe. The horse delighted in out running me—gaining and then leaving me in his dust, only to come back, begging for another match. After he cooled off, I led him back to the barn on his blind side, the back of my hand inside his halter for support. In his stall I brushed caked mud off of him from his jubilant rolling in the arena. Before I left I hugged his neck three times. He responded by bumping me with his head three times. It may have been a sign of affection.

"He wants to protect you," I heard someone say. The voice belonged to Maria, my two-stalls-down neighbor. "When we ride them, especially, they know it's their job to bring us home safe."

"It's been so long, I don't know if he even wants to be ridden?"

"Ask him."

"Ask him?'

"Sure. Talk to your horse. He understands every word."

Elbow-to-elbow we leaned over Tyson's stall door.

"I lost my horse, Jeremy, two years ago," Maria confided. "He put on a 'game face' for me after he colicked. I'd stay with him for hours at the clinic but I always took breaks so he could let down, have his real face. He didn't want to show me the pain."

We moved over to her horse's stall, watched Gnomey, her Friesian, eating hay.

"After Jeremy died, I went over to Holland and looked at a hundred horses, but this one—"

"What does he think his job is?"

"Eating!" She laughed, as the coal-black horse with a thick braided mane buried his nose deeper in a pile of alfalfa. "No, he knows he's here to fix my broken heart."

"He seems to be doing a good job."

"Yes, he is." She said. "He knows. They all know."

February 3, 2008 10:00 p.m.

God, in His sweeping, easy way, has made it rain. And He has made the winds to blow. The jacaranda is being testing for elasticity. More winds of change.

I dusted off my saddle, and tried it on Tyson's back today. It's been ten years since we rode. He stood quietly, attentively, ears flicking back and forth, telling me he's ready for work.

"Look! You're still the same size!"

Test run. No rush. We'd get to this tomorrow. He seemed a bit surprised when I unbuckled the girth, slid it off.

"That's all you have to today." I told him. "Good job."

It's different this time. Now it's more about "What do you want to do, horse?" Not like years ago when it was, "Here's what you have to do—for me." Tonight Tyson told me he wants to go back to work. He's ready for a job again. My stallion, at almost thirty years old, is about to make a comeback.

These winds are howling, blowing things all over the place. It looks like a tornado out there, leaves blowing by. My insides are constantly surging, tumultuous; how can I keep Riverview?

Maybe God and Tony can help?

I threw a jacket on and sought out his street light. Under that lamp and the moon I asked, "Tony, is it going to be okay? I have two roommates now. A guy's renting the guest house. Now there's almost as much coming in as is going out. They're all ignoring the 'for sale' sign. It's like no one can see it. Tony, I'm thinkin', maybe I can stick this out? Could you put in a word with God? I'm thinking of taking that fucking sign down tomorrow. What do you think?"

The lamp flickered, winked on and off, then came back on.

Opened to: *A man can receive nothing unless it is given to him from heaven.*

July 15, 2008 11:00 p.m.

Jack dipped the end of his corned beef sandwich into a shallow dish of Thousand Island dressing.

"You need two deals."

"Two deals?"

"Two—million-dollar deals."

"Even five grand, anything would help." I shrugged.

Jack ordered a Reuben, steak fries, well done. I went the "seasoned curly" route. Our discussion corralled the grim world of real estate.

"I prefer this kind of market," he chewed, swallowing. "That other kind, you're looking for property for everyone—not many of those buyers we found stuff for, bought. They'd say, 'I'll wait for the prices to go down.'"

"And you'd say, 'This is California. Prices (probably) aren't going down!'"

"Right."

"You always say that."

Jack had his favorite shut-you-up-before-you-ask-it quips. That was one of them. In fatter times he and I sold commercial buildings, recording studios, warehouses big enough to house airplanes. Jack was waiting the market out like a lion in the shade. Only his eyes and tail were moving.

He knew I was "lean" in more ways than one. Maybe it was the way my voice cracked when he called and asked if I was okay?

"Meet me at Tiny Marbles," he'd ordered in the gruff way he has of disguising concern.

"I know a broker who lost all three of her houses in the last crash," he remembered.

"How does that happen? Wasn't the idea, the big idea, my parents, their parents—the golden underlying rule, the Thirteenth commandment: 'If you have enough real estate you will never starve?'"

He dipped the sandwich again.

"All three. She didn't have a prudent reserve."

"Oh, that?" Did Jack notice my face singing to crimson? I made a confession. "I buried St. Joseph in front of my rentals."

"Upside down?"

"Saint Joseph or the market?"

We always made each other laugh, turned the light on in the hallway. In life and with real estate, it seems, there are a lot of waiting rooms, forced isolations.

"I feel guilty," I told my friend.

"Have the fries—all of them."

"No, it's not about the fries. I'm a part of this. I don't think it's a recession, I think—"

"Oh, it's a *Depression*, all right. We're going to crash—Soon. The difference is we have credit, so not as many people are starving!"

"I feel guilty because I got buyers into houses with almost no money down—stated income."

"What was the motto? "If they can smoke a mirror, they get funded?" And then they got cash back from the seller for non-recurring closing costs. "

"Right! They got paid to buy a house! I did it. Jack, we all did it!"

"You did nothing illegal. You gave them a start. "

"A launch. I figured if I got them in, the Universe would help them prosper."

"You like your Reuben?"

"Great. This place is great."

"You were just trying to make a living."

"So were the speculators, the people who bundled mortgages, who didn't know anyone, who didn't see anyone's face? That's the real crime, Jack. The one no one wants to talk about—people being ground into equations. What did Jimmy Stewart say? We have to know each other's story—"

"You gave those buyers a start."

"I guess I—I buy real estate and worry about food later?"

"I noticed." Jack said. "Finish the fries."

August 10, 2008 9:00 p.m.

"Lynn, has our lawyer been peppering you with phone calls?"

"All week! 'Three and four times a day. I'm sure he's been bought off by Cow Horn—probably getting a cut from every lawsuit he makes 'disappear'."

"He's offering me five grand to drop my case."

"Me, too. Fuck him. Fuck the bastards. They're trying to bury this under all that dirt out there."

"Are you going to take the money?"

"Hell, no! If I sign off, I won't be able to sue Cow Horn with the next lawyer—once this guy gets dropped. Trust me, my gut's telling me—he's taking a big percentage from each of us, plus a huge amount from Cow Horn—and he's got a deadline—before they dump him!"

"That money would pay my mortgage this month." I said, grimacing in pain." I'm thinking about it."

An hour later, Mr. Kleinshmidt, my perspiring lawyer and I, were seated across from each other at my dining room table, his shirt buttons straining over a round stomach. It was too hot for a suit jacket. The man looked like he needed a drink. I offered ice water. He never touched the glass. I guess he just happened to be in the neighborhood on a Sunday, knocking on all of my neighbor's doors in ninety degree heat—the ones who are suing Cow Horn Productions—that is? It's not often you see a lawyer on a dedicated mission like this—flying down to Los Angeles from San Francisco to walk streets, stay closer to his clients?

"Would you have any objection to signing this release form?" He led off, unscrewing the cap of his golden fountain pen, sliding it and a piece of paper over to my side of the table. "This is a guarantee. We'll have funds wired into your account by Wednesday."

I picked up the pen and was surprised to discover how heavy it felt.

"May I ask you a question?"

He folded his hands. "Of course."

"Why five thousand when this toxic waste—chromium six and mercury—has gone on for decades? When my health and my property value are jeopardized? Why only five thousand when Cow Horn has billions in assets?"

"I—we fought hard with their lawyers and we are up against years of court battles, delays, stalling. I came down here, today, to expedite this because I care. I know you want closure. It's in your best interest, I'm sure you agree—to—to move on. So, what are you going to do with all your cash?"

I was about to say, "Pay the mortgage," when another question over rode.

"And—if I sign, am I allowed to say or write anything I want about Cow Horn after this?"

He pointed to a paragraph on the page. "There is a confidentiality clause."

"This isn't my world. What does that mean?"

"It means—those rights would be relinquished."

So Lynn was right. Why was I feeling like a rag was being stuffed into my mouth? I watched my hand relinquish the pen. Freeing myself, I stood up, began walking away.

"I'll tell you what," I said, opening my front door. "I want to sign a different form. I want one that says, "I am no longer seeking representation from you or your firm in any capacity regarding Cow Horn Productions—here and hereafter.""

"And—what about the compensation?" He pursued, teetering over the threshold, one foot outside the door. "You're going to pass—on all that money? I could make this go away for you."

"You going make the pollution go away? I presume you're leaving that here? No, thanks. You keep it. I don't want Cow Horn's money."

"It's not Cow Horn's money."

"Really? It's Cow Horn's poison. I guess—how could anyone say "No" to Cow Horn, the 'big king' in the castle? Thank you for your time, Mr. Kleinschmidt. I don't want the money. I don't care whose it is. Can you get that form to me—tomorrow?"

September 29, 2008 11:50 p.m.

We were the last two patrons in the checkout line at Pavilions. Quiet night, deadly night, you might say. The man ahead of me had grey skin, like someone or something had drained him of blood, or life, or both. He paid cash for his gallon of Jack Daniel's. The checkout lady clipped off the lock, dropped the bottle into a plastic bag.

Looking like a bartender, hands on the grocery belt, she addressed us both.

"So, what do you think about the crash?"

"The stock market?" I asked.

The man turned to me in his ashen way, clutching the alcohol to his chest.

"I lost everything today. All my money's in stocks."

"Oh," I said, "All my money's in real estate."

ONE YEAR LATER

I AM HOUSE

I am house
I am home

She is frightened of
The paper what they
Chisel on it like it was stone
Threats that they will take me away

She doesn't eat much after
The envelope opens
She stands
Still

Nails need wood
Roofs need walls I
Need her to hear my voice
Tell her they cannot I will not

Be
Moved
I AM HOUSE
I AM YOUR HOUSE

CHAPTER TWENTY-FOUR

David vs. Goliath

September 20, 2009 9:00 p.m.

I could tell he didn't take shit. Vahe Parsinighian didn't need a gun or a dog. He had the law. He didn't sit. He paced. I sat. Not comfortably, but I sat. He had a marker board assisting him on an easel. He jotted notes on things I said. Boyfriends come and go in L.A., but a good lawyer who agrees to give you a free one-hour consult is hard to find.

"So, you took out an equity line on the first house in 2005, but they mistakenly put it on the other house, right?" He made some scratches, wrote "2005 #1," crossed it out, wrote "EL on #2."

"Right. For 370 K—but I didn't know that until I put House #1 on the market, thinking it had those two loans on it—expecting that it was a short sale."

"Why didn't you know about this until now?"

"I always made the payments! I asked them repeatedly to charge the address of record to the first house, but they never did. I always assumed the 370 was on #1."

"Now what are they saying?"

"They're saying—well, look." I slid a letter to his side of the black granite desk. "They're pursuing me to the full extent of the law if they don't get all their money. The biggest bank in the country."

Vahe squinted, thought for a moment, breathed through his nose in a way that had me expecting smoke to pour out.

"What's your plan?"

"I have to sell the first home. It has no kitchen sink. I was going to remodel, can't finish it—so I have an all cash buyer."

"Good."

"I've gone twice in person, to ask the manager at that bank to get someone to put the loan back on the right house, the first house. Then I could sell #1, be done with it, keep #2. Emailed them, too. They're saying they can't move that fast. Now I have to sell #2! I wanted to keep that one forever."

"What's it worth?"

"Six and change. But with the 370, it has nine-plus on it. I want to keep the profit on #1. I don't want to be this honest."

"Maybe you will get to keep the money. You'll wait too long to get nine on the other one. Our investments are supposed to pay us."

"I don't know why I never think that way. Probably because I think I have to take care of everyone else first—even houses!"

Vahe capped the red marker, placing it in the tray carefully. Everything he did was premeditated, like he was coiled, ready to strike. Overlooking events, the battlefield, he directed, "There are things you can do to delay—about three things, Chapter 11, B.K., but what I suggest you do right now—is nothing."

"Nothing?"

"Wait them out. You don't have to make a move—until they do. It's *their* mistake."

"Why do I always forget that?" I bellowed. "Why do I always think it's *my* error?"

"However—" he pivoted, hands in the pockets of his knife-pleated navy gabardine trousers. "From now on, I want you to do everything—all your transactions—cash, cashier's checks, no deposits. The less you have record of, on hand, the easier it will be if we have to confront them on assets, liabilities later."

"Vahe, they scare me."

"They want to scare you."

"They look like a very big Goliath."

"You've got a rock," he said. "We're just not going to throw it unless we have to."

September 21, 2009 7:00 a.m. meditation

"They're the biggest bank in the country and they're out to get me."

God didn't look up right away. He seemed much more interested in the arm of His chair. He nodded. Then He nodded again. "Talk about it."

"They said they're going to pursue me to the full extent of the law. They said they are going to use all their legal power to get that money."

He nodded again, made a fanning motion with his hand. "Talk more about it. Keep talking."

"Ah, they have all those lawyers and three hundred seventy thousand dollars is a shitload—"I'm scared. They're coming. It's a big army."

He took me in like only He can do—like He's seeing the inside and the outside at the same time— and led me out to the patio, to that view. Two seagulls flew by, eye level, checking us out.

"Do those birds look afraid to you?"

"No. Hungry, maybe? Not afraid."

"I know you may find this hard to believe, but I know how to run My business."

"Your business?"

"The world. You don't need an army. You've got Me. I already went ahead of you. Go fly free, like those birds are doing. Let the dust settle. How much can you send that bank today?"

"About five dollars?"

"Okay, send them a fin. Tell them it's all you have, that you'll send them five dollars every month—until it's resolved. Be accountable. Don't shrink from them—and watch what I'm going to do." Then He laughed. God really, really laughed. Like He had a secret that no one else knew about.

September 30, 2009 11:00 p.m.

When Jack isn't chewing, something really has his attention.

"I know of people who've stayed in their homes for thirty-six months without making payments," he mentioned, nonchalantly. "How many months is it?"

"Six." But I didn't have to tell him. I wear a look when I can't make the mortgage like some people do when they're about to divorce

"Did they file a Notice of Default yet?"

"No, just a million threats about foreclosure. Then last month I did get a notice. They're selling my loan to Sunbrite."

"Sunbrite?"

"Uh-huh."

"Hyenas. They'll crush your bones."

"Thanks for sharing, Jack. I feel—this hurts. I feel hunted."

"Don't you love real estate?"

"Jack, with all due respect—fuck you."

"Are you eating? Do you have food?"

"I know how to make soup. I'm painting House #2, the one with the pool, myself, selling it short sale. I keep saying, 'I want to cut the grass at Riverview more than Sunbrite does, I want to cut the grass at Riverview more than Sunbrite does.' I'm babbling," I apologized. "I had to evict the tenants. They couldn't pay and they got verbally abusive with me. They owe me seven K."

"You'll never see it."

"Oh, I'll see it. Just not from them! The universe has a lot of cash on hand. I'm going to paint it myself. Did I say that? Sorry, I—"

Jack pushed his plate away slowly.

"So, no N.O.D. yet? Why is the second one short? I thought the first was the short sale?"

"There are two scoops on this sundae. The bank, which was supposed to record the 370 second on the first house, put it on the other one—by mistake—and they're pursuing."

Jack removed his glasses, rubbed the bridge of his nose, crushed his napkin like he wanted to get juice out of it.

"Why didn't you—what picture—what house—was on the appraisal report?"

"The wrong one. The second one. I don't know how I missed that?"

"I saw it, too. I remember. How did I miss—?"

"Now I'm underground, stuffing a mattress. I'm all cash, baby, in case they—Jack, with all due respect," I confided, feeling something rising in my throat. "Thank you for being my friend—through this."

"Try and keep the big one," he nodded. "That's the one you gotta try and keep— Riverview."

October 5, 2009 11:30 p.m.

The foal was the size of a baby goat. "Be careful," Gloria warned. "They can kick."

But the miniature horse didn't move. He tucked the top of his fuzzy head under my chin, more like a puppy than a horse.

"What does he weigh?"

"Fifteen pounds? He'll put on weight, fast. He's what? Twenty-four hours old? I came in and there he was. I tore the sac open, toweled him off. Now it's another mouth to feed!"

"I'll never be able to hold a horse in my arms again, will I?"

"I'm calling him 'Stewart Little,'" she said, rubbing the foal's velvet nose. "I asked them if that mare was pregnant when I rescued her. They said, 'Oh, no!' Yeah, right!"

"Stewart Little," I repeated as I set him down next to his mother. "Nice handle."

October 8, 2009 11:00 p.m.

It's rule number one when you work with farm animals: "Close the gate behind you." Tonight I screwed up. Big-time. I closed the gate behind me, alright, but I couldn't see—didn't close the second gate on the other side of the corral. And my horse ran out. Horses in stalls began to neigh as my half-blind stallion was picking up speed, tail waving like a banner, across an open field.

"Gramps!" I prayed, "Help! Stop my horse!"

"Whoa!" I yelled. Instantly, unbelievably, Tyson skidded to a halt. I ran to his side, saying "Whoa!" about a million times. He didn't move. I haltered him and took the deepest breath ever known to a human—the one that comes after you know the herd is home, safe.

"Don't ever do that again!" I remarked to the black horse, whites showing in his eyes, prancing at my side. "Jeese!"

When he was safely in his stall I bolted the latch, leaned on the door and thanked my grandfather.

"Gramps, I know you're here. I know you're probably here every night with me when you don't have things to do over there, when you're not driving a big Percheron up Lake Shore Drive. Thank you, Gramps, for saving my horse—for saving our horse."

When Tyson's nose was deep in sweet feed, I heard myself ask my horse a question.

"Teach me how to read your mind." I said. "I want to talk with you. I need help not being so limited, so human. I'm—I can only hear with my ears and not with my heart. Would you teach me?"

Chewing stopped. Tyson turned his head and focused on me, as if to say, "Finally, you're ready."

I lingered, pressed to his side, my cheek cradled behind his shoulder, left arm over his back, and noticed my breathing change. Was Tyson drawing the fear of losing Riverview out of me? Horses communicate with thoughts, read “pictures” like movies in our minds, and live on elevated alpha waves. Horses don’t need words. Horses are in the business of healing. Horses know. They all know.

“Come on, big horse, help this feeble little human.” I begged. “Let me trust, house or no house, it’s going to be all right.”

October 15, 2009 midnight

I bolted next door to get Dorrie.

“I smell gas in the kitchen! Can you come?”

We dared no farther than the front door of my rental. Inhaling, she grabbed my arm, instinctively holding her hand over her nose and mouth, yanking me away.

“This is bad! Call the gas company!”

As soon as Vladimir the technician walked in, his clicking sensor erupted. From behind the stove his thick Polish accent called out, “Dis leak would have blown up any minute, for sure!”

“So what are you going to do now?” Dorrie asked half an hour later, setting a squat glass of orange juice on my side of her red oak table.

“The tenants wanted to pay up and stay. I let them have another month. The truth is I’d used their security. I hoped that they could pull it together. But then they disrespected me, Dorrie. She got verbally abusive more than once. Even if they paid up—” I shook my head. “Every time I would’ve taken their check, I would’ve felt like a whore. “Sure, beat me, do anything—as long as you pay me.” I have a new rule: “I’m not going to help you hurt me today.””

“Whatever we do as landlords, they hate us. Get used to it.”

“Isn’t it weird? Because I stood up for myself, they’re all OK. They’re alive. If I’d caved, let them stay, the house might have—they might dead. Life is so odd.”

She sighed, her hands rolling the glass between her palms like dough. "I miss having you next door."

Halloween Eve, 2009 10:30 p.m.

Stewart's home always smells like food—a turkey cooking, a ham bathed in pineapple and brown sugar, rice bubbling on the stove. Tonight, sounding urgent, he invited me over for garlic roast chicken,

"Unless you have something else to do?"

"So, how much do you think this place is worth?" he asked, throwing the question and a single dart at the board on his kitchen door. No bull's-eye. Stewart hit yellow.

I'd been seeing him abandoning piles of items at the curb for weeks—props from films, dishes, posters. Some had gone home with me, like that terra cotta pot, the white platter shaped like a salmon, and a Corning ware casserole. Stewart was acting like a captain throwing ballast off of a sinking ship.

I didn't get to answer. Holding a chicken thighbone up like a knife, he announced, "I'm not selling this house! Those motherfuckers who aren't giving me a loan mod—they can go fuck themselves! I have guns in my safe. No one's taking me out of here—alive!"

I said nothing. A caged animal is not one you want to pet.

"There was a time when I could have paid cash for this house, paid it all down, but hey, we partied a lot then—on location—women, blow, hey, those were the days! It was great. It was all "green," you know? All—flowing. We had so much money. We had so much hair." Swallowing the last of his glass of white wine, dropping the naked bone onto his plate, he asked, "Did you have enough? Would you like some more mashed potatoes?"

Tonight a band of teenagers is over at Stewart's house helping him build a very accurate graveyard on the hillside. I didn't think that they were going to get to it this year. Skull-faced zombies are sitting up at attention in coffins under Spanish moss dangling off the Chinese elm. They're over there, popping cans, hooting like owls. The swamp tape of crickets and frogs is rolling down to my side of the street along with smoke from the fog machine. A rotund fiberglass pumpkin has taken center stage in the bay window under spotlights where the skeleton family dined last year.

It's eat, drink, and be scary on Riverview tonight.

CHAPTER TWENTY-FIVE

Perfect Horse

I AM HOUSE

I am house
I am home

The Black
Carries her like he
Used to behind me on
The trails through the weeds

They are
One body his
Legs her eyes
She smiles often

Limps now
Needs the
Horse and
Me to feel strong

Against the no faces
Who scream from pages like
Demons because she
Cannot pay

November 6, 2009 10:00 p.m. meditation

"It's all too much! I'm getting pounded! Why did You tell me it was okay to buy both of those houses and Riverview? The shooting star—remember? I did what You said! What I thought You wanted. Now I have to sell them both! This wasn't my plan!"

God contained me in His arms.

"Whose houses are they?" I heard without judgment, as the handkerchief appeared.

"Yours," I choked. "But my parents said if you have enough houses, it will all be—the houses would always take care of you—you wouldn't have to worry. It would all be—"

"What do you really want?"

"I guess, to live in Riverview and write and ride Tyson and not worry about money."

"Do you think I'm able to do that for you?"

I wiped my eyes, mopped my nose.

"I can't make the payments! I'm falling behind, more and more—"

Softly He repeated, "Do you think I am able to do this for you?"

"Y-y-yes."

"Do you think that I *will* do this for you?" He waited. "This is important. Do you think that I *will* do this for you?"

"I couldn't trust anyone—"

"I know that. I'm not anyone. I am The One."

"How do I—how do I trust You? I don't know?"

"Ask Me. I'll help you."

"What?"

"You can ask Me for that, too."

"What? I can ask You for the trust to trust You?"

"You bet." He waited again.

"I just say, "God help me?""

"I'm in." Was all He said.

Then the real truth came out, unveiled: "I just want to come home, and be home and—"

"And?"

"And feel safe."

"Done."

"And I want the four poster Restoration Hardware bed," I sniveled. "The cherry one."

He smiled. "Are you hungry?"

"I'm always hungry."

"Join me for breakfast?"

The table on the patio was set with white linen. Not far away was a helicopter. A helicopter?

"First, would you like to go on a ride with Me?"

I strapped myself into a harness next to Him. He handed me a set of headphones. I couldn't believe that the thing had no steering wheel, just a stick and a lot of foot levers. Oh, well, if you crash and God is driving, what's there to worry about? In front of dials and instruments, behind plastic doors that were much too thin, we took off, slowly droning over the ocean along shoreline until we were above long buildings shaped like sound stages with my name—KATHY O'BRIEN—painted on them in huge letters. There were at least thirty. I stopped trying to count.

"I thought it was time you knew about this." He offered, banking the helicopter to give a better view. "I have so much to give you, so much. I don't want to overwhelm—Don't worry, it's all on hold until you're ready."

My mouth didn't seem to want to close. I almost had to lift my jaw with my hand.

"That's all for me? What's in there?"

"Most if it's ideas." He said. "Ideas bring everything else, you know? You're going to have—we're going to make some good projects together, you'll see. Now," He offered, checking the dials, moving the stick. "Ready for breakfast?"

November 18, 2009 8:30 p.m.

The two men who I brought did not expect a woman to climb up the ladder of the dumpster, first.

"Bring the truck alongside!" I called.

Everything that I'd grown, the women and children, plants that had fed, shaded me were been cut down, dismembered, shriveling under my feet—Valencia oranges, Black Pines, ferns, jasmine, roses.

Another crew in front of the house, some holding shovels, one on a Bobcat, watched as I dropped armfuls of camellias and iris down into the truck bed.

I wasn't going to be able to save them all—or the topsoil I'd built from sand to loam for twenty years. Because the first house, the Mother House, who gave birth to House #2 and Riverview, wasn't mine anymore. She lay butchered, gutted, bleeding, stripped bare. A carcass.

My workers reluctantly climbed up behind me. Quickly the half-ton mounded with rescues. There was no time to weep.

Dorrie, walking past on the sidewalk, had to stop.

"Taking what you can?"

Our eyes met. She turned to see barren, scraped earth around a house that had bloomed like an oasis twelve months of the year. Then she looked past me, squared her shoulders, and moved on.

December 1, 2009 9:30 p.m.

He still bites. It's a stallion thing, I know. In a herd the stallion usually brings up the rear, the savvy lead mare sets course. Stallions drive, keep stragglers from falling behind. Tyson evidently feels a need to "drive" me.

I, being that alpha mare, the one on the leading end of the rope, am not supposed to put up with this. When he bites, or tries to bite, I pull on the stud chain, back him up a few steps, establishing order. Being a stallion he wants proof, body language that I can handle my job.

Evidently, he's not sure about that or about something else. He continues to bite. I continue to establish order. There is dissent. I left the barn last night, questioning, "What is biting? Yes, it's about control but could it be—fear?"

The idea came to me as my eyes flooded. Of course—he's had a transient life up to now of being left behind by everyone—especially me. Before I bought him, he'd gone from place to place to be ridden by "trainers," some, who the former owner told me, used "pizza cutter" spurs on him. There are people come at horses with sharp weapons.

I do not ride with spurs. They are not the issue. Could it be abandonment? I moved him three times after I bought him. The last time was seventeen years ago. I visited. I came. And sometimes there were long periods, months, when I did not.

"I'll come back to get you," I promised almost twenty years ago, when we turned him loose in that corral, as he reared like a wild mustang. "I'll come back and get you—"

He waited. Seventeen years. Winters. Summers. In rain, storms. No human would have done that. I was one hundred miles away. I had things to do, men to chase. I was busy.

"He's okay out there," I told myself about ten times a day. "Mary blankets him at night. He's got all that space. He can look over at his mares, all day. He's fine without me. He's just fine without me."

Maybe he wasn't just fine without me? Tonight, while Tyson dove into sweet feed, after I brushed, toweled his coat soft and clean, I heard myself say, "You're home. You're not going anywhere."

He continued chewing, his right ear flipped towards me.

"If it comes between you and my house," I pledged, "I'll find another place to live."

December 2, 2009 10:00 p.m.

The biting stopped! Today when I went to see him, after I haltered I expected the turn, the nip, like he always does. But he stood calm, and still. When we came back in the stall, and I dropped the halter, Tyson did nothing.

No biting.

He stood there, ears at attention, turning to take me in with a soft brown eye.

December 15, 2009 11 p.m.

There were more neighbors jammed into that ballroom at the Holiday Inn than on a lawn for a good yard sale. Diana and I took second row seats. Pillars of the community, Florina, Larry Dennison, sat center front. At least fifty others crowded in. No one was late. An air of festivity prevailed—to hear a lawyer talk about pollution?

David Smithson is the second or third counsel to take on the case about Cow Field. No one knows what happened to the others. Jaded eyes, crossed arms, heard him out. His team believed that there was a case against Cow Horn Productions. He wanted to contact us individually, later. They had flown all the way from Sacramento because of the "gravity" of the case.

"Our Company has a history of successful resolutions regarding Toxic Waste." was his lead in. "This production facility, we believe, will be proven guilty for polluting Cow Field for decades with high levels of chromium six, mercury, and other chemicals with run off from their film vaults' cooling system."

When he opened the floor to questions, stories flew.

"My horse died of cancer of the sheath," a woman in a cowboy hat said. "I rode him there every day."

"My dog died of cancer of the face," a man added. "We always went there."

But the question, the idea most voiced was, "How do we make Cow Field safe?" All the community wanted was for their "secret" park to be the sanctuary that they always *thought* it was.

When it was done, Diana and I pushed through the crowd, headed straight to Denny's, and ordered lemonades. I don't know why it felt like we'd just come from a funeral? We were so thirsty.

December 21, 2009 9:30 p.m.

I'm getting it down to a science. I know what forms, profit and loss, the way these bankers want to see money—or the lack of it—for a loan modification.

I know they'll reject me—because they had 'insufficient information' or 'insufficient disposable income.' I get that they'll lose this 72-page fax and the next. This is my other job, compiling numbers for a loan mod. Because the payments are killing me and my house is slipping away like a sand castle at high tide.

Today I called the 888 number and went on endless hold, not expecting a person to answer. A man named Roger conducted the interview. This time I only waited an hour to speak with a human being.

"Do you have any expenses for home maintenance? Gardener? Pool service?"

"I am the gardener. My pool is a pond."

"Okay. And this, on line 32, is this all that you spend on food each month?"

"I don't go out. I'm growing my own vegetables."

Roger went silent for what felt like another hour. "This is the second time you've applied?"

"Yes."

"Our department will forward this to underwriting now."

"And then when will I have an answer?"

"I hope, four to six weeks. Check in every week."

"Thank you," I said, throwing myself around the stranger's ankles, not letting go. Forget dignity.

Just give me the house.

"We have thousands of applications coming in from around the country. We have—one thousand calls, waiting."

"I know. I'm sure you do," I swallowed, seeing people desperately clinging to tiny rafts of hope.

Would I survive this shipwreck? Or would I drown?

I think I thanked Roger again. I don't remember. Then I hung up and walked around my kitchen like a prisoner in a cell.

December 23, 2009 9:00 p.m.

Even if I had money for dance lessons, I can't dance. 'Tendons are shot, stretched too far and too long from decades of being up in heels. Now it even hurts to walk.

But it doesn't hurt to ride. When I'm upon Tyson, my foot doesn't hurt. When he's carrying me, I can fly—and it feels like we're dancing. People didn't expect that we would do anything, not with him almost thirty-two years old. That's like being one hundred in human years. He's a freak of nature. When we ride through Cow Field, I point at the back of my house and tell him, "Look, I live there now. Remember when we used to ride here, twenty years ago? And I said, wouldn't it be great to live there?"

When we're out, I see the looks, feel the judgment—people saying it's too dangerous to ride an animal that old. But

Tyson's faking some of them out—like the man on a buckskin quarter horse last week who asked how old my "baby" was?

"Oh, you mean, my horse?"

"Yeah, he's a beauty. How old? Four?"

Without any urging from me, Tyson walked around the man and his horse like he wanted to give them a better view. "He's thirty-one." I laughed. "Almost thirty-two. And he's showing off for you, I think!"

"He's amazing." The guy said. "Amazing."

Off the record, Dr. Banning confided, horseman-to-horseman, "You gotta keep riding him. If you don't ride him, he'll die. Give him a job. Everyone needs a job. And get him on glucosamine and MSM—see what happens. What have you got to lose?"

"Look!" I said to my stallion tonight as I was limping, leading him to an open paddock after our ride, my right hand guiding his blind side. "Look! We're back together. Just in time—when I need your legs and you need my eyes!"

Then I stripped him of all tack and delighted to watch him race over to a big chestnut thoroughbred mare in a corral next to his. Neck arched, tail curling, five years old again, he pranced, slow motion, nickering to her. Ears back, the mare threw a sullen glance and headed in the opposite direction.

"Not me, dude. Not today. Go light someone else's cigarette."

Unfazed, Tyson pursued, dropping his entire manhood in display. 'Still no response? When I returned with his halter and cooler, he'd run so much that steam was rising off of his back in hot grey tendrils.

By then the situation had changed. Some mares only come in season when a stallion is present. Evidently she was one of them. Suddenly she was calling, running the fence. I thought my horse would join her, courting. Instead he turned his rump towards the mare, walked up to me for his halter, and waited to be covered with his red cooler. I left with an available man and that bitch was shit out of luck.

Christmas Day, 2009 10:45 p.m.

The last red flax plant was going in. Teddy ran the hose while I stomped a deep "well" around it.

"So now," I directed, "When you water, it'll go straight down to the roots, not run away, down your hill! And your plants will thank you."

"Where did you learn all this?" she asked, watching water pooling, soaking down into soil.

"My mother, a long time ago, and then trial and error? Plants tell you what they want. They're very smart. Like houses, like horses, I guess. They—whisper their ideas. I don't know? I don't know anything. One thing I do know, even with all this going down about Riverview, foreclosure pending, I'm glad I went for it—that I'm not driving past it saying, "I wish I would have bought that house.""

Teddy got right in my face.

"It's gonna be okay. Trust and believe," she said, running her hand over her own scarred forearms. "God has you. He has this. If I can get through a fire, you can get through this. Damn," she remarked, taking in the entire the front yard. "My house looks so much better! You're a magician! This is the best Christmas I ever had!"

I had nothing to say.

Teddy filled in the silence. "You're here, on Christmas Day, making my house look—it's so much better. This was all just—dirt. Now look! Amazing!"

"You're going to have the' Hanging Gardens of Babylon'!" I teased, feeling guilty that I was spinning inside, thinking about Riverview—how to keep it—that every sentence I uttered ended silently with "But I might lose my house."

"This is the best Christmas I ever had," she repeated. "No fights. With my family, it was always drinking and fights."

I shrugged. I had no idea that showing up on Christmas Day would mean that much to her.

"I know you're worried about making the payments," she said. Then she had the audacity to laugh in the face of my fear. While she coiled the hose, she chuckled, "What do you always remind me about God?"

"I forget. When I'm scared, I—I can't think."

"He has all the money. He owns all the real estate. He knows all the people."

"Did I say that?"

"Yep. 'More than once."

"Say it again?"

"He has all the money. He owns all the real estate. He knows all the people."

Opened to: *"And I will carry you away, beyond Babylon."*

January 16, 2009 Midnight

He fell in the wash rack. Tyson fell and he couldn't—he couldn't get his legs under himself. The cement was wet, slick as oil. He struggled and struggled, then gave up. I called to a woman who ran over up to help.

"Downer in the wash rack!" She called.

Instantly people appeared.

"Horse down in the wash rack!" A man echoed as men in cowboy hats, women, and girls came running out of trailers from the Western show two barns over. A girl offered a pink towel to place under his head. Someone else threw a horse blanket over him. He'd fallen blind side up. All Tyson had to go on was touch, my voice, and what he could glimpse when he tried to lift his head.

The veterinarian on call was our Dr. Banning, a Western cowboy with Eastern ideas. He asked permission to place needles along Tyson's spine to open blood flow?

"He's strained so hard, the nerves are in shock here," he pointed, "Here, and here. Tell him what we're going to do."

"T, we're going to give you little shots now," I said, running my hands along his back.

One by one, the doctor inserted needles, twisting them. Where blood flowed, it was a good indicator. The dry areas needed more needles.

"Now his spine has 'communication,'" he said, removing them a while later. "Can we move him? Get him over to gravel?"

By then a crowd of at least twenty-five people had walled in around us.

"We can move him!" A man said. "Anybody got rope?"

Anybody got rope? At a Western horse show? Are you kidding?

Within minutes, ropes and lead lines wrapped in rags and men's shirts went around my horse's legs like a web.

"T, we're going to move you. It's okay," I said as I stroked my horse's neck.

"First, let's roll him!" the lead man called. "On 'three!'"

It took three pulls to get fourteen hundred pounds to roll over, another three tries and a dozen men to pull Tyson off of wet cement to gravel and sand where he got covered with more blankets. The girl with the pink towel inched along, keeping it in place while the men leveraged.

Maybe an hour passed. The street lights came on. No one left. I faced the crowd.

"My name is Kathy. This is Tyson. He's thirty-one. I know it's Friday night and it's a show, and you all have—"

"We got nothin' better to do, ma'am," answered a man leaning on a barn wall. "Y'all just take your time."

"Tyson and I thank you," I said, as my horse began to sit up.

"Look!" Dr. Banning said. "He's trying!"

Tyson was about to make a move.

"Slide a rope under him," a man directed.

Another brave person shot stiff rope under Tyson's partially raised chest before he collapsed again.

And then I got an idea—because I could tell my horse was gathering strength. But he needed incentive. I could see it in his eye.

"Is there a mare in the house?"

"I'll bring Cherry!" Gloria's voice called from the back of the crowd.

"Cherry" is a sorrel quarter horse mare who lives four stalls down from Tyson. Every day when she's walked past Tyson and Flash, they erupt. It's "so close yet so far." Cherry is their movie star. My horse wanted her, big time. Come to find out, he has a thing for redheads. Twice a day, every day, he screams after her perfection.

When Gloria led the mare over, Cherry lowered her head, sniffing the ground as if to ask, "Hey, Big Guy, why are you so short? What happened?"

Tyson's head shot up. He rolled onto his belly, back legs folded like springs. Gloria brought Cherry closer.

Tyson nickered.

Cherry answered.

"Get ready!" I warned.

In one huge effort, Tyson pushed up, and then fell back to his side. Cherry held still, ears moving. This party was not over.

Tyson took her in, began to push.

"Now!" a man directed his pals, as Tyson lurched, scrambled, started to fall until—men rushed in on both sides, holding, pushing—and he was up! Not only was he on his feet, he was trotting after Cherry, lead dangling!

"Stop him!" Gloria yelled over her shoulder, bolting ahead with the mare. One of the men ran after Tyson, grabbed his lead line, but there was no holding him back.

Half an hour later I walked my stallion past the crowd, staying on, now in their third hour, celebrating, laughing, tipping cans of beer, opening bottles.

I was yelling, "Thank you so much!" when my stallion halted on his own, took them all in, turning in a circle, neighing three times, head held high.

Everyone erupted in wild clapping. Then Tyson pulled, began leading me through the crowd—right up to the girl holding the pink towel—and bowed his head.

She started to cry.

"No, thank you," she said, placing her hand on his white star.

More applause rose up like music. As we walked away I was waving, they were waving. And the girl with the pink towel was waving it, high.

Resurrection *is* my horse's middle name.

January 17, 2010 9:00 p.m.

The maps were rolled out on Lynn's dining room table, layered like blueprints. He was there with Edith, and a man everyone calls "Slick." Slick is not his real name, but no one seems to care what his real name is. Tall, with thinning blond hair, once very handsome, he never took the dark aviators off. I guess it's a "Hollywood" thing. No one knows what Slick does for a living other than marry tall ex-super models who have a lot of finances of their own. What everyone does know is that Slick knows everyone, and everyone knows him. If you want the backstage "dirt," the scoop, on anything, you call Slick. We never shook hands. He was in the midst of explaining the aerial views when I walked in.

"The chemicals flowed down the street to the cul-de-sac—you can see the white areas—and the overflow footprint—how it formed "ponds" in Cow Field. Here's another view, later. We estimate that the river carried it downstream before the freeway was built, so that means all along the banks for miles was probably contaminated. But no one said anything. "He smiled, disdaining against the idea that it would have been any other way. "Because it was Cow Horn Productions"

Then he turned to me and fired. "Are you in a lawsuit against Cow Horn?"

"No, I cancelled. I didn't want a gag order, and I didn't like the lawyer."

Later, when I returned to Lynn's to bring Jasper some table scraps, he and I compared notes on the evening. Sometimes you can talk something to death. I wasn't sure that this issue was ready to roll over and die.

"Slick had his home office broken into—All his hard drives, disks, were stolen. He kept the Cow Horn files offsite. He had a hunch. He's made arrangements in case something happens to him. But he's not stopping the investigation."

"Wasn't he standing next to Danielle when the mayor said that the city couldn't build the sewage treatment plant there—because it was 'too toxic'?"

"He and another neighbor paid for the core samples."

"This wasn't what I expected when I bought my Dream House."

"You going to sell?"

"I'm—I'm not being directed to do that. I'm supposed to ride this pony out."

January 18, 2010 10:00 p.m.

Of course I had to ride him. Yes, a mounting block was required to get up on a horse that tall. For sure I felt him limping.

"They pulled his shoes," I told my accomplice, Lisa, twenty five years ago on that drive home after buying my horse. "He's thin. They were done spending money on him." Then I jeered, "It's all *your* fault! Yesterday you asked me what my 'dream horse' was and I told you."

"Hanoverian Stallion, black, four whites and a star, right?"

"And there he was, that night, in the *Recycler* newspaper. The *Recycler*? Right after—"Pygmy goats for sale"? There was the ad—"Hanoverian stallion, black four whites and a star"."

Lisa already had her dream horse—a half Arabian, half Quarter horse-fast-as-shit-corner-like-a-Porsche barrel racer named Shawna—a mare with one fatal flaw—she didn't always stop when you asked. Oh well, no one's perfect.

"How much will it take to buy this horse—*today*?" I asked the very obese lady owner after a handler led Tyson back to his stall. Three hours later I was counting twenties and fifties in piles on the front seat of her dusty pick up. She raised thoroughbreds for the track. Obviously, she wasn't about riding. She was about money. And this warm blood stallion, left over livestock from a failed business partnership, wasn't making her a dime.

The stallion looked through me that day—until the money went into her hands, and she'd signed the transfer of sale. Horses are like houses, they feel change when they have a new owner. As I led him into the arena, unbuckled his halter, said "Go!" Tyson launched into a gallop, tearing up the dirt like he was at war with it. On about the fourth lap, I had one thought as the locomotive ran, full-speed, straight at me—"Oh God, I hope he stops!"

I extended my arms like a cross. A few yards in front of me he skidded to a halt, spraying me with dust. About a year later… no, I'm kidding, I took a breath.

"No one 'plays' with him," my sidekick, Lisa, yelled from the safety of the top rail of a fence. "You should have a whip or something."

Slowly, deliberately, I lowered my arms, extended my closed fist. The horse walked forward, sniffing, curious.

"I'm 'it,' Chief," I said. "You and me—we're all we've got."

The only problem with taking your last four thousand dollars and spending it on a horse is there might not be any money left to board him somewhere?

"I guess he could live in my backyard with Shawna," Lisa offered. "We'll keep him as far away from her as possible. I don't need any baby horses."

Lisa's house was in Palmdale, an hour's drive away, fringed in open desert. One day in that open country I let my stallion run as fast and as far as he wanted to go.

"Come on, horse!"

I urged, setting my calves on his sides. That day, twenty years ago, Tyson showed me what "fast as the wind" means.

When times and money got better, I was able to move him to a barn a mile away from my house. That meant I saw him every day, sometimes two or three times a day. He filled out, became a vision of health. People seeing me ride him up on the mountain would comment, "What a gorgeous horse."

When money ran out again and my divorce became final, in desperation I ran an ad offering his stud services. That was when Mary called, a woman with a pasture full of warm blood mares and no stallion to cover them. Miraculously, within three days, on my birthday, she pulled up in a six horse rig to pick up a stallion she had never seen from a person she had never met.

"He's D-line Hanoverian. His name is' Das Nureyev Tanz'. Why did you give him the barn name, 'Tyson'?" she asked, going over the pedigree.

"Because he's big and black and I thought he'd be a champion."

Ironically, the stallion did stand and throw punches in the air when we let him loose that first day in his new paddock at their ranch in Palm Springs.

"I see what you mean about the boxing." Mary laughed. "I'll take care of him, breed him to my Trakaener mares. Let's see what kind of babies we get."

I don't know why I was thinking about all of this tonight

as I brought a tube of salve up next to my horse's eye. When he pulled back, I explained, "I have to put this in your eye. You scraped it when you fell." I let him sniff the tube, held it next to my own eye so he'd know the agenda. Reluctantly, he allowed me to squeeze the antibiotic in, and close his eyelid.

Then I noticed something in his eye, in the way he looked at me—not matter, not a particle. It was a deep sorrow, a doubt. Did Tyson want to know—was he being punished? And there was something else behind that, a shadow, a scar, that he had carried for a long time. Did he, could he, think that *he* had done something wrong and that's why everyone always sent him away?

"You are 'Perfect Horse!'" I countered, near his face, hand on his neck. "You were always 'Perfect Horse.' When I took you to Mary's, it was because I didn't have the money to keep you here. It. Wasn't. Your. Fault. *I*—stayed away too long. It was wrong of me, T. I—I didn't think I deserved you. I never think I deserve good things!"

There was no point in stopping the tears. My face found a home in his neck.

"I thought you didn't need me. I didn't know—you do need me—and I need you. I could have, should have… You are Perfect Horse. Perfect Horse. Perfect Horse."

CHAPTER TWENTY-SIX

ANGEL'S TRUMPET

I AM HOUSE

I am house
I am home

I spent years staring
Out the window
At nothing not
Seeing my daughter

I am here now Baby
Girl the one by her
Bed says I am here
Now I love you I see you

When I drank I told her
You don't deserve good who
Do you think you
Are because I didn't

Have nice things a
Childhood safe I was
Jealous of her my own blood I
Could have should have

January 20, 2010 10:30 p.m.

"Courage is not particularly well dressed."

The words swirled down like the cold winds off of the skyscrapers, piercing through like needles.

"Courage is not particularly well dressed. Courage is not particularly well dressed."

Why didn't I bring a sweater? The walk was farther than I thought. My dress was thin. The soles on my cheap plastic shoes were thin. The only thick thing was the brown accordion file under my arm.

"So, you tried to modify your home loan how many times?" The man asked.

"Twice, I think."

"No success?"

I smiled bravely. "They filed a N.O.D. I have ninety days."

Juan Lopez at Operation Help was my last thread of hope. In his thirties, wearing a white button-down collared shirt, patriotic red-white-and-blue tie, khaki trousers, and a tiny American flag on his lapel, he brought my stacks of paper to his side of the glass conference table.

"I know it's a long-shot. I know. Just—tell me what you want it to look like."

I bowed my head, folded my hands in my lap. Could he see? Did he notice that my knuckles were bloody and raw from knocking on every door, every bank, every lender that I could find?

"I've done everything you said to do and I—"

"Sure, sure," Juan said in his best counselor's voice, dragging a box of tissues to my side of the table. I was there because the under-earner in me, the small, frightened one, afraid to be heard, the beaten one who pulls back at the moment of triumph, who lets someone else claim the prize and settles for crumbs, couldn't run or hide anymore. I needed help.

"Let me get another client's profit and loss sheet," he calmed, gently rising. "I can't pick up a pen because if something goes wrong—"

"I know. I know."

Juan left me alone in that glass-walled room thirty stories above the City of Angels. Miles away, close enough to touch, was my mountain decorated with the Hollywood sign. If someone dropped me up there somewhere near that landmark, I knew how to climb to the other side, follow the trails down to the barn where Tyson is, and walk the last three blocks to the cats, to Sarge, to my house.

I bowed my head.

"God, help me."

It was a prayer said on the tip of a sword.

Juan appeared with his client's sheet. I copied the set up.

"'Just this? Only this?'

"Just like that. It's all I want. A lot of people don't do what I ask. Then I can't help them. One man said, 'They won't sell my house.' Then he called me one day, said, 'They're selling my house tomorrow. What do I do?' "'Got boxes?" I said. I would have a 'Plan B.' Sell the rentals if you have to."

"I am."

January 21, 2010 5:55 a.m.

I set the Christmas tree, crispy and wan, in the trash can. Sooner or later everything becomes compost.

"Okay, Christmas, 'see you next year!" I said to what was left of the tree. "I have a feeling it'll be in this house. I can't tell you why."

I was about to close the lid when I heard a voice—a muffled one.

"Hey! I'm in here!"

The one I didn't expect to unearth today was Frosty. A shadow of his former self, he'd flattened, melted away, unrecognizable from his softer, puffier days. Do you bury a sponge? Cremation? I think not.

"So," he asked, his voice sounding raspy. "Did you find the Big Guy?"

"Yeah, yeah I did. I think so."

"Now you don't need to talk to me, you can talk to Him! It's good for you, now, isn't it?"

"I—yeah, Frosty. I don't know. I still don't know if—what's going to happen? They filed on me. They're going to foreclose in ninety days."

"This house is crazy out of its mind for you. Anyone else would have torn it down."

"This is a lot to do," I sighed, feeling calmer because we were back together again, Frosty and me, old friends, talking.

"You're home," he reminded. "You're not going anywhere."

Then Frosty expired, right there in my palm. It was time. He was all washed up.

January 27, 2010 11:35 p.m.

"They said 'No.' They reviewed your file they're not going to approve the modification."

Something fell hard around me like plates breaking. So close, yet so far. Operation Help was my last straw. Thoughts blew in, one after the other.

"I guess the book ends differently?"

"Should I post a 'for sale' sign or not?"

"It'll be a short sale."

"Keep watering—the trees, the grass—keep telling the universe you intend to be here."

Doesn't the Universe "get" intent?

One last Voice took over above all the others:

"Get clarity: You have a right to ask for what you want."

"Juan," I ventured, "Could you find out why they declined?"

In fifteen minutes he called back.

"They didn't think profit and loss were up to date. The rental income showed less than bank deposits. They want to know if you'd like them to re-open the file?"

"YES!" I shouted, sprinting to the bathroom. Because, evidently, my stomach liked the idea before my head did. "I'll recalculate. I'll get the numbers to you today!"

It figures that I'd undercut myself. 'Less than my deposits? Now the Universe is giving me a second chance to trust that the truth is enough.

February 1, 2010 10:00 p.m.

I let Tyson walk back and forth on the other side of the pipe corral, sniffing at baby Stewart Little, blocking the colt's attempts to bite him with deftly executed adult head butts. This is a daily routine. The biggest horse and the smallest horse have become best friends. The child relentlessly challenges his elder, acting way too aggressively with his sharp baby teeth. Every time the stallion disciplines, Stewart responds with "baby talk," chewing in the air like he's trying to say something. Tyson's kind eye tells me that he's adopted the foal as his new "charge." He's trying to give the baby previews of coming attractions.

"Okay, kid, here's the deal. You have to—"

I need comic relief. I need distraction. Paranoia is closing in on me, showing fangs, cornering me in the belief that everything is futile, that I'm not good at anything, couldn't hold a "regular" job if I tried. Why not give up? I'm losing my house, everything I worked for. There's no answer yet about the loan mod. Everything's on hold. My entire life is suspended.

And I'm losing my horse. He's weaker every day, stumbles

often, leaks urine all the time. I hose his legs to help keep him clean. Didn't this happen to Tony? My horse is dying before my eyes. And there's nothing I can do about—"

Didn't my mother reach for a blade when she felt annihilation like this? When she was under attack, stripped of her dreams, her true home, the second one, when she had no safe place to hide? Did she feel like evil forces were stalking her, whispering things to her like they are to me?

"You know you're going to lose everything? You failed. It's all over. Give up. Wouldn't it be better if you ended it, quietly? Why don't you just kill yourself? "

I'm trying to stay strong, put on a game face for my horse. He needs me. But the nights go on forever. They are so black. It's when I have least defense, when the fears crowd me, close in, when I sink, have no place to hide.

Resolved: No more razor blades. No more shotguns.

Now what?

"Help me!" I prayed on my knees in the dark. "Help me, God, please! Someone, something, is coming up from a dark place, telling me I'm losing everything, that I shouldn't even be alive—help me!"

February 2, 2010 4:00 a.m. meditation

I never got to tell Him about the horrible dream where men with bulldozers were digging up all the soil around Riverview like they did at the Mother House, because God was having a nightmare of His own.

"They—they almost had you!" He was pacing, looking like He wanted to spit something bitter out of His mouth.

"Them?"

"All the dark ones have free will. Lucifer has free will. I gave everyone free will. It was good when we were all together. Then he got jealous. I guess I'm a little too 'human' for his taste? They were with Me, you know—before they—" He was churning, trying to put something to rest. "Why do they make Me out to be the bad guy? Lucifer was jealous of all My human babies. He thought he wasn't enough, that I would drop him. So he left. That's what he's infecting you with—fear that you're not enough. He wants you worn down. He wants you thinking I'll drop you. He wants you to not trust Me. He wants you—out." Then God stopped still. "I don't cause the dark. I *surmount* it. That's what I'm good at. I sent My Son, you, all my babies, to prove—how human I am. All I ask—is that you ask Me to help you. You asked! You were in the big house and you asked—"

He made no attempt effort to quell the water coming down His cheeks.

"My morning star, when he left, and he took the others, what was I going to do? Hold him down, foot on his throat; say 'Love Me or I'll kill you?' I could do that. But that's not Me."

I picked up the crystal lamp, pulled the plug out of the wall, offered it. He hugged me, laying it on the sofa.

"I'll tell you one thing." He erupted. "I'm brighter than any of them. Kathy, we can use them. We can use them to help you get you closer to Me. I will never let you be tempted beyond what you can handle. When they try to take you down, to lie to you, tell you it's hopeless—keep coming back to Me, to my Son, to us. You're in the family now, Babe. We got you. You tell them—"Game on!" Deal?"

"Deal." I nodded. We shook on it.

He sighed and the room quaked. Lamps on tables trembled. "All I ask—is that you keep asking. I can rearrange events, do things…but…" He pulled out a handkerchief for Himself. I—will *never* fail you. Anyone who wants to get at you has to go through Me first!"

I didn't know what to do. How do you console—God?

"I love you," He said.

Finally, I believed Him.

"I don't want to leave you. What's happening to me?" I asked. "I don't want to go back home?"

"You don't have to." He extended a hand, leading us upstairs where He nodded at a door with a carved brass knob. I opened it.

Inside was my bedroom, the library, the bed side tables, my desk with all the chapters, the books I'm writing, and the bed, my vision, deep, rich, and cherry red.

"My bed?" was all I could say.

"Everything. Everything—for you."

"So, I'm home?"

"You're always home."

"You sound like the Good Witch of the North![5]"

He laughed, long and low, a rumbling sound like a river going over boulders—until my fear of losing Riverview was washed downstream.

I began leaping around the room. Did David feel this way when he was chiseled out of the stone? "This feels so good! I had no idea! But—I can rent a room from a friend, take the animals if I have to sell—"

We stood there, smiling. And then I answered my own question—because I knew where I really lived. Whatever else was happening in life was—surface. My soul had permanent lodging: I was home. I wasn't going anywhere.

"Relax," He said. "Write. Ride. I'll take care of the rest."

Opened to: *He shall give His angels charge over you to keep you—lest you dash your foot against a stone.*

---

5. *The Wonderful Wizard of Oz*, L. Frank Baum.

February 4, 2010 9:00 p.m.

"I did something. I know I wasn't supposed to. Can you meet me by the swinging gate?"

Larry Dennison had to talk to someone.

"I did an interview about Cow Field," he blurted when we met at the end of the street, overlooking Cow Field's eleven acres.

"Really?"

"The timing was right. It was with a reporter from a big network. I checked him out. Gus Matthews. He won a Peabody. He used to work with the CIA, so I know he knows how to investigate!" Larry took a fast breath to deliver the rest. "It's going to be on TV next week."

"Really?"

"But executives from the network and their lawyers are talking with the show and protesting. The show's producers are saying, 'This is First Amendment. If we cave into bullying, into your fear of sponsor pull out, we're not bringing the news, we're running from it.'"

I probably said, "Really?" one more time. I know I did offer—"I want to watch it with you."

"If Danielle were here, she'd be happy about all of this." Larry said. "She wanted—resolve.

"I feel her around sometimes."

"I do, too. But—"he confessed, "I'm thinking—I've been thinking of moving to Newport—near my boat."

"Water's nice," I agreed, foot up on the gate. "Water's nice, but personally, I'm all about 'the land.' Isn't the field lovely?"

Grasses were growing tall from the rains, sporting flower hats. At the far end of the meadow three children on horses were raising clouds of dust in a full gallop.

"It really is lovely, isn't it?" I said. "It's green, like Ireland."

"Have you ever been to Ireland?

"No, but this is what I think it should look like!"

"I know," Dennis confirmed. "Bucolic."

March 4, 2010 8:00 p.m.

I didn't want to open the envelope. I knew it was another threat. For sure it had to do with the sale of the second rental, the pool house. It was that bank's corporate address—New York City. And I knew that they had me in their cross hairs for $370,000.

"Yes, I know I owe you $370,000. Yes, I know you're sicking your dogs on me. I get it. How many pounds of flesh do you want? "

"If they could only see that it was their fault!" I admitted to Serena, the short sale coordinator, when we were finally in escrow with a buyer. "I tried to get that bank to move it to the first house, the right one—"

"Let me see what I can do." Serena said, heading down the road like a messenger.

Ms. Serena isn't about pomp or circumstance. She wears Keds sneakers and old jeans to work, doesn't care about looking good. She cares about doing good. In this deal Serena was the voice, the mortar holding stones together—doing the improbable—convincing banks to compromise.

I slit the envelope.

I had to read it three times.

They forgave the $370,000. They admitted that as of March 1, 2010, the debt was "forgiven."

FORGIVEN?

Serena was my first call.

"Is this a joke? A scam?"

"No," she chuckled. "I talked with the new underwriter, but you never know. I told him the story. He checked it out, saw that it was their mistake. I didn't say anything to you because I didn't know—"

"How can I ever thank you?"

She laughed again.

"I'm happy, too. Now can we close this dog and pony show?"

$370,000. Forgiven.

Opened to: *Believe on the Lord Jesus Christ and you will be saved—you and your household.*

March 6, 2010 8:00 p.m.

"I hit him in the face, Betty."

"Oh—"

"I hit him on his blind side."

"Oh, honey."

"I hit him in the stall because he wouldn't calm down and I wanted to bridle—ride with my friends. I thought it might be the last time I—"

"Oh, honey, I know how you feel. Come in. Come inside." She was holding her front door open.

Crushed against the wall, the confession came out. "I don't feel like I have a right to *be*— but if I kill myself, then who does my horse have? No one!"

"No, no, no! Oh, honey, I love you so much."

"This—is unforgiveable."

"Oh, sweetie, my little peanut—"

"I went down on my knees in front of Tyson. I told him I didn't think I deserved to be his owner. I said I was wrong. Do you know what he did? He sniffed the top of my head and looked down at me like, "What are you doing down there?""

"I know how much you're hurting. You are not alone! I love you."

"I am unlovable! I don't feel like I deserve to be on this planet. Betty—oh, God," I folded, my legs melting in shame. "Have I become my father?"

"No!" she closed in. "You are in recovery! You're willing to let God change things."

"I am powerless over rage, Betty. 'Fucking powerless."

"Now—He can help you. That's when He always helps me—when I can't."

"Oh, God, Betty—"

"You have a big God! He can make anything right, anything! Do you think you're the only one who ever made a mistake? Who didn't stop and think? I made mistakes with my kids. None of us walk a perfect path. None of us! You're human! You're just—one of us! I love you, honey. You have to forgive yourself. You know, why don't we forgive your father while we're at it? We don't have to like him, we just have to turn him over—let God deal with him."

"Okay."

"Let's say, we forgive the S.O.B. He's just a man, huh?"

"Okay," I whispered. "I forgive my father. God, You take care of this." Then I stood up and I hugged her. "When I came over it was so bad, I wanted to kill myself?"

"I don't think you were mad at your horse." Betty said. "I think you're angry at death."

March 7, 2010 6:00 a.m. meditation

I came down the stairs, and met Him in the big room. I don't have to enter through the front door anymore. Not when I live here. He was reading *National Geographic*.

"Yes?" He peered over His glasses, patting the sofa next to Him.

"His eye, the left eye, the blind one, went white in the past two days. He's having trouble walking on the left rear. I rode yesterday. He tried hard to trot, but it was off. These—are his most magnificent days. But it's costing Tyson to do this for me. I'm losing my boy. Oh, God, I'm losing my boy! Two weeks ago, he worked like a pro. He's going down, fast. I don't know what to do with my—with a heart this broken. I might have to give him back to You. I might have to give Your horse back, soon—"

"Hey—" He pulled me into His side, covering me with His arm like a wing. "He's *your* horse. I might have to take him back for a little while, but he's your horse. I'll bring him back to you."

"How would You—"

He looked into my eyes. "I told you. Death is a front."

"I don't feel like I deserve him after I—"

"It's okay. You're okay."

"I don't feel like I…After I…"

"You are mine, my daughter. My grace solved it. You were forgiven before it happened. It's done, finished. And there's nothing you can do about it! And, ah, he'll tell you it's him. When I bring him back, he'll tell you three times. You'll see."

Right about then I noticed boxes lining the foyer, stacked floor-to-ceiling—Hundreds and hundreds of boxes. I walked to one of the cardboard towers, reached in, pulled out a sealed envelope. The address was someone I never heard of. The return address read: "G.O.D."

"What are these?"

"I'm shipping them to people so they'll know about your books."

"But they have no stamps."

"They don't need stamps. I'm mailing to their subconscious."

April 10, 2010 2:15 a.m.

"A man called me from Texas about my house today, T," I told my stallion after it was all over, when it was just us—him and me—laying under his blanket, my head resting on his neck, my back warming against his chest. It slipped my mind to call, to tell anyone about the underwriter—too much for one day—for two hands, for one heart, to hold.

"He told me they approved my loan modification and he wanted to read the terms to me."

Night was falling fast like it was tired, in a hurry to have the day gone. Pigeons cooed, and then quieted. Canadian geese trumpeted overhead.

I still have sawdust in my bra. I was on the stall floor with him for a long time. His lungs stopped first. His heart took about a year.

My horse didn't want to leave me.

Tonight I understood. I am that important. I always was that important. Now I know what being loved feels like.

Tyson fought to stay. He kicked, twice, after the first injection, the one that relaxes, the shot that let his bladder finally release. He sighed deeply, his head against my thigh.

"Perfect Horse," I said, at least a thousand times. The last thing he saw was me, the last thing he felt was my touch, and the last sound he heard was my voice. "Perfect Horse… Perfect Horse… Perfect Horse…" During the endless passage our eyes never left each other. Tyson ceased being a horse. We melted into an eternal world. And I heard the music of the other place.

"We made it this time." I told him. "I'm right here. Perfect horse. Perfect horse."

This morning was the first time he didn't walk out of the stall right away. I opened the door, dropped his lead. He took me in and didn't move. Minutes later, Stewart Little whinnied from the corral. Tyson's ears went up. His head turned. He managed one giant, clumsy step. His hips were sinking, wobbling. He didn't know why the disobedient left rear was dragging. With monumental effort he began hobbling, taking step after shaky step.

When he met the baby nose-to-nose at the fence, Stewart circled, bucked, and reared. Tyson lowered his head, tried to calm the colt, stared into the foal's eyes, blowing into his nostrils with his own. Back and forth the anxious baby went. Whenever the colt reared, struck out, Tyson raised his head, came down soundly on the baby's nose. Someone needed to discipline this kid. Then there was a long period when they stood close, breathing in each other's noses. Tyson, I thought, had a lot to tell the little one. And not much time.

"Be patient with the human ones, they have a lot to learn from us—"

Stewart's bottlebrush tail switched as they languished—Tyson with his front feet planted wide. Then he began to sway. I leaned on him, full weight, arms straight on his left shoulder, the way the men had held him up at the wash rack. But there was only one of me and my horse was falling.

"T, what do you want to do? I can't hold you up—"

The stallion licked the baby horse's nose and began the immense task of turning on three legs. People walking by, a blacksmith pounding an anvil, stopped as he weaved up the aisle.

I left his stall once to run to the ladies room, was leaning on the fence, praying for strength, when I felt Maria at my side.

"He needs you now," she winced, looking concerned.

Tyson had broken into a spin in his stall, circling right, then left, like he'd probably done all night, determined to outrun death. I watched him fall. Frantic, he was struggling to his feet. I ran in, held my hands on either side of his neck.

"Don't get up. Relax." I told my horse. He settled, dropping his head in exhaustion. "Maria, call the vet. We need help."

"You want to do this now?" Dr. Banning asked minutes later, kneeling next to us, black gym bag in his left hand.

"Yes, we're ready."

"This is a sedative," he explained as he knelt on Tyson's other side, filling the largest syringe I ever saw, setting it deep in the jugular vein. "The next two take relaxation deeper."

We waited. My horse began to take deep, easy breaths.

"I don't think we'll need a third."

"He can live through these," he explained, as thick red

blood began to flow down his neck. Tyson kicked, struck out two or three more times, letting death know he wasn't going easily.

After the third injection I asked Dr. Banning to clear the barn.

Decades came and went like film clips—T and me, galloping across miles of open desert, T and me, twenty years ago on the top of the mountain in Griffith Park, overlooking the San Fernando Valley, our kingdom.

After a long time in the quiet, when I could feel no more pulse, as I was stroking his shoulder, steam began rising off of his side.

"But he's not hot," I questioned. Why is heat coming up now?" More vapors began to lift off of his hips, ascending slowly, like smoke.

I'm seeing things, was what I thought.

And then I knew.

I *was* seeing things.

"It's so small for something so big," I marveled, as the cloud hovered over him, began circling aimlessly like the dragonflies. Waking, rising, moving higher, gaining momentum, it grew dense, floating out into the aisle, clearly silhouetted against a dark stall. Collecting, swirling, silvery, alive, it formed into the shape of a tornado, then into a tube—and shot up straight through the roof of the barn toward the sun.

Flash nickered.

More geese flew over, calling.

"I will watch for you in the eyes of a foal." I said. "Or in a two year old." Because in that second, I knew that nothing was going to come between me and my horse. I had God's word on it. Didn't He say, "I'll bring him back to you?"

"I don't want you to be here when the truck comes," Maria suggested when she returned hours later to turn lights on, check on me. "You don't want to be here for that. It will haunt you. Sid's going to take you out to dinner."

I barely remember pasta being served as Sid, Maria's husband, made small talk, conversation that slid past me. When we returned Tyson's stall was clean and clear except for his water bucket, now clipped to the outside of the stall, cascading with white lilies and fat red roses.

Maria and Gloria greeted me, standing much too close.

"We'll expect to see you here, tomorrow." Maria led off, "In britches and boots."

Gloria closed with, "We have a lot of horses here that need riding."

It's different walking your backyard when you know you don't have to move.

It's different walking your backyard when you know you've been chosen to witness a miracle.

"Gramps," I threatened, standing next to the old shed, my finger raised at the stars. "You better take care of my horse. Show him—he might not know—where the good pastures are. He's got four whites and a star—a lotta chrome—so you can see him in the dark."

Then a scent interrupted. The Angel's Trumpet announced itself, reaching over from another realm, holding me hostage with its perfume. It smelled so sweet, it hurt.

THE END

With Special Thanks

To Dawn Huber, who retyped my manuscript by hand and `brought it to flash drive; to Edyta Salak, artist and friend, who gifted me with the art work, the jewel, the cover of covers; to Mayaprina Long, who created cover copy/design and interior format; to Natali Toth, my computer wrangler; to Anne Stockwell, who helped originate cover copy; to Libbe HaLevy, for her direction at the start; to Lloyd J. Jassin, Jassin and Associates, New York, New York, for his guidance and legal advice; to Bill Toth, my broker, for his review and support; to Cynthia Frank for her expertise and unfailing direction, and all of her Cypress House professionals; to Al Canton and Alice Walker at New Media Create, for his website design; to Betty, who protects my heart; and to everyone who reads this book and holds it close, I say, "Thank you."

About the Author

Johnny@Johnnyolsen.com

Okay, so, it's like this: Madonna wasn't going to be a writer. Let's get that out there, first. Writing was not the plan. International runway modeling, stalking catwalks in New York, Italy, Germany, appearing in New York theatre, those were priorities. Yes, applause is a good thing. Bring on those stage lights. Everything changed when she began drafting scenes for fellow actors in a class and discovered that she had a spiritual gift. Plays, books, and a tour of duty as a newspaper reporter followed.

I AM HOUSE is Madonna's debut novel. *Princess, Underground*, and *Princess, Underground II*—modern trilogy fairy tales about a princess, lost in Hollywood, in search of her prince and happily ever after are scheduled for release soon.

Madonna is also a licensed realtor. She lives in Southern California surrounded by many animals and quite a few zany friends.

CPSIA information can be obtained
at www.ICGtesting.com
Printed in the USA
FSHW021635220921